P9-BBN-055

### *"This shouldn't have happened."*

Nothing Michael said could have hurt Alexandria more. He already regretted their wonderful lovemaking. How could he regret something that was so beautiful, so right? Tears filled her eyes but she blinked them away, unwilling to let him see her pain. She couldn't understand why he was treating her like this. Her heart ached in a way it never had.

"You're right," she said quietly, grabbing her nightgown and slipping it on. "This was a mistake, Michael, but you couldn't possibly be as sorry as I am."

Michael nearly flinched at the look in her eyes. But it was for the best. She had to know the truth up front. He had nothing to offer her. It was time she learned that he was a man without a heart, without a soul. He was merely...lost.

Dear Reader,

Welcome to Silhouette **Special Edition**...welcome to romance. This month we have six wonderful books to celebrate Valentine's Day just right!

Premiering this month is our newest promotion. THAT'S MY BABY! will alternate with THAT SPECIAL WOMAN! and will feature stories from some of your favorite authors. Marking this very special debut is *The Cowboy and His Baby* by Sherryl Woods. It's the third book of her heartwarming series AND BABY MAKES THREE.

Reader favorite Christine Rimmer returns to North Magdalene for another tale of THE JONES GANG in her book, *The Man, The Moon and The Marriage Vow*. The wonderful Joan Elliott Pickart continues her newest series, THE BABY BET, in Special Edition this month. *Friends, Lovers...and Babies!* is book two of the MacAllister family series. Also in February, Pamela Toth introduces the Buchanan Brothers in *Buchanan's Bride*— it's the first book in her series, BUCKLES & BRONCOS. Sharon De Vita's *Child of Midnight* is her first for Special Edition, a passionate story about a runaway boy, a caring woman and the renegade cop who loves them both. And finally, Kelly Jamison's *The Wedding Contract* is a marriage-of-convenience story not to be missed!

So join us for an unforgettable February! I hope you enjoy all these stories!

Sincerely,

Tara Gavin
Senior Editor

Please address questions and book requests to:
Silhouette Reader Service
U.S.: 3010 Walden Ave., P.O. Box 1325, Buffalo, NY 14269
Canadian: P.O. Box 609, Fort Erie, Ont. L2A 5X3

# SHARON DE VITA
## CHILD OF MIDNIGHT

*Silhouette*®

SPECIAL EDITION®

Published by Silhouette Books
**America's Publisher of Contemporary Romance**

If you purchased this book without a cover you should be aware
that this book is stolen property. It was reported as "unsold and
destroyed" to the publisher, and neither the author nor the
publisher has received any payment for this "stripped book."

This book is dedicated to two men who have blessed my life:
My lawyer, Frank R. Curtis—thanks for your support, for sharing your
brilliance, and especially for honoring me with your friendship.
Moses, you're one in a million.
Michael Barry Joyce, #23, fellow Irishman, gifted writer,
seasoned traveler, but more importantly, my friend, for more
than words can ever say.
Thanks Moses, thanks Michael, for proving the
Three Wise Men weren't the last.

 SILHOUETTE BOOKS

ISBN 0-373-24013-9

CHILD OF MIDNIGHT

Copyright © 1996 by Sharon De Vita

All rights reserved. Except for use in any review, the reproduction
or utilization of this work in whole or in part in any form by any
electronic, mechanical or other means, now known or hereafter
invented, including xerography, photocopying and recording, or in
any information storage or retrieval system, is forbidden without
the written permission of the editorial office, Silhouette Books,
300 East 42nd Street, New York, NY 10017 U.S.A.

All characters in this book have no existence outside the imagination of
the author and have no relation whatsoever to anyone bearing the same
name or names. They are not even distantly inspired by any individual
known or unknown to the author, and all incidents are pure invention.

This edition published by arrangement with Harlequin Books S.A.

® and TM are trademarks of Harlequin Books S.A., used under
license. Trademarks indicated with ® are registered in the United States
Patent and Trademark Office, the Canadian Trade Marks Office and in
other countries.

Printed in U.S.A.

**Books by Sharon De Vita**

Silhouette Special Edition

*Child of Midnight* #1013

Silhouette Romance

*Heavenly Match* #475
*Lady and the Legend* #498
*Kane and Mabel* #545
*Baby Makes Three* #573
*Sherlock's Home* #593
*Italian Knights* #610
*Sweet Adeline* #693

## SHARON DE VITA

is an award-winning author of numerous works of fiction and nonfiction. Her first novel won a national writing competition for Best Unpublished Romance Novel of 1985. This award-winning book, *Heavenly Match,* was subsequently published by Silhouette in 1986.

A frequent guest speaker and lecturer at conferences and seminars across the country, Sharon is currently an Adjunct Professor of Literature and Communications at a private college in the Midwest. With over one million copies of her novels in print, Sharon's professional credentials have earned her a place in *Who's Who in American Authors, Editors and Poets* as well as the *International Who's Who of Authors.* In 1987, Sharon was the proud recipient of the *Romantic Times* Lifetime Achievement Award for Excellence in Writing.

She currently makes her home in a small suburb of Chicago, with her two college-aged daughters, and her teenage son.

Hey Tyler;
I'm living with Alex now. It's
not so bad evin if she makes me
brush my teeth twice a day
and eat slimee green vegtubles.
If your gonna hang around you
better bring your toothbrush and
maybee a dog to eat the
vegtubles.

GABriel

# Chapter One

Police Lieutenant Michael Tyler decided he needed a strong drink and a willing woman, but not necessarily in that order. He'd gone far too long without either, he decided as he stared bleakly out the window.

It was three days before Christmas and he was in a foul mood. It wasn't so much the fact that he'd been denying himself two of life's pleasurable necessities as it was the fact that he *hated* Christmas.

And he hated Christmas carols.

Outside the police station, snow was falling like pennies from heaven, and he could hear the awful racket the Christmas carolers—kids—were making, screeching out sappy songs about joy and love and being home for Christmas.

Michael scowled. If the carolers were so intent on everyone being home for Christmas, why didn't they go *home* and leave him alone?

"Tyler!" Captain Philip Sims's growl was unmistakable, interrupting Michael's thoughts.

"Yo?" Michael dragged his gaze from the window, and swiveled around, propping his feet atop his cluttered desk. His six-foot-four frame was sprawled haphazardly in his chair, which produced an annoying squeak every time he moved. Absently, he arched his left leg, pressing the heel of his hand to his aching knee—a souvenir of a bullet he'd taken years ago. The bullet was gone, but the memory and the pain remained, especially when it was cold and damp, like tonight, or when he was tired, like tonight. Then it ached like crazy, certainly not improving his mood.

"Something you should know." Captain Philip Sims shifted his massive weight. He looked at Michael gravely. "Remember James Webster?"

Michael was thoughtful for a moment, his memory on search. Suddenly his scowl deepened and he slowly nodded in recognition.

"Yeah, I remember him. A real piece of work." Michael rubbed his aching knee, making his chair squeak. "Murder one. Killed a kid named Paco Ramirez. Got thirty-five to life, as I recall." Remembering the sentence, Michael almost smiled, pleased he'd had a part in it.

"Yeah, you recall fine, Tyler." Captain Sims sighed heavily, dragging a hand back and forth across his flattop. "But I thought you should know I just got word that his conviction's been overturned."

"What!" Michael's feet came off the desk. "What do you mean, the conviction's been overturned? We had him dead to rights." Michael's eyes darkened and his brows drew together. "We had an eyewitness. Someone who saw him kill that kid."

"I know, Tyler. I know." Captain Sims sighed wearily. "Webster's lawyer got the conviction overturned on a technicality." Shaking his head, Captain Sims frowned. "Damned exclusionary rule again. His lawyer took it all the way to the Supreme Court and they threw the whole case out because of it."

Michael slouched even lower in the chair, but his nonchalance was feigned—he was suddenly wound up tighter than a Slinky. His eyes narrowed suspiciously. There was more here than the captain was letting on. He had a feeling the other shoe was about to drop.

One dark eyebrow arched. "And?"

"And Webster's out." Sighing yet again, the captain rubbed his stomach, ignoring the fire that lit Michael's eyes. "They let him out on bail pending a new trial." Captain Sims glanced at his watch. "He got out about two hours ago."

Muttering a string of expletives, Michael surged to his feet, nearly knocking his chair over backward.

"They let that killer out?" Fury tightened his words.

James Webster was a criminal who disguised himself as a respectable businessman, when in reality he made his living pushing drugs to street kids, getting them hooked, then recruiting them to push for him. By that point the kids had no choice. Once hooked, it was work for Webster, or else. And in this case, the "or else" was not pleasant.

"Yes, they let him out." The captain shook his head sadly. "We've got to start the whole ball of wax all over again. Since it was your case I figured you should know." The captain started to leave, then stopped, turning back to Michael with a confused frown. "The eyewitness we had, he was a kid, wasn't he?"

Michael's stomach coiled and he nodded his head slowly. "Yeah. Gabriel Sanchez. An eight-year-old runaway." Dragging a hand across his tired eyes, Michael sighed deeply, remembering. "Gabriel was with Paco when he was killed. Paco had been pushing for Webster, but decided to get out. But first he decided he'd help himself to a little of Webster's profits as traveling money. Unfortunately, before Paco could take off, Webster realized what had happened." Eyes cold, Michael shrugged. "Paco and Gabriel were in the school playground counting the cash when Webster found them."

Scowling suddenly, Michael shook his head. "Webster never did his own dirty work, always had his goons do it for him. That's why we could never nail him. But not this time.

This time he wanted to do it himself, to make Paco an example in case anyone else in the neighborhood decided to help themselves to his cash." Lips pursed, Michael absently rubbed his aching knee. "He walked right up to Paco in broad daylight—in a school yard, for Pete's sake—then slid a knife right through the kid's heart."

Michael's lips tightened and he shook his head. "Damn kid never had a chance. He was dead before he hit the ground." Closing his eyes, Michael tried to get a handle on his emotions. The anger he would deal with later; he needed it now to keep the other, unwelcome feelings at bay.

"The Sanchez kid saw the whole thing." The captain's voice was unusually quiet.

"Yeah. He saw the whole thing." Anger nudged Michael's other emotions, making his eyes almost black. "Gabriel ID'd Webster within twenty-four hours and I convinced his social worker to let him testify. That's how we finally put Webster away."

Wearily, Michael leaned back in his chair and closed his eyes, letting his anger take hold. An image of Gabriel Sanchez flitted through his mind.

Tough, rough, devoid of emotion, Gabriel pretended to be fearless. He acted the part, complete with the arrogant swagger and lip-curling sneer that would have looked ridiculous on any other eight-year-old, except when you looked into Gabriel's eyes and saw the bleakness, you realized *this* eight-year-old had somehow earned that bleakness. Battle scars, Michael thought absently. Nothing but battle scars.

He'd never forgotten Gabriel Sanchez. The kid was wise and weary beyond his years. But it was the kid's eyes that had haunted Michael. Huge, dark and desolate, they were filled with a hopelessness that you'd have to be blind not to see. He'd seen it and remembered it. No, his mind corrected, *recognized* it because it was the same bleak hopelessness he'd seen in his own eyes at that age. He still saw it in his eyes at *this* age.

No one that young should be that desolate and defeated, he thought grimly. *No one.* But especially not an eight-year-old who hadn't even had a chance yet, simply because no one had cared enough to give him a chance.

By the time he'd met Gabriel, the kid had a litany of juvenile crimes behind him. He was a pint-size holy terror. A child of the streets, by eight he'd already learned that the world could be a pretty empty place if you didn't belong anywhere to anyone.

Michael sighed deeply. He knew the feeling; he'd felt the same way at that age. Perhaps that was why he remembered the Sanchez kid so well. Perhaps that was why the kid touched something deep inside him, something he never let anyone see, let alone touch or reach. Sanchez reminded him of himself.

Bitter bile rose in Michael's throat, but he angrily forced it back as he shifted his weight, trying to ease the ache in his knee as well as the silent ache in his empty heart. By eight, he, too, had learned how cruel the world could be. By twelve he'd accepted that he belonged nowhere to no one, and probably never would. By fifteen, he'd started making and breaking his own rules. At eighteen, he was headed on a fast track to big trouble—until fate intervened.

Sitting forward suddenly, Michael glanced at the man standing in the doorway of his office, wondering if the captain even knew how much he appreciated all that he'd done for him? He looked away, feeling self-conscious. Without Captain Philip Sims, Michael might have ended up a whole lot differently. He owed the captain big time. That thought came suddenly, as well as the realization that he'd probably never even voiced his appreciation. Soon, he thought. Maybe he'd be able to do it soon.

"Tyler?"

The captain waited for Michael's gaze to meet his. "With Webster out, that kind of puts the Sanchez kid behind the eight ball, don't you think?"

"What's your point, Captain?" Frustrated and suddenly furious at himself and the system that said if you played by the rules, good things would follow, Michael shoved his fists into the pockets of his jeans, fearing if he didn't he just might shove his fist through a wall. He'd never dealt with futility or frustration well, which was probably why he'd been on probation so many times.

Where were the good things the system promised Gabriel Sanchez? he wondered angrily. Where were all the good things little kids were supposed to have, *entitled* to have—like a home, a family, love, safety, security? Where were all those things for Gabriel?

Where the hell had all those things been for him?

Frustrated, Michael shifted his thoughts with a sigh, unwilling to meander down memory lane right now. He had more important things to think about. Like the Sanchez kid. And his own guilt.

*He'd* been the one to convince Gabriel to testify. *He'd* been the one to cajole and nearly blackmail Sanchez's caseworker into letting the kid testify, promising her that nothing would happen to him. He'd given her his word, and he'd never gone back on his word to anyone. *Ever.* One thing the captain had taught him was that a man—a real man—was only as good as his word. And he prided himself on making sure his word was as good as gold.

With Webster out, and Sanchez once again in danger, what did that make his word worth? Muttering an expletive, Michael dragged a hand across his face again, cursing Webster, the system and everything in between.

"Tyler." Captain Sims shifted his weight. "We're going to need the Sanchez kid to testify again, especially now that the murder weapon has been ruled inadmissible. Sanchez is all we've got." The captain shrugged. "Without him, there's no case." He paused to take a puff on his cigar. "Webster will walk if Sanchez doesn't testify." The captain's world-weary eyes were steady on Michael's, the message in them clear. "It would be nice if Sanchez was alive to do it." The captain's eyes continued to bore into him. "You get my drift, Tyler?"

"I get your drift, Captain." His voice was a combination of insolence, arrogance and bitterness. There were days he hated this job, and this was one of them.

"Handle it, Tyler. Pronto. We need that kid alive and well to testify. Find him."

Michael dug his fists deeper into his pockets. "Piece of cake, Captain."

"Right." The captain looked at him skeptically. "Just make sure you don't bite off more of this cake than you can chew, Tyler. Webster's desperate. That kid is all that's standing between him and life." Shrugging, the captain stuck his cigar in his mouth and bit down hard. "Who knows what Webster will do? You know how long it took us to nab him on something we could make stick. We've been after him for years."

"Yeah, yeah, I know." Years that Michael had personally waited for him to slip up so he could nab him. Now that he had, the system had once again screwed things up. Was it any wonder the system was such a mess and kids like Paco and Gabriel fell through the cracks?

"Just make sure you're careful." There was a bit of paternal worry in the captain's voice.

Michael's face was dour, although his eyes lit with a wicked gleam. "Now, Captain, why would I want to be careful?" And who cared if he wasn't, Michael wondered grimly as he watched the captain's retreating back.

Suddenly feeling very alone, Michael turned and scanned the street below, his gaze finally landing back on the children. They were still standing in the falling snow, singing their hearts out about love and joy and happiness. Just the sight of them annoyed him, reminding him that another kid was out there in the cold and snow, but this one, unlike the carolers, was in danger—grave danger. And it was all his fault. Michael shook his head. If anything happened to Gabriel he'd never forgive himself. He *had* to find that kid fast—before Webster did.

Michael swore softly. He didn't even know where the Sanchez kid was. After the trial, his caseworker had placed

him in a foster home. But where? Out of habit, and a real
strong sense of survival, Michael hadn't stuck around long
enough to find out.

With a sigh, he pulled one fist from his jeans, and withdrew a cigarette from the pocket of his shirt, fingering it.
He'd quit smoking years ago, but had gotten used to the
habit of keeping a pack in his pocket. In times of extreme
stress, like now, he simply slipped one out of the pack and
held it. An adult version of a pacifier, he thought in wry
amusement.

Never taking his eyes off the children caroling outside,
Michael absently fingered the unlit cigarette, trying not to
scowl. He really did not want to tangle with Gabriel's social worker again. Once was enough. But tangle with her he
would. He'd do whatever was necessary to protect Gabriel; and this time, nothing was going to screw things up.
Not even Ms. Alexandria Kent.

Absently, Michael shook his head, a hint of amusement
on his face. Now, Lord, if that name wasn't a mouthful.
And if she wasn't a sassy, stubborn handful.

Thinking of her, a flash of something resembling pain
settled in his gut, gnawing at him, but he forced himself to
ignore it because he knew he couldn't—wouldn't—deal
with it. Not now. Probably not ever. He couldn't deal with
the emotions Alexandria had brought to the surface, emotions he'd successfully kept buried for a lifetime.

Until he'd met *her*.

Narrowing his gaze, Michael continued to stare out the
window, not seeing the children anymore, but something—or rather *someone* else. His memory of her hadn't
dimmed one bit in two years. Michael sighed heavily.

The moment he'd laid eyes on Alexandria the only thing
he could think of was hopping into bed.

With her.

But it was more than just testosterone calling—much
more. There was something about her; not just a physical
awareness, but this unique emotional connection between
them, like there was some kind of invisible thread running

from him to her. He'd never felt it with anyone else before—especially a woman. It was the most unusual thing he'd ever experienced. He knew what she was thinking before she said a word; knew what she was feeling by merely looking into her eyes; knew what she was going to say a moment before the words popped out of her mouth. And he had the uncanny feeling she knew all the same things about him.

And it had scared the hell out of him.

Tension suddenly tore through Michael, and one hand balled into a fist. The unlit cigarette in his hand broke in half but he didn't notice. He hadn't seen Alexandria in two years. Not since the last night of the trial. He was no fool. He'd spent a lifetime learning when to advance and retreat, and he knew the moment the trial was over he had to retreat. Or surrender. The last wasn't an option, not for him. So he'd bolted without so much as a backward glance the moment he knew Webster was under wraps and Gabriel was safe. And he never looked back.

But it had all been in vain. Now, he had to start the whole damn process all over again. Michael's shoulders hunched wearily. He did not particularly want to see or deal with Alexandria again.

He just didn't trust himself with her. She was the kind of woman that burrowed under a man's skin and stayed there, making him lie awake sweating at night, which was why he'd deliberately walked away from her two years ago, and stayed away. He knew better than to play with fire; all it got you was burned. And Ms. Alexandria Kent was the kind of woman that could burn a man. Badly.

Shifting his weight, Michael sighed heavily. In spite of the connection between them, they were exact opposites in almost every way. She cared about everything and everyone. He cared about nothing and no one. She did everything by the book, while he'd never even opened *that* book—the one with all of life's rules and regulations. The one she studiously followed. They'd disagreed constantly from the moment they'd laid eyes on each other, and yet it hadn't diminished the awareness humming between them, nor did it do anything to lessen the emotional connection. If anything, all it did was increase the tension and the awareness, until his aching body and empty heart were nearly thrumming with it. And so he'd fled, certain he could run from her—and his feelings and emotions—and never have to look back.

Unfortunately, once again fate intervened.

As he scratched his stubbled chin thoughtfully, a deep frown creased Michael's brow. Like it or not, he was going to have to deal with Alexandria. And he was going to have to control his feelings and emotions. Piece of cake, he thought wryly, simply because he'd gotten so very good at it over the years. In fact, he'd been controlling his feelings and emotions for so long he could be considered an expert.

Michael's scowl deepened. He could control his emotions as long as he didn't see her, but he wasn't quite so confident he could control himself when she was in his line of vision, close enough to see, to touch, to *want*.

Muttering a string of curses, Michael tightened his fist. This was business, he reminded himself, and he'd keep it business. He'd gotten too involved with her once, and he was a man who never made the same mistake twice.

He'd do whatever he had to if it meant he'd be able to keep Gabriel safe in order to put Webster away for good, but he wasn't getting involved with Alexandria. His jaw clenched as his lips pursed. Not a chance.

Never again.

Michael continued to scowl at the singing children. Snow fell and blew around them, settling on their knit caps and scarfs. They didn't even have enough sense to come out of the cold. And where were their parents? he wondered furiously. It had to be close to ten below, with a blizzard on the way. Even *he* knew that wasn't any kind of weather for a kid to be out in, no matter how well they were bundled up.

Silently cursing stupid parents, Mother Nature, Christmas, and life in general, Michael leaned his forehead against the cold pane of glass and sighed wearily, feeling more alone than ever, and wondering why it was bothering him so much today. But he knew why: Christmas. His eyes slid closed for a moment. He just couldn't deal with it. Never had been able to deal with it. It brought back too many memories. Empty, lonely memories of a little boy left all alone in a world where everyone belonged somewhere to someone.

*Everyone except him.*

He banished those memories and took a slow, deep breath, trying to ease the ache in his empty heart. His breath frosted on the glass, then quickly evaporated. One of the children below spotted him and waved, nearly tumbling backward in her eagerness. His scowl deepened. She was so little that if she'd fallen backward, she would have been buried in snow. For a moment, he was tempted to go downstairs and haul her inside. She had no business being out on a night like this. It was too damn cold and treacherous for anyone, let alone a little bitty tyke who was nearly up to her eyeballs in snow. And where was her mother? Or father? Or someone who cared about her?

Smiling up at him, the child lifted one oversize mittened hand and waved again, her too-big glove flapping gaily in the breeze. She almost lost her balance again, making Michael swear under his breath. She was going to get frostbite if she didn't get out of the cold. He scowled. Why didn't someone take care of her, protect her? She wasn't big enough to be out there braving the elements by herself. She belonged indoors, wrapped in warm clothes sipping hot chocolate in front of a fireplace while someone read her a story. He had a good mind to charge outside and hustle the little tyke inside the warmth and safety of the station. But one look at him and the poor little thing would probably be scared to death. He couldn't help but think of another child out there, all alone, braving the elements, but there was no one to protect that child or take care of him.

Clenching his jaw, Michael turned away unable to watch the children any longer.

Yes there was.
He had to find Gabriel. Now.

The snow just kept coming.
She was cold and wet and if she didn't get her panty hose off soon—real soon—she was going to scream! Huddling deeper inside her coat, Alexandria locked her car door behind her, wearily shifting her purse to one arm and her briefcase to the other, urging her feet forward with the promise of freedom from her high heels. And her dreaded panty hose.

Exhausted, Alexandria looked longingly at her gaily lit second-floor condo hovering just in the distance. If she could make it across the street, through the doorway and up the stairs, she'd be home free.

Well, she'd be home anyhow, she amended with a delicate little frown, glancing both ways on the deserted street before crossing. She still had hours of paperwork ahead of her.

Looking up in the eerie darkness, Alexandria noted one of the streetlights was out again. It was still snowing heavily and a brisk gust of Lake Michigan wind caught some debris from the cluttered street, picking it up and sending it sailing through the air, causing her to shiver.

She was dead tired. Three days before Christmas and the agency was as busy as a department store running a half-price sale. Alexandria shook her head, wishing she had a free hand to brush away the limp, damp strands of blond hair clinging to her face. What happened to people at Christmas? she wondered with a weary sigh. It was supposed to be the most joyous of seasons, and yet some people acted as if they had been injected with a kind of ornery potion.

And unfortunately their children paid.

Blinking rapidly, she dislodged a snowflake that had settled on her lashes, then stepped up onto the curb, coaxing herself forward toward her brightly lit doorway, which stood like a welcoming beacon in the dark night.

Today the agency had ten new cases of abuse or neglect. Fifteen children had to be removed from their parental homes and placed in the agency's protective custody for their own safety. Alexandria shook her head sadly, causing her shoulder-length blond hair to sway in the brisk wind. It had to be something about Christmas, she thought, feeling sorry for people who couldn't just relax and enjoy the wonderful, innocent beauty of the season.

Absorbed in her thoughts, she didn't see him step out of the shadows. When his hand landed heavily on her shoulder, she screamed, whirling around and instinctively swinging her purse high in the air. She hadn't lived and worked in the city of Chicago for ten years without knowing how to take care of herself. Her purse caught him flush on the chin with enough force to send him arching backward.

"Damn!" Michael let out a yelp, clutching his face. He'd forgotten the lady could take care of herself. She might look like a fragile little thing, but she was strong as iron inside. "Are you crazy?" he demanded, his voice rising in the thin night air.

Alexandria's eyes widened in shock. That low, gravelly masculine voice was familiar. Too familiar. Taking a step closer in the shadowy darkness, she narrowed her gaze and her breath came out in a rush.

*Michael Tyler.*

His name whispered through her mind like a sad, haunting melody. Her heart tumbled over unexpectedly as her dazed gaze connected with his. Even after all this time, just the sight of him still had the power to take her breath away. He was the only man who'd ever been able to do that, and it still stunned and annoyed her. She couldn't have been more surprised if Santa Claus himself had shown up on her doorstep.

*Two years.*

She hadn't seen or heard from him in two years. Not one word. Two long, lonely years and she simply couldn't believe he was here now actually standing in front of her, bold as brass, as if it had been two hours instead of two years.

She didn't know whether to hug him or hit him.

Emotions swarmed over her, rocking her. They came so fast she couldn't control them, didn't even try. Relief came first—relief that he was safe and apparently well, judging by the looks of him. Anger quickly followed, simmering just below the surface. How dare he show up here after walking out on her without so much as a goodbye! The pain came last, and lingered. Pain that what they'd had and could have shared had meant so very little to him, he could simply walk away from her without even bothering to look back.

Gathering her dignity and her galloping emotions, she allowed her gaze to drink him in. He hadn't changed that much, she thought, letting her eyes do a quick, visual inventory. He still looked tough, rugged ... *dangerous*.

His blue black hair obviously hadn't had any kind of relationship with a barber in a good long time. It was shoulder length, and he still wore it slicked back in a ponytail that she was certain women found blatantly sexy. At the moment, she thought acidly, the only thing she'd like to find him was a barber with a very sharp pair of scissors.

She'd almost forgotten how tall he was—mammoth, she'd always thought; probably at least six feet ... something. She couldn't see that high without a stepladder. And he had a chiseled face that was far too craggy to be handsome, but she supposed some women found it fatally attractive. His mouth was full and lush, and looked unbearably soft. It was a mouth that had haunted her dreams when she thought of all the things that mouth was capable of doing to her.

It wasn't his face that got to her, but his eyes. Those sad, desolate eyes. Huge and heart-stopping blue, those eyes had haunted her, tugging at her tender heart and making her wonder what had caused such sadness, such desolation. But there was also something else there, an invisible steel veil that seemed permanently slammed shut so that nothing and no one could penetrate it.

Especially her.

During the time she had been forced to deal with Michael Tyler she had learned he was a man who guarded himself and his emotions as if everyone—including her—was a thief. And she'd just spent two long years doing penance for some unknown crime she hadn't even realized she'd committed.

"What the hell is wrong with you?" Michael demanded, rubbing his chin and gingerly testing his jaw to see if it still moved. It did—painfully.

"Me?" The disappointment she hadn't allowed herself to feel came quickly, followed by a quick bubble of anger. After her former husband's betrayal she never thought she'd be able to trust another man. But she had. Michael. She'd blindly given her trust, only to once again be betrayed. The realization only intensified her anger.

Taking another step closer, she momentarily forgot her weariness as she tipped her head back and glared up at him. "*Me!* What the heck are *you* doing sneaking around in the dark, preying on unsuspecting women?"

"Preying?" His voice rose to a level that matched hers and he stepped forward, still rubbing his aching chin. Their eyes met and held. The air between them suddenly crackled with shared memories and enough electricity to cause a power surge in three counties.

"Preying!" Michael bellowed, trying to dispel some of the tension that was suddenly tearing through him. He'd thought the chemistry between them would have dissipated with time.

It hadn't.

He thought he'd imagined the impact she had on him.

He hadn't.

And it only further blackened his mood.

"I'm a cop, remember?" Michael's voice rose in frustration. He wondered why the mere presence of this particular little spitfire had the ability to raise his blood pressure.

"I'm *supposed* to be sneaking around in the dark, preying on people," he growled, leaning down until he was nose to nose with her. *Mistake,* his mind screamed. He was too close to her. Far too close. He caught the soft, feminine scent of her. He'd forgotten how wonderful she smelled. Her scent seemed to swirl around him, ensnaring him, angering him. "Lady, I get *paid* to sneak around in the dark."

"Then you're overpaid...." Alexandria snapped, turning on her heel simply because having him so near made her incredibly nervous. No, she mentally corrected, scrupulously honest to the end. Being so close to him didn't make her nervous, it made her *aware,* far too aware—of his intense masculinity, and the unbearable feelings he'd always aroused in her. Intensely female feelings that she didn't have the faintest idea what to do with, especially now.

She didn't know how to respond to him, what to say to him. Words and logic seemed to have deserted her. Over the past two years, she'd spent hours and hours rehearsing what she'd say to him if he ever dared show his face again. The words had alternated between soft and tender, and fast and furious, yet now, she couldn't remember a single word, a single sentence. It was as if his mere presence had emptied her mind of any logical thought, and that irritated her.

She was not the kind of woman who allowed a man— *any* man—to make her behave like a blustering female idiot. She considered herself bright, intelligent and capable, certainly not the simpering kind of clingy woman who had to have a man, *any* man, to make her life complete.

She'd always thought her life *was* complete until two years ago, when the bold, brazen Michael Tyler had breezed into her life—no, she mentally corrected again—*bullied* his way into her life, making her realize for the first time just how lonely she'd been. It had been an utter shock. Michael had filled a gap she hadn't even known was there before she'd met him. Then he'd fled without a word or a backward glance, making her acutely aware of how empty her life was without him.

And she was still very angry about it.

Yet now, face-to-face with him, she realized in spite of time, she was still undeniably drawn to him and it didn't make her happy. Maybe it was because he was just so completely different from any man she'd ever encountered.

She'd devoted herself to her career and her charges, which didn't leave much time for a personal life. Her work was very important to her, so important, in fact, that for the past five years it had been her *whole* life. It gave her a feeling of importance, of being needed because she knew she was doing something good and worthwhile for so many kids.

But lately she had begun to wonder if there wasn't more to life than work. It wasn't that she wasn't interested in men, it was just that most of the men she met simply didn't interest her. They either bored or annoyed her.

In spite of her petite size, and perhaps because of her job and her no-nonsense attitude about it, men were generally intimidated by her. Men saw her as strong, determined and fiercely loyal to her charges, willing to take on anything and anyone to protect them, and protect them she did. For some reason her strength of purpose seemed to intimidate most men. Fools, for sure. But not Michael Tyler. He was neither a fool nor intimidated—by anything. Especially her. And she'd admired him for it, finding herself more and more fascinated.

The men she met were usually so caught up with what possessions they had, or how much money they had, they left her cold. When, she wondered, did it suddenly become important to measure a man's worth by his pocketbook? Evidently some time when she wasn't looking.

But money had never interested her. It wasn't the size of a man's bank account that was important, but the size of his heart. Although, if past experience was anything to go by, she wasn't entirely certain Lieutenant Michael Tyler had a heart.

He was like one of those many-faceted little cubes. She'd enjoyed probing and exploring him, had enjoyed the verbal sparring that left them both weak, weary and inexplicably exhilarated. They'd argued and they'd fought, and they had talked. Lord, how they'd talked. About everything and anything. There was something about him, despite the cold harshness, that made her want to talk to him, to confide in him, to trust him, to *reach him*.

She'd often wondered what it would take to get through to him. He'd buried his emotions between layers of resentment, then covered the whole mess up with a steel veil that nothing seemed to penetrate, which only made her want to try harder to penetrate that invisible barrier that held everyone at bay.

Looking at him now, shadowed in darkness, she realized his impact on her hadn't diminished with time. She'd never met a man who made her ache for his touch. And there were times when she'd wanted to touch *him* so badly that she feared she might have to hog-tie her hands, simply because Michael Tyler clearly had "untouchable" written all over him.

In some ways, he reminded her of one of her charges, the ones who had been pushed around and abused, and no longer trusted or cared about anything or anyone. Nothing could have touched or ensnared her heart more.

But Michael wasn't one of her charges, and she wasn't looking to get hurt again. He'd hurt her once; she'd never give him the opportunity again. She'd given him something she'd never given any other man: her complete trust. And he'd carelessly taken it, then abused it, using her merely for his own personal gains, then walking away from her without thought or explanation.

But she was smarter now.

Alexandria blinked in the shifting darkness.

She hoped.

Drawing a deep breath, Alexandria steeled her defenses and leveled her chin. She had no idea what Michael Tyler wanted this time, but she knew what he didn't want.

*Her.*

He'd made that abundantly clear.

She'd had no choice but to live with it. She was far too proud to chase him or call him. If he wanted her, he knew where to find her. But he hadn't until now.

Now, when she'd almost forgotten him and his sad eyes, he'd stepped out of the shadows and touched her, renewing all the old feelings of longing and wanting once again.

But she could resist him, *had* to resist him, for her own well-being and peace of mind. Besides, tonight she was simply too exhausted to go another round with him. Her defenses were depleted. She'd been giving so much to everyone else that she had nothing left to give to anyone—especially tonight.

Alexandria heaved a weary sigh. There were just some things a woman shouldn't have to do twice in her lifetime, and putting up with a renegade cop who looked like he belonged *behind* bars instead of in front of them was something *this* woman definitely was *not* going to do twice in her life.

At least not while she had a shred of sanity left.

Self-protective to the end, without a word, Alexandria turned away from him and continued toward her condo.

"Wait." Michael dropped his hand to her shoulder, leaning away from her just in case she started swinging again. His hand tightened and then he immediately loosened his hold. He'd forgotten how small she was; even in her heels she barely came up to his shoulder. But what she lacked in stature she made up for in spit and vinegar. She had a mouth that wouldn't quit and she didn't take guff from anyone, not even him. No wonder she was so good with kids. You'd have to be blind, deaf and dumb to try and take her on when she was trying to protect one of her charges, and protect them she did, Michael remembered, with a hint of fondness.

And she was one of the few people in the world who couldn't have cared less about his perpetually sullen mood. She just said her piece, spoke her mind—all of it—standing up to him, going toe to toe on whatever issue she was being righteously indignant about on that particular day. Michael almost smiled. He'd forgotten how much he'd come to enjoy their verbal bantering as each tried to outdo the other.

The little spitfire almost always left him in her dust.

Watching as she turned back to him, her eyes shooting sparks, he realized how much he'd missed her; and he'd never missed anyone in his life, simply because there'd never been anyone to miss. The thought would have scared the hell out of him had he paused to consider it. But he didn't. He had far more important things on his mind.

"Alex." His voice had dropped to a husky whisper that stopped her in her tracks. "I need to talk to you."

She narrowed her gaze on him, shivering a bit as the wind whipped about her stockinged legs. Absently she wondered if it was the cold, the wind, or him that was making her shiver. Instantly her defenses went up another notch. He was up to something.

"Lieutenant," she said coldly, using his title so that it sounded like an insult. "You may need to talk to me, but I can assure you I don't need to listen."

"Come on, Al," Michael coaxed, giving her shoulder a little squeeze. The snow fell faster, the wind seemed to pick up strength, blowing harder in the dark night. "Why don't we let bygones be bygones?"

One blond brow rose in the darkness. "Al?"

She'd forgotten his disgusting fondness for pet names, abbreviating hers, she was certain, simply to annoy her. Something she remembered he enjoyed doing—with relish.

"All right." He sighed. "Would you prefer Alex?"

"Actually, I'd prefer it if you leave." Her gaze boldly, defiantly met his.

The lady still had that sassy mouth, he thought, with an admiring shake of his dark head. The faint hint of a smile curled his lips. He had a feeling it was going to be an interesting few days.

Alex blinked, not certain she wasn't seeing a mirage. Lieutenant Michael Tyler had almost—*almost*—smiled! She couldn't ever remember Michael Tyler *almost* smiling before. It was one of the things that had bothered her about him. The man never smiled. Never. She couldn't help but wonder why, or what had caused an *almost* smile now. Whatever it was, she wished it would happen again because an *almost* smiling Michael Tyler was an amazing sight.

Tucking his chin against the blowing wind, Michael fisted his bare hand, then blew on it for warmth. She resisted the urge to scold him for not wearing gloves. The man had the sense of a five-year-old.

"I'd like to accommodate you and leave, but not tonight. Not a chance, Alexandria," he said, deliberately using her given name so as not to rile her any further. He needed her help and annoying her wasn't going to help. Not that the thought of annoying her didn't amuse and fascinate him. "Like I said, I need to talk to you." The clock was ticking, and the candle was burning at both ends. Webster was out there...somewhere. And so was little Gabriel Sanchez. He had to find the kid before Webster did. And in order to do that, he needed her help. And she *was* going to help him; she just didn't know it yet.

"Why?" One eyebrow rose and she stared at him suspiciously, wondering what kind of craziness he was trying to drag her into this time. "Why do you need to talk to me?" The last time he'd "talked" to her, he'd managed to convince her to let little Gabriel testify for him. Something she'd regretted to this day. She still wasn't certain she'd performed her duties as prescribed—which required she put a child's needs first—or if she'd merely been swept away by the charm of one renegade cop with sad eyes and some kind of inexplicable hold on her heart.

The lieutenant had conned, connived and convinced her into believing that having Gabriel testify was in everyone's best interests, although looking back on it now, she probably should have asked for a list of everyone, because as far as she could tell, "everyone" amounted to *him*.

But, she'd reluctantly had to admit his assurances that the child would be safe—he had given her his personal guarantee—had been good. In spite of her misgivings, in spite of the fact that the man took great pain and pleasure in doing things in any other but the prescribed way, there was something about the man that had made her believe and trust him.

Alex shook her head.

It must have been a lapse in sanity.

She had a feeling that Michael Tyler had merely used Gabriel to further his own goals, and had used *her* to get to Gabriel. She did not like being used.

Exasperated, Alex blew a damp wad of hair off her face and tried to stop shivering as she dropped her purse and briefcase to the ground, too tired and weary to hold them any longer. The snow wouldn't do much damage since she couldn't afford anything but imitation leather anyway. And she knew if she didn't stay and let him speak his piece, she wouldn't get any peace. She raised belligerent eyes to his.

"All right, Lieutenant. You have my undivided attention. Talk." She drew up the cuff of her coat and glanced at her watch. It had stopped running. Probably days ago, but she'd been far too busy to notice. "You have exactly five minutes. That's all the time I can spare." It was all the time she could afford to be in his company. She didn't trust herself with him longer than that. Besides, in five minutes she was going to collapse in a frozen, exhausted heap.

Michael rubbed his aching jaw. "You're generous, Alex, but I need more than five minutes." He held up his hand as she opened her mouth. "All right, all right. I'll talk fast. Do you remember Gabriel Sanchez?"

She hesitated, her eyes narrowing for a moment. Fear prickled at every nerve ending, but she desperately tried not to show it. Telling herself to relax, she took a deep breath, then cautiously met his dark gaze.

"Of course, I remember him. I remember all my charges." She looked at him suspiciously. "Why are you interested in Gabriel Sanchez all of a sudden?" Another skitter of fear rushed over her. "Or should I say again?"

"Well…" Michael hesitated, knowing how protective she was of her charges. She reminded him of a mother hen, hovering over all her wounded little chicks, making sure one and all were safe, well and protected. It was one of the things he liked about her. She might be a sassy, stubborn little spitfire, but she *really* cared, and there weren't many people in the world who did anymore.

"Do you…uh…remember you agreed to let Gabriel Sanchez testify for the state in that murder trial?"

"I remember, Lieutenant." She angled her chin and dug her gloved hands into her coat pockets for warmth. "Although, as I recall, I didn't have much choice in the matter. Seems to me you went over my head to my superiors, and mentioned something about obstruction-of-justice charges if I didn't." Her voice had grown just a bit icier at the memory. She didn't like being "handled," and Michael Tyler had tried every trick in the book to "handle" her, from his eschewed version of charm to gentle persuasion, to common sense, which surprised her, since she would have bet money that the man didn't have any sense, common or otherwise.

Michael glanced away, his gaze scanning the deserted street again. He scowled at the lavish display of Christmas lights that dotted the neighborhood. Some fool had actually wasted time stringing lights on all the bare-branched trees, making the entire block look like a Christmas postcard. It was a shame people didn't have better things to do with their time and money.

"Yeah, Alex, well, we all do what we gotta do." His face and voice were grim.

"And I suppose," she said acidly, "that's supposed to make sense to me?"

He was still staring at the Christmas lights and a vague, empty feeling seemed to blossom and grow inside him. Ignoring it, he stamped his feet on the ground for warmth and cursed softly at Mother Nature. It had to be close to ten below, with a windchill hovering at about forty below. If it kept snowing, things were going to be a real mess. Eighteen inches were predicted before morning.

"Yeah. Whatever." He swung his gaze back to hers and shifted his weight, turning the collar of his leather jacket up to prevent snow from sneaking down his back. "Look, Alex, I'm freezing my buns off here. Why don't we go inside and I'll explain the whole story to you."

"No!" The word came out with more force than she intended. Fear skittered along her nerves again. The last thing she wanted was Michael Tyler in her apartment. "My—my apartment's a mess," she lied, deliberately avoiding his gaze. He looked at her suspiciously. Knowing how meticulous she was about every area of her life, he had a hard time believing her apartment would be a mess.

Determination lifted her chin. "Just give me the abbreviated version of this story, Lieutenant."

"You know the guy Gabriel testified against?"

She looked confused for a moment. "You mean…" She searched her memory, frowning. "Webster. James Webster?" She'd never forgotten the man's name, even though she had deliberately tried to put him and the entire episode out of her mind.

"Yeah, that's him. Well, about three hours ago I found out that his conviction was overturned." He started talking fast at the look on her face. "His hotshot lawyers took it all the way to the Supreme Court and they won. Threw the case out on a technicality."

She looked at him curiously, studying the play of light and shadow on the chiseled angles of his face, wondering if he knew how appealing he looked. Or how much she'd missed him.

"And this news is supposed to be of interest to me?" she asked in confusion.

Michael glanced away again; looking into her eyes did something to him. "Yeah, well, it means we'll have to re-try the case."

"How nice for you." Her patience and her nerves strained, Alex grabbed up her bags and turned away from him, certain this had nothing to do with her. He caught her elbow, stopping her.

"Alex, wait... there's more." The softness of his voice stopped her. She couldn't ever remember him using that tone with her before. It almost sounded like a caress; the sound a lover would make during the intimacy of night when there was nothing in the world but him and her and an hour's worth of sultry memories.

Pushing the unbidden thought away, she sighed heavily. She couldn't turn to look at him, couldn't face those sad eyes, or the pull they had on her. Couldn't face what she was feeling, wanting, or needing. Not now, when her de-fenses were depleted and she had nothing left.

Drawing a deep breath, Alex forced herself to distance herself from him, and her own feelings. Lifting her gaze, she looked at her gaily lit apartment. It seemed to beckon to her, drawing her closer.

Just like Michael Tyler.

Alex swore softly—a luxury she rarely allowed herself. Gathering her wits, she took a deep breath, trying to con-centrate on her thoughts, and not on her feelings.

"Now why doesn't it surprise me that there's more?" she muttered into the spiraling breeze, but still she didn't turn to face him.

"Alex, since Webster's conviction was overturned, we're going to have to bring him to trial again." Michael's voice was soft, mixing with the sounds of the night. Slowly, she turned to look at him, her stomach coiling into a sick, tight knot. Her eyes carefully searched his.

"And?"

"And... well... Gabriel's going to have to testify." He hesitated. "Again." Michael met her gaze head-on, trying to ignore the impact her pale blue eyes had on him.

Stunned, Alex stared at him for a moment. Blue eyes warred with even bluer ones. His eyes, sad and sullen, seemed to be pleading for understanding. Hers were fierce, determined, not willing to give an inch. Not now. Not on this point. Not ever again.

Alex drew in a deep shaky breath, her personal feelings forgotten. The transition from woman to social worker came quickly, instinctively. This time he'd gone too far. Pushed her too far. She would never again live with the memory of putting a child in jeopardy, not even for sad, sullen eyes. And if this man even entertained the merest hint of a thought that she would, he was going to have to get some new thoughts. Quickly.

Digging deep for strength, she angled her chin, thrusting her fists deeper in her pockets to prevent herself from pushing one into his nose.

"No." The word was cold and clipped, leaving no room for argument. Michael Tyler had just crossed a line.

He swore under his breath. Snow swirled around them, enveloping them in a white winter land. The wind blew with gusto while they merely glared at each other.

"Come on, Alex," he coaxed. "Help me out here?"

"No." Her voice was sure, steady, and confident, laced with steel. It was a tone he had come to know very well and it annoyed the hell out of him.

Alex dragged her gaze from his, then turned on her heel, determined to forget this night, and especially this man and his absolutely, utterly ridiculous request. She'd put Gabriel in danger for him once. But never, ever again. No matter what he aroused in her.

"Alex, wait, you don't understand." He put a hand on her shoulder to halt her movement, unprepared when she whirled around to face him, shrugging off his hand. Her eyes were glinting with genuine fury.

"No, Lieutenant, *you* don't understand." Glaring, she tilted her head to look at him, blinking back tears of anger and utter frustration. "Do I look like a bozo to you?"

Absently, he scratched his eyebrow, trying not to grin. He pretended to stare at her as if he'd never seen her before. "Uh...no, Alex," he said in utter seriousness as he leaned closer, annoying her further. "If I recall, Bozo had red hair and a red nose." He cast a quick glance downward. "Much bigger shoes, too. Your hair's blond, not a wild red," he remarked seriously, "but I'll bet at the moment, your nose could give Bozo a run for his money." Absently, Michael lifted his finger and ran it down the length of her cold, red nose. She jerked her head away, stunned by her reaction to his touch, and furious. Furious that he still had the power to cause such a reaction in her. Even after two years.

"Cute," she snapped. "I'm dead on my feet and nearly frozen half to death and you're making jokes," she muttered, hiking the strap of her briefcase higher.

He caught her elbow with a bit more force, stopping her before she could storm away. He didn't know why but there was something about this starchy little lady that demanded he harass her. Maybe because it was the only way he could keep her at bay. But when he spoke this time his voice was soft, sincere.

"Alex, listen. I don't like this any better than you. I'm not real partial to putting anyone in danger, especially a little kid." He stared at a flake of snow that was stubbornly clinging to her long, dark lashes. His fingers itched to brush it away.

Her chin went up. "You could have fooled me, Lieutenant. And would you please release my arm?" Furious, she tried to jerk free of him, almost losing her balance and landing in the snow on her delicate rear end. A frustrated sigh lifted her slender shoulders. "I'm cold and exhausted, not to mention starving since I haven't had a morsel of food all day." It took the last of her energy, but she stubbornly angled her chin. "I'd like to go in now, and I'd prefer to do it without dragging a deranged detective with me." Her defiant eyes met his in the darkness. "Release me, please." Her gaze drifted to his bare hand, still holding on to her. She was tempted again to scold him for not wearing gloves, but thought better of it. She just kept staring at his hand holding her.

She'd forgotten that Michael Tyler had an annoying habit of manhandling her, but not in a forceful way; in a very male way that made her much more aware of him. Didn't the man have any idea what his touch did to her?

"Not yet, Alex. There's more." Michael held on to her, and she sighed in exasperation, struggling deep for patience, something she seemed to do regularly whenever he was around.

"Then get on with it, please." She glanced away from him. His touch seemed to be awakening emotions and feelings she wasn't up to dealing with at the moment; emotions and feelings she thought she'd successfully forgotten. One look at him, and she realized how wrong she'd been. Michael Tyler wasn't a man a woman forgot.

He glanced away from her, unwilling to respond to the messages her eyes, her body were sending him.

He needed to keep her at a distance for both their sakes.

Shifting his weight, he dug his other fist deeper into the pocket of his jeans for warmth and held on to her with the other, stalling for time and unwilling to let her go, unwilling to break the connection between them.

He knew when she heard the next little tidbit of news she was going to let him have it. And he'd rather be holding on to her arm than have it swinging in his direction, he assured himself, knowing it was a bold-faced lie. Taking a deep breath, Michael looked at her, his voice as grim as his face.

"Alex, Webster's out."

## Chapter Two

"**O**ut?" Not following his drift, Alex frowned in confusion, blinking in the swirling snow. "Lieutenant, what are you talking ab—"

"Out of prison, Alex," he clarified, watching the color drain from her face. Her eyes widened, and two twin spots of color rose high on her cheekbones. "Webster's out of prison."

"Oh, my God," she murmured, dropping her chin to her chest and feeling the last of her energy seep away. "Oh, my God," she said again.

Frowning, Michael laid a comforting hand on her shoulder. She'd begun to shake.

Her head suddenly reared up and her eyes blazed at him. "How could Webster get out of prison? He *murdered* someone," she cried. "How could you just let him out of prison?"

"I didn't let him out, Alex," he said bitterly. "If it were up to me, he'd rot there."

She looked up at him. The aching fear and sudden vulnerability in her face ate at the hole inside him.

"But you promised me if Gabriel testified, the man would never go free. That...that he'd be punished for what he did. That testifying would guarantee Gabriel's safety." She was babbling and she knew it. But she couldn't believe James Webster was free. The whole purpose in having Gabriel testify, in putting the child in jeopardy in the first place, was so that he would be completely safe from the man. Now she realized how futile it had all been. Dazed, Alex shook her head.

"Why on earth would they let him out of prison?"

Shrugging his massive shoulders, Michael watched her. Seeing the fear and accusations on her face caused another ache, knowing he had caused it. He'd never intended to let her or Gabriel down, would never have been so insistent on the kid testifying had he known this was going to happen.

As a cop, he always knew it was a possibility; the system stank, and no one knew it better than him. But until something better came along, the system was all they had to work with. He sighed heavily, his breath frosting rapidly in the cold air.

"Webster's lawyer got the case thrown out of court because of a technicality." He shrugged again. "He's been in the joint for two years, so they let him out on bail pending a new trial."

Eyes blazing, she glared at him as if he were personally responsible for opening the cell door. "That's the most ridiculous thing I've ever heard."

She was entitled to her anger, he figured, turning his head to check the street again. He didn't like her standing out here in the open, exposed. It made him nervous.

Watching him, Alex was suddenly suspicious. Narrowing her gaze, she glared up at him. "Lieutenant, is there more to this?" Forgetting herself, she took a step closer to him, her fury taking hold, banishing for a moment some of her fear. "Have you told me everything?"

He cleared his throat. "Uh . . . not exactly." He paused. Alex watched him carefully. His long, lean body was as tense as a cat ready to pounce. And why did he keep twisting his head, checking out the street as if he was looking for something or waiting for someone? It was making her nervous.

"How much more 'exactly' is there, Lieutenant?" she demanded. "And what kind of technicality allows a murderer to walk free?"

Suddenly Michael's narrowed gaze swept the vacant street again, searching, assessing. Trying to hide his sudden tension, he turned back to Alex. His eyes were so dark, so dangerous, she shivered, and it had nothing to do with the cold.

Michael's senses were screaming. He glanced up and down the street again. He'd feel better if she was in the protective safety of four walls. But he couldn't tell her that, or why—yet. So he'd simply have to improvise.

He moved so fast it was as if he'd been shot out of a cannon. Grabbing her elbow, he quickly hustled her across the street, nearly pulling her out of her shoes in his haste. "If we can't go up to your apartment, the least we can do is go inside the vestibule so we don't freeze to death." He yanked open the outer door of her building, and a gust of warm, welcome air buffeted them as he pulled her inside, then leaned against the closed door, taking a deep breath in relief before she had a chance to open her mouth.

"Al, I want you to listen to me." The tone of his voice stopped the heated words forming in her mouth. He laid his hands on her shoulders so she'd stay put. "The technicality Webster got out on is called the exclusionary rule."

"And I suppose," she snapped, glaring up at him, "that's supposed to make sense to me? I'm a social worker, Lieutenant, not a damn lawyer. You're going to have to explain that to me—in English," she clarified, lest he decided to be cute and use some other language.

"What it means, Al, is the cops confiscated evidence—in this case the murder weapon, Webster's knife—without a proper search warrant and the judge overturned the conviction because of it. He ruled we can't use the knife as evidence since it was obtained improperly. So we have to start the whole ball of wax all over again. Until then, Webster's a free man.'' She opened her mouth to say something—again—but he didn't give her a chance. He rushed on. ''It's a safe bet Webster's going to come after Gabriel because without the murder weapon, Gabriel's testimony is all that's standing between Webster and a life of freedom.'' His voice was low and deep, vibrating with an intense sense of urgency that had her shivering in fear again. ''So it makes sense for Webster to come after him.'' He looked at her carefully, noting how pale she was; she resembled a poor little rabbit stuck in the glare of someone's headlights. ''And I can't let that happen. I've got to find Gabriel before Webster does, and like it or not, you're going to have to help me.''

Alex just stared up at him, trying to comprehend all of this.

''You...you...'' Words failed her and she whacked him. Hard. ''How dare you put Gabriel in jeopardy again! How dare you!'' Tears of fury and frustration burned her eyes. This was the final straw in an already infuriating, exhausting day. ''Lieutenant, you promised! You gave me your word that Gabriel would never be in jeopardy if he testified.'' She shook her head as tears slid down her already damp cheeks.

''You lied to me, Lieutenant!'' she cried, her tears coming faster. ''You lied!'' She impotently whacked him on the chest again, but she had little strength left. Fear and exhaustion had sapped it. ''Don't you have even an ounce of decency or common sense?'' Her voice broke, and Michael realized that in spite of her facade of cool control, she was just as vulnerable as everyone else when she cared about something, especially when it came to her charges, although she tried very hard not to show it. Maybe he saw it because he knew a little bit about putting up barriers.

"He's just a little boy," she whispered. Her huge eyes, glittering with tears, met his. "How could you do this to him?" Her voice cracked. She was so cold and tired, so unhinged by Michael's sudden appearance—which, she realized now, had nothing to do with her but everything to do with her cooperation, again—she couldn't hold back the tears.

He'd done it to her again. She'd trusted him and he'd let her down. But this was worse. This wasn't personal, this was professional; and it wasn't just her heart that was at stake this time, but something far more important—Gabriel's life.

"Aw, damn," Michael said in disgust, balling his hands in his pockets in an effort to stop himself from reaching for her. He'd never touched her. Deliberately. He knew better; knew that if he touched her, he might never want to stop. He hated the weakness she brought out in him, the weakness that made him want, and need, and care, when he knew damn well he had no business wanting, needing or caring—especially about her.

Watching tears slide quietly down her already snow-dampened cheeks, he sighed in frustration. She wasn't nearly as tough as she thought, and seeing her standing here furious, crying, and looking more vulnerable than any woman had a right to look, filled his empty heart with the barest hint of tenderness. He suddenly realized that this fierce, spitting little tiger was really nothing but a tender little kitten after all. The thought thawed a bit more of the frost around his heart and he *almost* smiled.

"Don't cry," he ordered gruffly.

Ignoring her muttered protest, and knowing it was a mistake, he hauled her close, holding her against him. It was only his own guilt, he assured himself as he wrapped her tightly in his arms, allowing the soft warmth of her to engulf him. "Don't cry," he ordered again.

"I'm not crying," she lied, sniffling and pushing against his hard chest in an effort to free herself, mortally embarrassed that she *was* crying—all over him. She struggled to get free, but it did no good. He held her protectively in his arms until she sagged against him, too tired to do anything else.

"You lied to me," she repeated, her voice muffled against his chest. Lied in more ways than she cared to think about right now.

Michael shifted his weight because she was jamming her briefcase against his tender knee. And doing unbearable things to the rest of his aching body.

"You couldn't care less about Gabriel or anyone else." She sniffled, unaware how deeply her words cut him. "All you care about is getting your own way."

"That's not true, Alex," he said gently, wishing she knew just how much he cared; but it was a luxury he couldn't afford. "I've got a job to do, just like you, and I try to do it the best way I know how." He shrugged. "Sometimes even my best just isn't good enough." There was a hint of bitterness in his tone. Michael drew back, his gaze finding hers. The weariness in her face caused him to soften his words and his tone. She looked dead on her feet. "And I never lied to you, Alex. I told you the truth—at the time." He kept his arms around her, liking the way they fit together. Liking the way her feminine curves snuggled against him. Even through her coat, he could feel her softness, her warmth.

He'd almost forgotten how soft and warm a woman could be. Maybe because it had been a long, long time since he'd held a woman, at least in comfort. Usually, the only thing he was interested in was a quick tumble, and comfort was the last thing on his mind.

But he'd known instinctively Alex wasn't the kind of woman who was interested in a quick tumble. No, she was the type who wanted everything. Or nothing. Which was why she was so dangerous to him, and why he'd fled two years ago. He didn't have room in his life or his heart for this kind of woman—the kind who could touch his emotions and wind him into a tight knot of feelings. He knew what he was capable of and with whom, and he kept to what he knew. It was a lot safer that way.

"I'd never lie to anyone about anything," he finally said quietly, resisting the urge to lay his chin on the top of her silky head and just rest. "Especially a kid. I had no idea Webster was going to get out on a damn technicality." He ran a hand up her back, aching to run it over other, softer places. "Cold?"

Unconsciously, Alex shivered against him, wondering how it was possible to be so cold and yet so very, very warm at the same time. It was a warmth that made her legs weak and her body tremble.

Mistaking her trembling, Michael unzipped his leather jacket, then drew her closer, tucking her into it, once again wrapping his arms around her and drawing her close, encircling her with his warmth. The cold butt of his gun nudged against her rib cage, but she ignored it, too cold and grateful for his warmth and his arms to care.

Alex tilted her head to say something, suddenly realizing just how near he was. Words deserted her. The lean hardness of his hips pressed against her. Even through her coat she could feel the heat and power of him; the unleashed energy. Undeniably it drew her, causing her heart to beat wickedly beneath her breast.

She could feel every hard masculine inch of him, and an unbearable wanting seemed to coil deep within her. Trying to dispel the feeling, she took a deep breath, glancing at his face, her eyes finally settling on his mouth. She wondered what those soft, full lips would feel like on hers. It was something she'd wondered about for two years.

During the course of the months they'd been thrown together, he had hugged her affectionately, ruffled her hair playfully, and chucked her under the chin maddeningly, but never once had he touched her in the way a man touched a woman, in the way she wanted him to touch her.

And she'd always wondered why.

Occasionally, she'd catch him watching her intently, and then his slow, lazy gaze would drift to her mouth and she'd wondered—hoped he was going to kiss her. But he never did. Then she'd get so flustered she'd chew her lower lip to keep from leaning close and pressing her mouth to his, not knowing what his reaction would be.

Deliberately channeling her thoughts in another direction, Alex sighed wearily, realizing that was then, and this was now. Now, two years had passed and there was nothing between them except anger and mistrust. And lies. So many lies. It made her heart ache. For her. For him. And especially for Gabriel. She sniffled loudly, swiping her nose with her gloved hand.

"You're a cop, Lieutenant, you should have known this stupid technicality thing could happen." He should have known and let *her* know. It might have made a difference in her decision. But she'd trusted him with her heart and Gabriel's life and safety. It was a mistake she *would not* make again.

"Cops don't know everything, kid." She stiffened against him and he knew she was probably furious that he'd called her a kid. It was the only way he could think of to put some much-needed distance between them.

He shouldn't have taken her in his arms. He knew now it had been a mistake. But he'd wondered for two years how she would feel. Now he knew. They fit together perfectly. The moment he'd pulled her against him, he heard something inside click into place. It was as if two puzzle pieces had finally fit together, each in the right place. He tried not to think about it as her softness snuggled against him, nestling and nudging all the right male places, making his blood turn heavy and thick.

Deliberately, Michael shifted his weight, annoyed at himself. He couldn't let her get to him. Not again. And touching her sure as hell wasn't helping. He'd almost allowed her to get too close once, and couldn't afford to make that mistake again. He couldn't let *anyone* get to him. He'd learned a long, long time ago that there was no point standing in front of a bakery gawking when you knew you couldn't eat the sweets. And so he'd learned over the years to do without and live without all the things others took for granted.

*Love.*

*Affection.*

*Attention.*

*A sense of belonging somewhere to someone.*

Simple things. Everyday things. Things every human being had. Except him. He'd trained himself not to need anything, and had succeeded, until two years ago when he ran full tilt into a pint-size spitfire with more grit and guts than any one woman deserved to have. A woman, he was beginning to realize, that was far more dangerous than any of the cons he'd ever had to deal with.

He sighed wearily. "Listen, Al. If I'd had any idea they'd let Webster out, I never would have insisted Gabriel testify against him."

"But you did," she sniffled, stepping out of his arms, trying to stop the needs and desires sweeping over her. "And now Gabriel's in danger again." She wished she'd never allowed Gabriel to become involved with him to begin with. "This is all your fault," she accused with another sniff.

Michael heaved another sigh. "Yeah, kid, I know." It was the tone of his voice more than the words that made her realize something had pierced the veil that guarded his emotions. She could see the faint glimmer of grief in his eyes; it passed quickly, but not so quickly she didn't notice. Instantly remorseful, she realized she'd hurt him with her accusation.

"I'm sorry," she whispered softly, curling her gloved hands against his broad chest to stop their trembling. "It's just...just...I feel so helpless. So...responsible."

"Yeah, tell me about it," he said in disgust. He wanted to tell her for her own sake, that she'd better learn not to care so much—about everything and everyone—because it was a sure trip to heartache. But he had a feeling it wouldn't do any good. She was a born caretaker, a woman who didn't know how to do anything else but care about everything and everyone. But who took care of her? he wondered grimly. Hell, she needed his protection, if only from herself.

"I feel responsible, too," he admitted, instantly regretting the fact that he'd allowed her even that much. He didn't discuss feelings—his or anyone else's. Ever. With anyone. Or he hadn't until he'd met her. Maybe that was why she scared him so much. She had the power to get to him in ways no one else—especially a woman—ever had.

Michael shook his head, wondering if the snow and the cold had frozen his brain. "Regrets and recriminations aren't going to amount to a hill of beans right now."

"I know," she agreed wearily, rubbing her gloved hands together.

"So, Alex, I'm sure you understand why you're just going to have to tell me where Gabriel is."

She stiffened, then lifted her head. Slowly, very slowly, she licked her cold lips. Unconsciously, Michael watched the movement, wondering what she'd taste like, suddenly craving a kiss the way a thirsty man craved a drink.

"Lieutenant," she began slowly, matching his determined stare. "I have no intention of telling you where Gabriel is." He wasn't going to do this to her again. He'd used her once for his own selfish gains. She'd never let him do it again!

Michael swore under his breath. He should have known she was going to be her usual stubborn self.

"Alex, look, you've got no choice here. At the moment, I'm all that kid's got."

"I don't find that very comforting," she said with a frown. He ignored the insult, more intent on getting her cooperation.

"Comforting or not, Alex, you don't really have a choice. You *have* to tell me where to find the kid before Webster does. And we don't have a whole helluva lot of time, either."

His words caused a frisson of fear to skate over her and she shivered.

"Lieutenant," she continued slowly, her mind spinning. Logic overtook her emotions, suddenly making her clearheaded. "If you don't know where Gabriel is, what makes you think this Webster character does?" Gathering steam, she went on. "He's been in prison for the past two years. It's very unlikely he'll know where to find him." She realized a man like Webster would probably make it his business to know where to find someone who could put him away for life, but she was banking on the fact that two years might have put a dent in his memory.

"*How*, Alex," Michael corrected, realizing logic wasn't the way to go, either. "Webster doesn't have to know *where* to find Gabriel, all he has to know is *how* to find him. And I guarantee he'll remember the kid whose testimony put him away once and can very well do it again."

She groaned, clearly not understanding. "Back up a minute. What do you mean, *how?*"

Wearily, he ran a hand over his face. His skin was still tingling from the cold. "Alex, men like Webster don't do their own dirty work. It's a matter of public record that you were Gabriel's caseworker. You were in court every day. It shouldn't be too hard for him to find you."

Her eyes widened and her nerves felt as if someone had just touched her with a live wire. She tried to stop trembling, but simply couldn't manage it.

"Are you saying you think this Webster character will come after *me* to get to Gabriel?"

"You're the only one who knows where the kid was placed." Michael shrugged. "It's the most logical thing to do." He shrugged again, realizing he was scaring her, but if that was the only way to get her to cooperate, so be it. Better he scare her, than Webster or his goons. The mere thought caused his determination to rise. "It's what I'd do."

"If you're trying to comfort me, you're failing miserably." Unable to deal with the enormous and suddenly frightening possibilities, Alex closed her eyes, trying to absorb everything he'd told her. Her emotions were as tangled as a cat's ball of string. Finally, she opened her eyes and lifted her gaze to his. Her eyes were wide with fear and he silently cursed himself for scaring her, regardless of the reasons.

"Are you trying to tell me," she began softly, "that a murderer is after *me?*"

"Not trying to tell you, Alex. I just did."

"That's what you meant by how, right?" she asked dismally, and he nodded, hoping now that she knew the seriousness of the situation, she'd cooperate. Then again, knowing her, probably not.

"That's right," he said.

In spite of herself, she wished she were still wrapped in his arms if only for a moment. He was strong and steady, radiating heat, calm and confidence and right now she could use a little dose of each just until she gathered and recharged her resources.

"I'm the key then," she whispered softly. "If Webster finds me, he thinks I'll tell him where Gabriel is?" Her eyes searched his. "Right?"

He nodded slowly. "Bingo, Alex."

"Wrong! I'd never tell him anything, let alone where Gabriel is." Michael's heavy, frustrated sigh caused her to rush on, unwilling to listen to another sermon. "So what you're telling me, Lieutenant, is that Gabriel and I are both in danger from this lunatic?" Her worried gaze searched his.

Amusement lit his eyes. "Now don't panic, Alex, I've got the situation handled."

"Oh, Lord," she muttered, letting her head drop to the broad expanse of his chest. "I'm not certain I've got enough strength left to deal with your version of 'handling,' Lieutenant."

"Come on," he teased. "It's not that bad. I figured I'd just take you into protective custody." But who, he wondered suddenly, was going to protect him from her?

"Protective custody?" Her head came up and annoyance darkened her eyes. "In your dreams, Lieutenant. I can't just up and walk away from my life, my job and my responsibilities. It's three days before Christmas and—''

"What the hell does Christmas have to do with anything?" he thundered, his face darkening.

"Everything!" she shouted back. "Don't you like Christmas?" she asked incredulously.

"I *hate* Christmas," he said with more emphasis than necessary. "And crime doesn't stop just because of a stupid holiday. Lady, do you think we could get our priorities in order here? You're in danger and all you're worrying about is a damn holiday?''

"Don't swear at me." Her fists balled at his chest, and her eyes darkened as she met his angry gaze. "Do *not* swear at me!"

Shaking his head in supreme aggravation, and swallowing the hot words that burned his tongue and would surely burn her ears, he sighed. "All right, all right." He expelled a weary breath. "Arguing isn't going to get us anywhere."

"Neither is swearing," she retorted, finding it necessary to make her point.

"All right!" His eyes had grown hard. He was done pussyfooting around; she had to know how dangerous the situation was and how determined he was. She and Gabriel were in danger because of him, and now he was responsible for seeing to their safety and he took his responsibility seriously.

"Alex, you're just going to have to bite the bullet, forget your reservations and tell me where Gabriel is. *Right now*. And close your mouth," he ordered, tapping her gently under her chin to help her out. "And then—like it or not—I'm taking you into protective custody. Although with your mouth and disposition you just might give Webster and his men a run for their money." He glanced down at her, waiting until her gaze met his. "You got it, Alex?" Nothing—nothing was going to happen to her or Gabriel as long as there was a breath left in his battle-weary body. He'd protect her whether she wanted him to or not. She didn't have a choice in the matter, and the sooner she realized it, the sooner he could get back to doing his job.

"I got it, Lieutenant." Furious about his heavy-handed behavior, not to mention the seriousness of the situation and the thought of being forced into his "custody," Alex didn't even bother to try and bank down the fiery embers of her temper. Giving it free rein, she poked his chest with one long, gloved finger.

"Now you get this, Lieutenant. How dare you order me around! Who do you think you are?" Eyes blazing, she poked his chest again, nearly spearing his flesh with her nail. "For your information I have managed to take care of myself and survive for almost thirty-one years and I can assure you I can continue to do so on my own." She inhaled deeply, trying to bank the flare of temper his words ignited. Too late. She was furious and tired and decided to let it loose.

"I have no intention of allowing you or anyone else to take me into custody for some supposed or imagined danger. Not even for my own protection. Nor do I have any intention of telling you or anyone else where Gabriel is. So you can just forget it!" Her voice rose, echoing loudly through the silent hallway. Not caring that she was probably giving her nosy neighbors the best entertainment they'd had all year, Alex blazed on. "You promised me Gabriel would be safe the last time, and look what happened. I made the mistake of trusting you once, and I never make the same mistake twice."

With his own temper simmering, Michael swore softly. This woman was deliberately trying his patience, and patience was not something he was known for.

"It's not supposed or imagined danger, Alex," he countered wearily, trying without success to keep the sarcasm out of his voice. "The danger is real. Very real. To both you and Gabriel. Pride and stubbornness can only take you so far. And I guarantee you that Webster won't be nearly as polite as I've been, trying to find out where Gabriel is."

"This is your version of polite?" she snapped, trying to ignore the thread of terror his words had caused.

He glanced out the glass door at the dark, vacant street, scowling once again at the Christmas lights blinking in the darkness. Didn't people have better things to spend their money on? he wondered grimly, irritated more than he thought possible. Waste of perfectly good electricity.

His gaze swept the street again. His eyes were quick, thorough, searching, and assessing. For some reason the hair on the back of his neck was standing up, and he was on edge. He felt uneasy, and he didn't know why. But after twenty years as a cop, he knew well enough to heed his instincts.

Trying to hide his sudden tension, he turned back to Alex, ignoring the look of hurt in her eyes. He knew the trust she was talking about wasn't just about Gabriel, but he couldn't deal with it. Couldn't let her know how much she'd affected him. He had to keep this, and her, strictly business. For both their sakes. He'd never asked her to trust him, so why did she? And why did he feel responsible? Why did the look of hurt in her eyes bother him?

"Look, Alex, I know you have no reason to trust me, but you're just going to have to." His voice was gruff. "I promise if you tell me where Gabriel is, nothing will happen to him. I'll make sure he's protected until Webster is safely behind bars again." He didn't like the stubborn light in her eyes, or the angle of her chin. Nor did he like her words when she finally spoke.

"You've already made and broken that promise, Lieutenant, and we have nothing further to discuss. I have no intention of allowing Gabriel to testify again, so he's really in no danger." She held up her hand to stop his words, certain he could see the logic and reason of her argument. If he couldn't, it wasn't her problem.

"Nor am I telling you or anyone else where Gabriel is. I guarantee you he's someplace safe, with people who love him." She took a deep breath to calm herself. "Webster will never be able to find him. And neither will you. Gabriel's been adopted and his name is no longer even Sanchez. I will personally guarantee that neither you nor Webster will ever be able to discover where he's at. We have nothing further to discuss. Case closed. Good night." She turned on her heel and hurried up the steps before he could stop her.

"Alex, wait!" Michael watched her retreating back muttering a string of long, hot curses about stubborn, cantankerous women. He was just about to head up the steps after her when he heard her loud, bloodcurdling scream.

## Chapter Three

"Stay put," Michael whispered, shoving her behind him and shielding her with his big body. He had one hand on her, the other on his drawn gun. His senses were on red alert, his face grim, his body tight, poised for anything. When he'd heard her scream, everything inside him had stilled.

"Just where do you think I'd go?" she whispered back, her voice filled with a combination of fear and fury.

Fear because she hadn't taken him seriously. Fury that he'd put her and Gabriel in jeopardy. Again. If he hadn't gone over her head to her superiors, if he hadn't insisted Gabriel testify in the first place, none of this would have happened. She'd thought he was dramatizing the situation just to con her into telling him where Gabriel was. Now she knew differently. And she couldn't help but feel a little angry at herself for not taking him seriously.

Looking at her wide-open apartment door, Alex's eyes slid closed and she swayed, her knees nearly buckling when she thought about what could have happened had she been there alone when her apartment had been broken into. An involuntary shudder racked her slender body and she inched closer to him.

Thank goodness she had worked late, and that Michael had detained her, or she could have been just as broken as the lock hanging haphazardly from her door. The thought made her stomach curl into a hard little ball of fear.

Clutching the back of his jacket more tightly in her fist, Alex tried to peek around him and into her apartment. He nudged her back behind him, then sighed heavily.

"Alex, do me a favor," he murmured out of the side of his mouth. His eyes never strayed from the open apartment door. Adrenaline was surging through him. "Just this once, do as you're told. Stay here, and stay still. A little quiet right now wouldn't hurt, either." He didn't want to have to fight with her and whoever might be waiting for him inside her apartment. There was only so much a man could take.

She nodded, clamping her teeth tightly together to prevent herself from telling him exactly what she thought of his high-handed orders. But at the moment, she was too frightened and grateful he was there. She'd yell at him later.

Michael's eyes swept the brightly lit hallway, quickly taking everything in. The door to her apartment had been jimmied, then left wide open. Obviously she'd had impatient, unexpected visitors. But what were they looking for? They surely wouldn't have broken into her apartment to get to her. No one could be that stupid. Had she been home, by the time it took them to jimmy the lock open, she would have been screaming the house down for the cops. Or her neighbors at the very least. They had to know that, and they wouldn't risk wanting to be seen or caught. These guys were pros, and they certainly weren't stupid—they played for keeps.

So what was the point?

Michael's eyes narrowed as his mind whirled, trying to make sense of this. It would have been much easier to just snatch her on her way to or from work. Or taking the garbage out. Or, as she was going to her car one morning or evening. The thought caused a string of soft curses to slip unheeded through his lips. Knowing how stubborn she was, he could just imagine how she'd react if someone tried to grab her. With her mouth and temper, he had no doubt she'd fight like a tiger, and like it or not, she was bound to find herself in over her head. Way over her head. These guys played hardball, and wouldn't hesitate to use whatever means necessary to get what they wanted. Now, if he could just get *her* to understand that, they just might have a chance.

Feeling an extreme bout of uneasiness, Michael glanced around again. They wouldn't have broken into her apartment unless they were looking for something. But what? Michael shook his head. He didn't know, but he was going to find out.

The moment he'd heard her scream, he'd nearly broken his legs racing up the stairs. With his gun already drawn, he'd taken the steps three at a time and found her standing stock-still, staring wide-eyed at her apartment door. Her briefcase and purse lay on the floor, carelessly dropped in her fright. Relief that she was safe flooded through him, almost weakening his knees. He tried to stay objective, professional, but inside he was seething.

The sight of her looking so ashen and terrified had made his insides coil. He'd almost dragged her to him them, but common sense and training prevailed. He had to keep this on a strictly professional level. He couldn't let his emotions interfere with his judgment. Especially now. His jaw clenched. But he hoped for their sake that whoever had broken into her apartment had the good sense to be gone, because if they weren't, he was going to make them sorry they were ever born.

So much for his objectivity, Michael thought in disgust.

"Stay put," he whispered again. "I'm going in."

"Alone?" Softly, her voice edged upward in panic and she clutched his jacket tighter, not certain which frightened her more—the fact that he was going to leave her alone, or the fact that he was going to venture into her apartment alone. She suddenly felt protective of him and clutched the back of his jacket even tighter, wanting to hold on to him to keep him safe.

"Yes, alone," he whispered, wondering why that one word almost made him smile. "I'm a cop, remember?" He turned his head to glance at her, not liking the look on her face. Her eyes were huge and wary, her face nearly devoid of color, except for those two twin spots high on her cheeks. He'd seen that look before and knew she was probably in a bit of shock, not to mention scared out of her mind. But naturally she was too proud to admit it. But the tightness with which she held him said more than words ever could. He cursed himself again for getting her into this mess. And cursed whoever had caused it. Why hadn't she listened to him? Stubbornness was one thing, stupidity was another. He'd deal with that and her... later.

"Please, don't do anything foolish." Clutching his jacket, her knees shaking, Alex moved closer to him, not certain if it was for his comfort or hers. She only knew that the closer he was, the safer she felt.

"Only foolish people do foolish things," he muttered, noting the way she'd moved toward him. He wasn't accustomed to having anyone console, comfort or worry about him. It was a bit startling, but nice, he decided. Real nice. For a brief moment, he felt a stirring of something deep inside him. Then he remembered it was her job; she was a professional comforter to all of life's strays. It didn't mean a thing, and he sure wasn't anyone's damn stray. Especially hers.

Annoyed at himself and his thoughts, Michael quickly surveyed the empty, well-lit hallway again. Nothing had moved or stirred since he'd bounded up the stairs. If anyone had heard her scream, they weren't letting on. All the doors around him remained closed and locked. He'd speak to the neighbors after he checked out her apartment.

"Don't move," he whispered, turning to her and lifting a finger to his lips to make sure she stayed silent. No sense announcing his arrival if someone was still inside. Surprise was his biggest weapon.

Michael's senses went into overdrive and his fingers tightened on his gun. Suddenly he grew so still, she wasn't even certain he was still breathing. Quietly, carefully, he stepped into the apartment. His stomach knotted with tension and he felt sweat bead on his forehead. It was simply a physical reaction to danger. He'd gotten used to it years ago. Silently, quickly, he kept moving, his gun poised, his stance ready, his ears open.

Whoever had been here apparently wasn't interested in anything of value. Nothing looked missing or out of place, he realized as he visually appraised the apartment. Slowly, he moved from room to room, making no sound. The entire apartment was neat as a pin, except for the jimmied door. They hadn't touched anything. For a moment, Michael stood still, listening, his mind whirling, trying to make sense of this.

What had they accomplished by breaking into her apartment when she wasn't even home? Perhaps they were merely trying to give her a message—a very frightening one.

But why would they announce their intentions?

Michael shook his head. This didn't make sense. Not at all. He'd have to sit down and figure this out—later. Right now he wanted Alex out of here and somewhere safe, just in case they decided to come back and pay her another visit.

After inspecting every room, closet and crevice—twice—Michael let out an uneasy breath. Whoever had been here was long gone. It was clear they'd made a thorough search of the apartment, yet it appeared that they'd not taken anything, at least nothing that he could see. He wouldn't know for sure until he had Alex take a closer look.

As he headed into the living room again, something stopped him in his tracks. He glanced around the spaciously neat living room with a frown. This was her idea of a mess? His gaze swept the room again and his frown deepened. Obviously she had some other reason for not wanting him in her apartment, but what? He'd been in her

apartment before. Two years ago, the first time he'd come
to see her about Gabriel testifying. So what was the big
deal? He didn't know, but it suddenly intrigued him and he
went through the apartment again, looking at everything
carefully. His brows drew together in a troubled frown as
he circled back to the expansive living room. Something
was definitely out of sync.

This room—as well as the entire apartment—was not
only spotless, it looked like a damn department-store display window. A huge advertisement for Christmas, he
thought with a scowl. There was a huge, elaborately decorated Christmas tree occupying one corner of the room.
Under it was a mound of presents wrapped in beautiful gold
and silver foil paper, each topped by a brilliant, matching
bow. Over the mantel of the fireplace, a garland hung,
dotted with gold and silver and strung with tiny, twinkling
Christmas lights.

He swiveled his head around, taking everything in. Every
nook, every cranny, every available space had some sort of
holiday decoration. A small manger was set up under the
tree, and around it was a toy electrical train that looked to
be a genuine antique.

Annoyed, Michael shook his head. Apparently this
woman took Christmas *seriously*. No wonder she was so
determined to not go anywhere three days before the happy
event. He scowled at the thought, then glanced around the
room again.

He made a mental note to ask her about all the decorations. They would have made Santa himself envious. He'd
ask her about it later. Once he got her safely out of here.
And once he found out the real reason she didn't want him
up here. His lips pursed in annoyance. Alex had lied to him,
and he did not like to be lied to.

He swiveled his head around again, taking everything in,
certain he was missing something. But what? He didn't
know and that bugged him. He prided himself on his instincts and his instincts were telling him there was more to
all of this than met the eye.

Something was definitely going on with her, and he damn well was going to find out.

"Is it safe?" Alex whispered, looking up at him as he holstered his gun and strode toward the doorway. Standing ramrod straight, she was absolutely still and stricken, but there was something in the depths of her eyes, something he almost didn't recognize because he'd rarely seen it. Then it hit him.

*Trust.*

He almost stopped in his tracks, stunned beyond comprehension. Damn! She *trusted* him. The thought shocked and almost humbled him. Considering the circumstances, considering what had happened between them in the past, she had absolutely no reason to trust him. But unless he was reading her wrong, she did, whether she realized it or not. And he found it touched something deep inside him, turning his anger at her to ashes.

Humbled, Michael realized he wanted—no, needed—her trust. A flitting moment of sweet satisfaction filtered through him, warming him and nudging aside the coldness inside. It suddenly mattered what this fiercely proud, unbearably stubborn woman thought of him.

It mattered.

A lot.

He couldn't remember the last time anyone had looked at him the way she was looking at him. Nor could he remember ever feeling the way he felt at this moment. But he knew *this* moment he'd remember. An invisible smile curled around his guarded heart, thawing it a bit more.

"It's safe," he said quietly, bending to pick up her purse and briefcase. "Whoever was here is long gone. Come on in, but don't touch anything." He ushered her into the apartment, staying close because she was still trembling but from fear now, not from the cold. He leaned her bags against the wall. "I want you to have a look around. I'll need to know what's missing."

Alex nodded, but didn't move. She just kept looking at him with those wide, scared eyes. His arms ached to hold her, to drag her close until the fear was replaced by passion, but he didn't. With supreme control he restrained himself.

Flustered, Alex finally shifted her gaze, letting it sweep over her home as if seeing it for the first time.

Michael watched her carefully. He'd worked robbery long enough, years ago, to know and understand what she was feeling. Finally, she lifted her hesitant gaze to his.

"I...I...just feel so..." Her voice trailed off. She couldn't put into words what she was feeling.

"Violated?"

Biting her lower lip, she nodded.

"It's natural." All cop now, his voice was soft and soothing. She needed his professional experience in order to get through this. And maybe, so did he. "Someone's invaded your territory without your permission. Gone through your things, invited themselves into your life as if they had the right." He was quiet for a moment, trying to bank down his personal feelings and keep things professional. "It will pass, Alex, I promise." But not for a while, he knew from experience. Not for a long while. "But I'm taking you into protective custody. *Now.*" His tone was low and controlled, but just barely. "Get some things." His eyes slid closed and he drew in a weary breath. "And please—please don't argue with me this time?"

"I won't." The softness of her voice startled him and he looked down at her carefully. She was looking incredibly vulnerable again. She was trying very hard to be strong, to be brave, but her hands were nervously twisting together as if she were wringing out an invisible mop.

"Oh, hell," he groaned, thoroughly disgusted with himself. Maybe if she wasn't trying so damn hard to be strong, to be brave, it wouldn't have mattered so much. But she was. And it did. "Come here," he ordered in a none-too-polite voice. She hesitated, her pride kicking in as her eyes flashed and her back went up.

"Alex," he encouraged softly, his voice a sultry caress. He was unwilling and unable to just stand by and watch fear consume her. He'd promised to protect her and keep her safe, and he was damn well going to keep his promise.

"Come here." Softening his stance, Michael slowly opened his arms to her. Hesitantly, she went, releasing a huge sigh of relief as his arms closed securely around her and he hauled her close.

Alex's lashes fluttered and she inhaled deeply of his warmth, his scent, his comfort, trying to stop the fear that swept over her like a tidal wave. Wrapped in his arms, she felt...safe—something that a few moments ago, when she'd walked in and found her apartment door ajar, she thought she'd never feel again. But wrapped in Michael's arms, she felt protected, so protected, as if nothing or no one could ever harm her. It was a welcome feeling and she luxuriated in it, knowing it was probably fleeting.

Tightening her arms around him, she tried to steady her breathing, grateful he was here now. She hated feeling weak, helpless, and had worked very hard to banish such feelings from ever invading her life again, but she was exhausted and scared. Usually she was far too proud to show such weakness, especially to a man, but not with Michael. Not tonight.

Not a woman prone to tears, Alex found herself crying from sheer weariness and fatigue for the second time that night. Two hours ago, all she wanted out of life was to escape from the cold, the snow, and her panty hose. Now it seemed as if her life had somehow spiraled out of control. Both she and Gabriel were in danger and the only thing they had to cling to was...Michael. He was a safe harbor from this nightmare that her life had suddenly become. And she wasn't certain she found the thought any more comforting now, than she did when he first stepped out of the darkness and back into her life.

"It's all right," he crooned, stroking her back. "You're safe now." At least for the moment, he thought, letting his gaze scan the apartment again just in case he'd missed something.

Clutching his back, she was surprised at how slender, yet strong he was. How hard he was against her softness. She brushed her fingers against the soft flannel of his shirt, clenching it tightly, grateful to have something and someone safe to hang on to.

Michael shifted his weight, bringing her closer, trying to ease the ache her nearness had caused, allowing the sweet feminine scent of her to tease his senses. His eyes slid closed and he allowed himself the pleasure of just *feeling* her.

The thought of someone violating her in any way, or scaring her made his gut tighten. Tonight, someone had deliberately done both. Seething, he clenched his teeth until they hurt. Whoever did this was going to pay. And the price would be high.

Michael shifted again as his body hardened even further in response. Lord, this woman was going to be trouble in more ways than one. He knew there was nothing he could do to prevent it, not at the moment. Not when she was warm and pliable in his arms.

"Michael?" Her whisper-soft voice startled him. She tilted her head to look up at him. Unable to resist, he looked down at her.

Their gazes met, held, clung.

Slowly, Michael drew in a deep, weary breath, trying to resist the urge to touch her.

He failed.

Feelings and needs surfaced so quickly they stunned him, momentarily throwing him off-balance.

Lifting a hand, he circled the curve of her neck. The tender skin there was smoother than he'd ever imagined; the strands of hair that caressed the back of his hand silkier than he'd ever thought possible. Seconds seemed to drag by, and still their gazes clung. Desire and need hit him hard and fast, and he drew her closer, then closer still until the mouth he had only kissed in his dreams was a scant few inches from his. Too far to touch, too close to resist.

There was something he'd been wondering about for the past two years, something he needed to know.

Now.

It couldn't wait any longer. He bent his head and covered her mouth with his. He heard her startled gasp, taking advantage of her open mouth to slowly slide his tongue between her silky lips. His pulse pounded through his aching body and he felt the heat sear him as he dragged her closer and off her feet, wanting to bury himself in her. He kissed her with the blatant hunger of a lost, lonely man.

Alex groaned softly, sinking into him, winding her arms around him, wanting to hold him close. She opened her mouth to his, felt the fierce touch of his tongue against hers, darting, dancing, telling her what he wanted to do—what she wanted him to do—with her body.

She'd always wondered, but had never expected anything like this... overwhelming heat and need. It hit her hard and fast, nearly taking her breath away.

The world felt as if it had suddenly tilted until there was nothing in it but Michael and his arms. And her own spiraling needs. From shoulders to hips she was pressed intimately against him, feeling his need, his desire. She responded honestly, openly, giving back all that she got, feeling the hot coil of desire curl deeper in the pit of her stomach. A yearning so strong, so powerful overtook her. She'd never felt this... this wild explosion of her senses before. Her heart was hammering, her breath scant and fast. Even through all the layers of material that separated them, she could feel every hard male inch of him and knew she desperately wanted—needed—more.

With a groan, Michael's hungry mouth took her deeper. One hand slid from her back to the curve of her buttocks, pulling her closer to his aching hardness. She moaned softly, arching against him. Her breasts were full, her nipples aching for his touch. She moaned softly again, the sound muffled by his lips, but it fed the wildness stirring inside him. He slid his other hand to her hair, tunneling his fingers through it, anchoring her mouth more tightly to his.

He'd expected her to be a lot of things, but not this... this... wild heat and need. It matched his own, frightening him. Perhaps that's why he'd always avoided touching her. Maybe somewhere deep inside he knew it would be like this. There had always been this heightened sense of awareness between them—an awareness he'd never allowed himself to act upon.

Until now.

Tormented by a flare of hope, Michael immediately knew this had been a mistake. With a muttered oath, he reluctantly dragged his mouth from hers, suddenly feeling bereft, the lost and lonely feeling engulfing him once again. He hugged her tightly to him, waiting for his breathing to calm and his emotions to stabilize. He'd been shaken right down to his boots. Shaken and *scared*. Maybe that's why he'd never been able to forget this woman; maybe that's why he'd also avoided her. She was the one person who had been able to storm his defenses and sneak through all the protective layers he'd erected over the years. With her storm-the-gates-and-let-the-consequences-be-damned attitude, and her compassion and caring, she'd touched him as no one had touched him. And just for a moment, he'd forgotten about all the things he could never have, and had let her slip through. And it scared the hell out of him because he knew, had learned over the years, that he couldn't have normal things, a normal life. He glanced down at her. A normal woman.

No, he knew what he was. And what she was: all the things he knew he could never have. But that hadn't stopped him from wanting her. Or letting her get to him.

But never again, he vowed, setting her gently back down on her feet, and trying to forget the longing inside him. *Never again.* He had to keep this on a strictly professional level. For his safety and sanity. And hers. He couldn't—wouldn't—allow anything more.

''Michael?'' Her voice was shaky and whisper soft. The sound of his name on her lips was almost too much for him. She hardly ever called him by his name, although, he reflected wryly, trying to get his emotions and his body under control, she'd called him a great many *other* things.

Shaken, Alex stood there, staring at him. Her mouth felt bruised and bereft, and she wondered how one kiss could completely shatter her cool, calm, empty world into so many pieces. It was so cold, yet she felt nothing but warmth, heat. His heat. And she knew she wanted more, needed more; perhaps more than he could ever give. What did she have to do to reach him? To pierce that veil of resentment and coldness? She didn't know. He was already withdrawing from her and she didn't know why or what to do about it.

"Michael?" she repeated softly, desperately wanting to reach him before he withdrew completely. She lifted a hand to his face. He looked at her for a long, silent moment, struggling to get his feelings and emotions under control. Her eyes were soft, vulnerable. Didn't she have an ounce of self-protectiveness in her? Everything she felt was in her eyes. He could read her as if her thoughts had sprouted legs and had begun two-stepping across her forehead. Michael glanced away, unable to watch the well of pain pool in her eyes. Lord, she needed a keeper if only to protect her from herself!

"Michael?" she whispered again, stroking her hand down the slope of his cheek. With great effort, Michael turned his head away, pretending what had just happened between them hadn't meant anything.

Alex found it hurt. Terribly. She withdrew her hand, stuffing it into her pocket, although she desperately wanted to stuff it in his nose, just to knock some sense into him.

With a weary sigh, Michael turned his head, his skin still burning from her touch. He couldn't remember anyone touching him with such care, such gentleness before, and it caused an ache deep inside—not a physical ache, but something much more powerful, and much more frightening. He had to put some emotional as well as physical distance between them.

Now.

"We'd better get out of here." His voice had changed. It was cold, distant; and she felt that coldness seep into her, chasing away all the warmth and comfort. Wearily she rubbed her hands up and down her arms. How could he dismiss what had happened just now as unimportant?

Easily, she realized sadly. Just as he had dismissed her two years ago. Without a thought. Without a care. Michael Tyler was a man who wasn't capable of caring about anything. And she'd had two years of hurt and humiliation to prove it. Why hadn't she remembered that?

Gathering her dignity, Alex glanced around her apartment, anxious to put things back on a more level footing.

"Do you think they'll come back?" she asked quietly. She couldn't bear to see that coldness in his eyes, couldn't bear the hurt it caused. She was no longer looking at the man she knew, but at a cop: a cool, calm, determined detective. All emotion had been wiped from his face, and he was once again all coldness and emptiness.

Michael hesitated for a moment, unsure how to answer. He never lied to anyone about anything, and didn't want to lie to her now, but he wasn't certain she was up to hearing the truth. He didn't want to frighten her any further, and decided hedging was his best bet.

"I'm not sure." He thought it sounded reasonable. Even plausible. Maybe.

"They didn't get what they came for." She tried to smile, but he noticed her lips, still damp and a bit swollen from their kiss, were trembling. Peeking around him, she glanced at her apartment. "They'll be back," she whispered firmly.

"Alex . . ." His voice trailed off. What could he say? She was right. They would be back until they got what they were after. But first they were going to have to go through him. "I doubt if they'll be back tonight. I need you to take a look around to see if anything's missing, then I want you out of here. Just grab what you'll need for a few days."

She nodded, and her gaze swept her home again. It had always seemed like such a safe haven, a place of peace and contentment. She'd worked so hard for it, worked to make it a real home so that the idea of feeling so scared and unsafe here was terribly unsettling. She looked around at her familiar surroundings, knowing she'd never feel safe here again. It made her furious and sad—unbearably, terribly sad. Now she knew how her charges felt when they were suddenly uprooted, removed from all that was comfortable and familiar. It made her empathy for them deepen.

Michael watched her. She was just standing there, hesitantly glancing around.

"Want me to go with you?"

She turned and looked at him, surprised that he seemed to understand how unsettled she felt. That was one of the things that had drawn her to him in the first place. He was the first and only man who seemed to be able to read her thoughts before she'd even expressed them; hear her words before she'd even said them. It had created some kind of emotional connection between them. Well, she amended, at least a one-sided emotional connection. She wasn't certain *he* was capable of feeling *anything* emotional or otherwise.

Not trusting herself to speak, she offered him a wan smile, but her hands were back to wringing out the invisible mop.

"Come on." He draped an arm around her slender shoulder and headed into the apartment. "Lead the way." Their hips bumped once and they both froze, their eyes meeting in an aware, uncomfortable gaze, remembering.

He stared at her, wondering how anyone could look so fragile, smell so good, and feel so soft, yet still be full of so much determination and stubbornness.

She stared at him, wondering how anyone so cranky and uncaring could be so calm, feel so hard, and yet feel so strong and comforting.

The moment seemed to stretch on, heartbeat after heartbeat, until Michael grew acutely uncomfortable. Finally he glanced away, breaking the invisible threads connecting them.

"See what's missing," he said quietly. Nodding, she walked the length of the rooms with Michael's arm tightly around her.

When they were back in the living room, she shook her head. "I don't think anything is missing."

Michael nodded, confused, but trying to make sense of this. "That's what I thought." Instinct made him cautious, as his gaze swiveled around again, knowing something was out of sync. This just didn't make sense. None of it.

"Go pack," he said wearily, realizing he wanted her out of here if only to keep her safe and calm her down. She hesitated, until he followed her to the bedroom. Michael stood in the doorway, watching, as she haphazardly threw clothes into a suitcase.

"Don't take anything fancy," he cautioned. "Just warm things. Jeans and stuff."

Nodding, she went to the closet, pulling clothes free and rapidly folding them into the suitcase. She just wanted to get out of here as quickly as possible. She felt creepy, knowing some stranger had gone through her personal belongings.

"I'm going to call this in." At her panicked look, Michael softened his expression. "Don't worry, Alex, I'll be right in the next room."

Hating the way she was feeling, Alex fought her fear and nodded. "Go on. I'll be fine." As if to prove it, she headed for the bathroom adjoining her bedroom to gather her toiletries, but her knees were knocking.

Michael went into the kitchen, grabbed his handkerchief out of his pocket and picked up the receiver, calling the nearest precinct. When he was finished, he wandered back toward her bedroom, pausing to once again examine the other rooms. Her home was beautifully decorated in differing shades of yellow. The colors reminded him of sunshine.

And her.

His gaze drifted from one elegant piece to another. It was clear she had decorated the place with a loving hand. He found a smile tugging at his mouth—and a hint of sadness tugging at his heart.

This was a real home, a place of warmth and welcome, a place for her to retire to, to find solace after the disappointments of the day.

It was something he'd never experienced.

He'd never had a home, at least not a real home: a place where he truly belonged. Even now, his apartment was simply a place to rest his weary head. He had no furniture. Other than a box spring and mattress, an old bureau he'd picked up at a flea market, and a battered kitchen set that had been left by the previous tenant, nothing about his apartment by any stretch of the imagination could be called a home. There was no warmth, no caring, only... emptiness. Just like the rest of his life.

But everything about this place screamed "home." Even the spare bedroom had been decorated with gaily colored hand-drawn pictures—from her charges, no doubt.

But now someone had violated her sanctuary. His jaw tightened. He might never have had a home, but that didn't mean he couldn't appreciate how much a safe one meant to someone. Or at least it had been safe until tonight.

Shaking his head, Michael balled his fists in frustration. He was determined something like this would never happen again.

He stood in the long hallway that connected the main rooms to the sleeping rooms, sweeping everything with a quick, thorough gaze. It was there again: that feeling that something wasn't right. It wasn't something he could put his finger on, but something abstract. Just a feeling, but after twenty years as a cop, he usually went with his gut feelings. They hadn't misled him yet.

A shiver crawled over his skin. Like it or not, there was something definitely wrong here. Now all he had to do was figure out what.

He waited until he had her suitcase safely tucked in the back seat, and her safely buckled in the front seat before even thinking about broaching the subject of Gabriel.

Gunning the motor to life, Michael abruptly pulled into the street. The snow was at least eight inches deep now and the plows hadn't been by, causing his tires to fishtail on the slippery road. He felt her fingers clutching his arm through his leather jacket, and instinctively lifted his foot off the accelerator a bit. He forgot that he drove like a madman sometimes. Came with the territory. There was rarely anyone else in the car with him. He was a loner who was used to being alone. He never had to worry about someone complaining or worrying about how he drove.

"Relax," he murmured, glancing at Alex. She was still clutching his leather-covered arm, her eyes wide as he got control of the car. He hadn't meant to frighten her, merely to get her away from her apartment as quickly as possible.

"Do you always drive as if the hounds of hell are after you?" Slowly she released his arm, and he almost smiled in the darkness. She was back to sass and spitfire again, so maybe she was going to be all right. He let out a relieved sigh.

"Yep." He glanced in his rearview mirror, checking to make sure they hadn't been followed. He frowned suddenly as he turned the corner. "Tell me something, Alex, do you ever bring files home with you?"

She hesitated a moment and a growing sense of unease crawled over her. "Sometimes." Taking a deep breath, she looked at him. The oncoming lights from other cars glowed against his profile. She could see his face was grim, his jaw set. "Why?"

He braked for a red light, flipped the heater up higher, then turned to her, rubbing his cold hands together. The low sweet sounds of a love song drifted from the slightly out-of-tune radio. "Because I can't figure out why they would break into your apartment but not take anything. They were obviously looking for something. Obviously they had to know you weren't home or you'd have screamed the joint down before they'd even gotten in the door. So what was the purpose of breaking in?" Confused, he shook his head. "It just doesn't make sense. They had to be looking for something." Blowing out an exasperated breath, Michael rubbed a hand across his stubbled chin as he glanced up at the light. It was still red. "Did you have any files at home tonight?"

She shook her head, deliberately avoiding his gaze. "No. It's against policy for me to keep files out of the office overnight."

"Then what could they have been looking for?" Exasperated, he turned back toward her as he waited for the light to change. "Do you have any idea?"

She was silent in the darkness and a feeling slowly unfurled in his gut. As soon as the light turned green, he jammed his foot down on the accelerator, then swerved around the corner, pulling to the curb and jamming the car into Park. Taking a deep breath, he clenched the steering wheel tightly, then turned to look at her.

"Alex, you're not being straight with me here."

"I—"

He raised his hand. "Don't lie to me." His voice was low and cold. "Just...don't...lie...to...me." He took a deep breath. "You lied to me once tonight already, and I guarantee you I am not in the mood to hear another one." He let his words hang in the still, cold air for a moment. "You know what they were looking for, don't you?" His eyes challenged her. Dark, intense, his gaze refused to release her and Alex almost shivered again, feeling a sense of apprehension.

How could she feel so safe with him one moment, and so uncomfortable with him the next? Michael Tyler had the ability to stir up myriad emotions within her, and she wasn't certain she liked all of them.

Long moments slowly ticked by as cold blue eyes warred with defiant bluer ones. The only sound was their mingled breathing. With the heater off it was getting cold in the car, and their breath became puffs of white smoke that drifted, then evaporated into the darkness.

Michael waited, hoping she'd volunteer the information, then scowled, his hands tightening on the steering wheel. He should have known better.

"Alex." His voice was low, anger and frustration vibrating through every syllable. He took a deep, slow breath, trying to calm his temper. "I can't protect you or Gabriel unless you tell me the truth. They broke into your apartment but they didn't take anything. You didn't want me in your apartment, but not because it was a mess, right?" His gaze bore into hers, waiting. Finally, she nodded wearily.

"You're right," she stammered, glancing down at her clenched hands.

"Why?" Even in the darkness she could see the veil snap down, shutting her out, closing off all of his emotions. It angered her all over again. "Why did you lie to me?"

She couldn't answer him. Instead, she turned and stared vacantly out the window. Snow was falling harder. It felt as if the temperature had dropped another ten degrees. The wind blew fast and furious, picking up the snow and sending it buffeting against the windows. It was so thick she could barely make out the building across the street.

"Alex." Taking a deep breath, Michael decided to try a different tactic. "Whoever broke into your apartment tonight was looking for something. You know what they were looking for, don't you?"

"Yes," she whispered. Her voice caught as she turned to face him again, trying to control her fear. Not for herself, but for Gabriel. As a social worker, she knew all too well how precarious adoptions of older children could be. They'd had a life previously, sometimes not a pretty life, and she wanted to be certain Gabriel started his new life with a clean slate. Knowing the circumstances of Gabriel's life and the danger that had preceded Gabriel's adoption, she had painstakingly made sure that she covered her tracks so that no one from Gabriel's former life would be able to find or trace him. He *was* safe, she reassured herself. Safe as he could be; safe as it was humanly possible for one little boy to be. No one knew where he was. *No one.* She'd made certain of that; had taken every precaution to make sure of it. Gabriel's safety had been her number one priority almost every waking moment of every day for the past two years. And she wasn't going to let Michael Tyler frighten her into believing anything different.

If the lieutenant had come to her to learn Gabriel's whereabouts, that meant that Webster probably hadn't and wouldn't be able to find him, either—at least not for a little while, which gave her some time. Time to think, and plan her next move.

Webster had only been out of jail for a few hours. He wasn't Superman. Surely not even he could have sifted through the legal paperwork that went into an adoption this quickly. Adoption records were sealed, and it would take a great deal of time and energy to untangle the trail. She'd covered her tracks well—very well—for Gabriel's sake, just in case something like this ever happened. The thought reassured her—but only momentarily. Then she was filled with a nagging sense of doubt.

"Now I'm only giving you one shot to be straight with me, Alex." He held up a finger. "Just one. What were they looking for?"

She turned away from his glance, curling her gloved hands into fists. Michael waited, praying for patience.

"Alex?"

When she turned to him, he could see the fierce determination in her eyes. She took a deep breath, realizing she had no choice now but to put her trust in him. Again. But she didn't have to like it. Trusting Michael Tyler had proved to be a very costly proposition, not just to her heart, and her life, but more important, to Gabriel. She was going to have to trust him, at least on this. But she hoped neither she nor Gabriel lived—or rather, died—to regret it.

"Alex, what were they looking for?"

"Gabriel." Her voice was so soft he could hardly hear her.

"What?"

"Gabriel." She sighed wearily. "They were looking for Gabriel."

Michael stared at her in confusion, not certain she was being straight with him. "What are you talking about?" He shook his head. "Why would they be looking for Gabriel in your apartment?" Obviously this puzzle was missing more than a few pieces. Bewildered, Michael watched her carefully.

Alex prayed she wasn't making a mistake. Finally, she released a slow, deep breath and boldly met his gaze. When she spoke her voice was eerily quiet.

"Gabriel's my son, Michael. I adopted him."

## Chapter Four

"What?" Michael merely stared at her, certain he hadn't heard her correctly.

"Gabriel's my son," she repeated grudgingly, unwilling to give him anything more. She was determined that nothing would harm Gabriel. *Nothing.* Not even Lieutenant Michael Tyler, no matter how good his intentions.

Ignoring his curious stare, Alex lifted the collar of her coat with trembling hands and ducked her chin into it. She was so cold and so tired, not to mention hungry, and now, in addition to everything else, terrified could be added to the list. And she had Michael Tyler to blame.

Stunned into silence, Michael never took his eyes off her. She had faint smudge lines of fatigue under her eyes, and she was shivering, although he wasn't certain if it was from the cold or fear.

"Gabriel's your son," he repeated, stunned beyond comprehension. He shook his head, running a weary hand over his eyes. "How? When? Why—?"

"The how, when and why should be very obvious, Lieutenant," she said haughtily, although some of the effect was lost by her chattering teeth. "How? The usual way, through legal channels. When? I began the process about a year and a half ago. The adoption was final four months ago." Her gaze pierced his and her voice remained cool. "And as for why, that question doesn't even deserve an answer." Furious she'd had to give him this much, Alex hunched deeper into her coat and turned away from him, watching her breath frost on the window, wishing she were anywhere but here.

Her eyes slid closed for a moment and she wished she were in a small cabin on the banks of Lake Geneva, Wisconsin, with a little boy who was eagerly and happily anticipating Christmas with his mother.

The thought of Gabriel brought silent tears to Alex's eyes and a shaft of pain to her heart. She loved him so very, very much. She couldn't bear the thought of anything happening to him. He'd been through so much already; he deserved some happiness, some . . . normalcy, just like every other little boy. And in the past two years she'd tried to give him just that. And she'd succeeded, until Michael Tyler had shown up tonight, bringing danger and deception with him, and shattering the calm, secure world she had built for Gabriel.

"Your son," Michael murmured softly, his mind and emotions in chaos. He'd taken her news like a drunk takes a punch, and he still hadn't quite recovered. Feelings came quickly, unexpectedly, shocking him, shaking his tight rein of control. His hands unconsciously tightened on the steering wheel in an effort to hold on to something solid.

*She'd adopted Gabriel!*

Michael numbly shook his head. He couldn't quite believe it. If he'd been a praying man, he would have said a prayer of thanks. His eyes slid closed for a moment and a rush of warmth unfurled slowly in his gut. He'd always known she was one special woman, but he'd never expected or anticipated this.

He couldn't stop the flood of feelings that suddenly warmed his cold heart. Gabriel had finally gotten that chance. Finally, the kid would have a shot at a life—a normal life, a life filled with love. And a home. A *real* home. He thought of all the things that came with it—knowing you belonged somewhere to someone. Knowing that you were loved, cared for. Knowing that you mattered, that you had a place in this cold, empty world.

And Gabriel's world was no longer cold or empty. Michael was certain of that. Not with Alex in it. Nothing could have made him happier. He turned to her, pinning her with his gaze.

"Alex?"

The tone of his voice, soft and sultry again, caused her to grow suspicious and she slowly turned to face him. Her eyes widened and shock almost knocked her socks off.

"You're smiling," she said, blinking once to clear her tears, then again just to make sure she wasn't seeing a mirage. His smile seemed to grow in proportion to her shock.

Reaching across the seat, Michael took her gloved hand in his, holding it gently. "You are something else, Ms. Alexandria Kent." His smile spread to his eyes, softening them. She merely stared at him, her own shock sapping her voice. "Something else, indeed." His throat was tight, his eyes stinging. All the control he valued was gone; it had slipped away under a barrage of feelings. He wasn't used to feeling, let alone putting those feelings into words.

The little spitfire almost—almost—made him believe in miracles.

Lifting a hand, he cupped her chin. Her eyes went even wider in shock. "Alex, that's the nicest thing I've ever heard."

"What?" she asked with a frown, still feeling resentful and unsettled. "That you're smiling?"

He shook his head. "No. That you've adopted Gabriel." Still smiling, he gave her hand a gentle squeeze, trying to impart all of the things he couldn't say into that one inadequate gesture.

Alex felt something tug at her cautious heart. A smiling Michael Tyler was a sight to behold; a sight no woman still breathing would ever be able to resist. It softened some of her anger and resentment toward him.

"You've given that kid more than a home, Alex. You've given him a chance." His voice, now soft, floated through the bitter cold air, wrapping her in a cocoon of warmth. "A chance to be normal, just a normal little kid, with a home and a family and...love." The last word came out a hushed whisper. "It's all a kid ever needs. Gabriel's a very lucky boy."

Watching him, watching the intense play of emotions on his face, in his voice, Alex suddenly realized the steel veil was gone. It was the first time she had ever seen Michael open himself up or reveal himself, and a flicker of hope was born. She realized she liked what she saw.

It was clear that Michael Tyler was a man of intense emotions and deep, deep feelings. She'd finally gotten a glimpse of the real man. No wonder he buried everything behind a thick veneer of control. She wondered if he even realized how much he cared, at least about Gabriel; and, she wondered, what else.

Thinking about his words, Alex suddenly wondered if Michael was talking about Gabriel.

Or himself.

The thought struck her like a blow. She suddenly realized she really didn't know much about Michael's background. He never talked about it—getting him to talk about anything personal was like trying to find a groundhog in the desert. Michael Tyler had never revealed any part of himself—not his past, not his present, not his emotions.

Until this moment.

She watched him carefully, remembering how well he'd gotten along with Gabriel. In spite of his gruffness Michael Tyler had a special affinity with kids; a special gift that allowed him to get through to even the toughest, most hardened child.

When she'd first met Gabriel he'd been scared and wary of her, so wary she could barely get through to him, but when Michael entered the picture, during the long months of the trial, he slowly built a special bond with Gabriel, gaining the child's trust.

For some reason Gabriel responded to Michael on a level where she couldn't reach him, at least not at that time. It was as if Michael knew exactly how Gabriel had felt and what he'd needed.

Until this moment, Alex had never really thought about it before. But one didn't develop those kinds of instincts about children from a book. No, there was something more to this. Something much more.

Michael Tyler had a special gift with lost, troubled children. An affinity toward them that seemed to give them the confidence they needed and the caring they craved. Alex wondered again if it was because he, too, had been a lost, troubled child with no one to turn to and nowhere to go. That thought brought a sharp slice of pain to her tender heart and she squeezed his hand, longing to reach him before the barriers slammed shut again.

His gaze never left hers, warm, seductive, mysterious. She felt as if she were being drawn into a deep well that was both frightening and fascinating. There were so many sides to Michael Tyler, so many emotions that he'd buried and controlled.

What would it take to break through all the barriers he'd erected?

What would it take to reach the man inside?

Until this moment, Alex had given up hope that she would ever be able to accomplish that, but now, watching the softening of his gaze, the loosening of his control, she felt a flicker of hope that maybe someday, she just might be able to break through all those barriers.

For a long moment, they sat in silence, holding hands, wrapped in solitude, the cold and their own thoughts, just looking at each other ensnared in something strong, powerful, seductive.

Like a lemming drawn to the sea, Alex was drawn to him. Even though she knew she shouldn't be she couldn't help herself. She just wanted to touch him; *had* to touch him. He'd touched her on so many levels, awakening so many feelings, impulsively, she lifted a gloved hand and gently laid it against his cheek. His gaze never left hers, and she felt as if those mercurial eyes could see all the way to her soul—all her secrets, all her dreams, her wants, her needs. She felt exposed, vulnerable, but she couldn't pull away; couldn't break the connection between them.

She wanted so much to reach him, to get through to him, to let him know she cared. But she knew she couldn't tell him, couldn't risk him withdrawing from her again. Not now. She needed him, needed his strength and his solidness and his protection—not just for herself, but for Gabriel, as well. Every time he withdrew from her it tore another little piece of her heart.

Michael nestled his cold cheek against her gloved hand, his eyes sliding closed for a moment. He knew he shouldn't allow this to continue. He had to break the emotional connection between them before it ensnared him in its trap. It was far too dangerous. If he let his feelings and emotions loose, he'd lose his hard edge of objectivity, and right now he needed that objectivity. It was the only thing that would keep her and Gabe safe.

But she'd thrown him for a loop with her confession about Gabriel, and he still hadn't quite recovered. He didn't know why he'd been so surprised. The little spitfire always did the unexpected and unconventional.

In some ways, they were very much alike. Except she wore her heart on her sleeve, exposing it to so many dangers, not caring that it might get ripped to shreds.

Damn fool woman!

Didn't she know that nothing could have touched him more? She was the kind of woman who saw a need and filled it. Saw a child and loved it. If she wasn't going to protect herself, then he was damn well just going to have to do it for her, if only for his *own* peace of mind.

But he was going to have to try to control his feelings and emotions. He simply *had* to do it. Not for himself, but for her, and Gabriel. He knew what happened when a cop lost his objectivity and got too emotionally involved. He made mistakes, and right now he couldn't afford to make any mistakes. Alex's and Gabe's lives were at stake.

Banking down the flood of emotions he'd allowed free rein, Michael glanced in the rearview mirror. Jerking away from Alex, he jammed the car into gear, uttering a string of curses that would have made a longshoreman proud.

The moment was abruptly shattered, leaving Alex with her mouth gaping open. Stunned, she blinked several times, trying to figure out what had just happened. "Michael, what—"

"Damn!" Ignoring her, he stomped on the accelerator, but the car only fishtailed, swerving crazily on the ice and snow as he fought with the steering wheel.

"What on earth are you doing?" Frightened by the way the car was careening across the street, Alex stared at Michael as if he'd lost his mind. Frightened, she grabbed his arm, unwilling to be a victim of his hounds-of-hell driving again.

"Get down," he barked, brushing off her arm and watching the headlights behind them in the rearview mirror draw closer as he tried to get the car under control.

"But what—"

"Down, damn it!" he ordered, pushing her head toward the seat. She bumped her nose on his thigh, then gave him a whack, furious at his manhandling.

"Will you please stop pushing me, shoving me, dragging me—"

"Someone's following us, Alex," he growled. "Now stay down and be quiet until I get us safely out of here." Michael jerked the wheel again, trying to keep his eyes on the car behind them and on the road in front of them. The car careened forward crazily, and for a moment, he feared they would sideswipe a telephone pole. Michael's teeth clenched. His face grew grim as he jerked the wheel, finally straightening the car and punching the accelerator again. The car skidded for a moment, then plowed forward, spewing dirty snow in their wake.

It took several minutes, several turns and Michael's full concentration before he lost their tail. Heaving a sigh of relief, he downshifted, then turned down a side street that he knew led to the expressway. Right now he needed to get Alex out and away from the city as fast as possible. With it looking as if the weatherman had underestimated the amount of snow they were to receive, the last thing he wanted was to have them stranded somewhere in the city. It would be far too easy to find her.

He swore softly under his breath, furious at himself. He'd allowed his own personal feelings and emotions to color his judgment and it had almost proved disastrous. If he'd been paying more attention to the job and less attention to the woman sitting next to him, they wouldn't be in this mess. He had to curb his feelings and emotions, especially now, if he wanted to keep Alex and Gabe safe. *No emotion,* he silently chanted to himself. Gabriel's and Alex's lives depended on him. He couldn't afford to slip up again.

"I think we lost them." He laid a hand on her head. The silkiness of her hair beneath his fingers reminded him of how she felt in his arms. He banished the memory to the dark recesses of his mind. He couldn't be thinking about having her in his arms right now—or ever.

"You can get up now." He paused, checking his rearview mirror one more time. Noting there was no one behind him, Michael's fingers relaxed somewhat on the wheel.

Alex sat up, brushing her hair off of her face. She glanced behind them nervously. "Is...is it safe?"

Michael's face was grim, his lips drawn into a tight line as he maneuvered the car. "For now." He glanced in the mirror again, grateful he saw only darkness. "We have to talk."

"I know." Taking a deep shaky breath, Alex tried to calm the fear that snaked through her. She crossed her arms across her breasts, huddling deeper into the seat. "Do you think it was Webster or his men?" She hated the way her voice shook with fear. She turned her head to look behind them again.

"No doubt about it." Michael glanced at her. She looked scared and pale, but maybe now she'd take this and him seriously. "Obviously they know a lot more than you think, Alex. If they broke into your house looking for Gabriel, that means they must know that you've adopted him."

"Impossible," she said. "You didn't even know," she argued—quite reasonably, she thought. "Adoption records are sealed. There's no way they could have known."

He shot her a look. "Do you have any idea how naive you sound?" Shaking his head, his mouth twisted. "Money opens any door. Including sealed adoption records."

"Are you saying Webster paid someone to learn who adopted Gabriel?" Her voice rose in indignation and his mouth quirked in humor.

"Either that, or dropping in on you this evening was just a lucky guess." She frowned, realizing he had a point. "Which means, if they know you've adopted Gabriel, sooner or later they'll find out where he is." Michael glanced at her. "Where *is* he, by the way? You still haven't told me."

Her chin went up. "I know, and I don't intend to."

Michael sighed, suddenly weary. His knee was killing him from his kamikaze driving, not to mention the fact that he'd been up and on it for close to eighteen hours.

"You're not going to start that again, are you?" He shook his head, never taking his eyes off the road as the car careened onto the expressway. It, at least, had been plowed. He steered the car into the farthest, fastest lane, then stomped on the accelerator. "Don't you realize how much danger you and Gabriel are both in? Especially now. Damn it Alex, don't be stubborn." His voice rose. "This is a race against time. I have to get to Gabriel before they do. I'm the only chance he has. It's either me or Webster and his goons. They already know more than is safe for either of you. So make up your mind. It's either trust me, or take your chances with them."

The way he said the words made her shiver and she realized he had a point. The break-in at her condo couldn't possibly have been a coincidence. It was all too neat and pat for that. It had to be Webster or his men. Realizing she had no choice in the matter, that she was going to have to trust Michael Tyler again, Alex heaved a weary sigh.

She was so cold and tired, not to mention hungry. A headache that had begun earlier in the evening, now erupted full-blown, pounding against her temple in a weary rhythm. Closing her eyes, she rubbed her temples, trying to think. She had no choice; she had to trust him. But she didn't have to like it.

"All right," she said softly, cringing as he passed a car with barely a hair of room between them. "I'll tell you where Gabriel's at, but don't get any ideas," she warned, not liking the look in his eye when he glanced at her. "Just because I've told you the truth about adopting Gabriel doesn't mean I've changed my mind." Her voice gathered steam and she shook her head. "He is *not* testifying for you again. And this time you can go to *my* superiors, *your* superiors, or *both* of our superiors and it won't do any good. This isn't professional any more, Lieutenant, this is personal. Gabriel is my son. Do you understand me?" She poked his arm, just in case he didn't. "And if you think I'd let you put him in danger again just to further your own aims, you're out of your mind."

"Fine, Alex. Fine." He checked his rearview mirror again. "Just tell me where he is."

Taking a deep breath, Alex said a silent prayer. "Gabriel's in Wisconsin with my parents."

"Wisconsin is a big state. Could you be a bit more specific here?"

"Lake Geneva. My parents have a home up there. Every Christmas the whole family converges there to celebrate the holiday." Alex smiled in the darkness, memories of her own happy childhood surfacing. "As soon as the kids get out of school for Christmas vacation, they head to Mom and Dad's. It's a very special time for them, and for Mom and Dad. They get to spend time alone with their grandkids. Dad takes them skiing, sledding and snowmobiling, while Mother puts them to work in the kitchen baking cookies and candy and wrapping presents. Then on Christmas Eve all the adults arrive and everyone decorates the Christmas tree." Smiling at the memory, Alex tucked her legs under her for warmth, snuggling deeper in the seat. "The first year Gabriel was so scared. He just stood in a corner, warily watching everyone. He'd never celebrated Christmas before. To him it was just another day."

"Yeah," Michael muttered glumly. "I know the feeling."

There was a bitterness in his words that even his tight control couldn't hide. A shadow of sadness seemed to fall over his features, piercing her heart and only further arousing her curiosity.

Without a word, she laid a comforting hand on his arm, remembering his earlier caustic comments about Christmas. He glanced briefly at her hand, then at her, but said nothing. Obviously, Christmas was something that held no joy for Michael, only painful memories. She wondered why, but decided not to ask. Not yet, anyway. Her curiosity could wait. Right now, she merely wanted him to know she was there, and that she cared.

"It took Gabriel a few days to get with the program," she added quietly, "but once he realized that everyone just accepted him as part of the family, that he was treated no differently than any of the other kids, he finally began to relax and join in the fun. The past two years, since Gabriel's become part of my life and our family, he's really blossomed, Michael." There was genuine joy in her voice, and Michael found himself glancing at her. "He loves going up there to be with his grandparents and his new cousins." Laughing softly, she squeezed his arm. "Gabriel couldn't wait for school to get out so he could head up there. He actually marked the days off on a calendar." Sighing, she laid her head back against the seat. She glanced at Michael, noted he was suddenly scowling.

"What?" she asked with a frown. "What are you scowling about now?"

Home. Family. Traditions. Celebrations. *Christmas.* Michael's scowl deepened. "You sound like a Currier & Ives commercial," he grumbled.

"Why is it that any mention of Christmas causes you to act like a bear with a burr in his belly?"

"No particular reason," he lied, ashamed to admit that what she'd described sounded like every Christmas he'd ever read about or dreamed about. The kind of Christmas he'd never had—would never have. "I just don't happen to like Christmas," he snapped. "Or any holiday, for that matter."

"Why?" Her voice was soft. She watched him carefully, knowing she was pushing him but unable to stop herself.

He let out a long, deep breath, desperately wishing for a cigarette. A *lit* cigarette. "No particular reason."

One slender blond eyebrow lifted in question. She knew he was lying to her, but decided not to press the issue just yet. "Gabriel loves Christmas," she said with more than a hint of pride. Emotions came suddenly, flooding over her, swamping her like a tidal wave. Her eyes suddenly swam with tears and her breath caught in a sob.

"Oh, God, Michael," she whispered, stricken with genuine fear. "I couldn't bear it if anything happened to him." Pressing a gloved hand to her mouth to stop the sobs that were threatening to break loose, she shook her head. "I just...couldn't...bear it." Her voice caught and she turned her head away.

Never taking his eyes off the snow-slicked road, Michael reached for her. Looping an arm around her shoulder, he drew her close until she buried her face in his shoulder. He could feel the sobs racking her slender body and cursed himself seven ways to Sunday.

"Don't cry, Alex," he whispered, wishing he could pull over and just hold her. But the snow was coming down faster, accumulating quickly, making even the snow-plowed expressway dangerous. They were going to have to stop somewhere soon. It was becoming much too treacherous to remain on the roads.

"Don't cry," he repeated, feeling totally inadequate in the face of her tears, but knowing he didn't want to see her frightened or worried. It did something to his insides; something he didn't entirely like, or know what to do about.

"I promise nothing is going to happen to Gabriel." Glancing down at her, his eyes were dark, fierce, determined. *"Nothing.* You got it?" Swiping at her tears, Alex nodded solemnly, snuggling closer to him, grateful for the warmth.

Even through the thick layers of their clothing, pressed against him, she felt that momentary flash of safety she'd felt back in the apartment and it somewhat soothed her nerves.

"I give you my word, Alex." Michael's face grew grim. "I may not be a by-the-book cop, but I *am* a damn good cop."

"I know that," she whispered softly, watching as he shot up a ramp that connected with another expressway. She knew all about his citations and decorations. Knew his file backward and forward, had made it her business to know his professional background the moment he had become involved in Gabriel's case. What she knew didn't always comfort her, since he really wasn't a by-the-book cop, and had numerous suspensions on his record to prove it. But he did get the job done. And he had kept his promise to her.

When she'd agreed to allow Gabriel to testify for him, he'd given her his personal guarantee that Gabriel would be safe. And he had been. If she was honest with herself, she knew she really couldn't blame Michael for their current circumstances.

He glanced at her. "Please, just try to trust me. Do you think you can do that?" Looking at him, Alex couldn't help but nod. She had no choice in the matter; she *had* to trust him.

"I'll try." Her words brought on another brief smile that warmed and comforted her. Certain she would stay put, Michael unwound his arm from around her and held tightly to the steering wheel, concentrating on his driving. Alex frowned suddenly.

"Where are we going, Michael?" She looked out the window, realizing she didn't have the faintest idea where they were. Calmer now, she tried to move away, but he held her in place, liking the feel of her next to him, wanting to keep her close, not certain if it was for her comfort. Or his.

"Wisconsin. Lake Geneva, to be precise." Michael's brow drew into a concerned frown. "But I don't think we're going to be able to make it up there tonight. The snow's picking up. Another couple of hours and these roads will be completely impassable."

"But what about Gabriel?" Fear laced her words and she trembled against him, curling her fingers into her palms to stop their trembling.

He sighed heavily, his mind on overdrive. "Alex, we probably have a head start on them. If they were tailing us, it's a good bet they don't know where Gabriel is—yet—so I figure we've got a few hours' lead time, which is an enormous advantage, especially in this weather. And if we know exactly where he is, but can't get to him because of the snow, I'm betting they won't be able to get to him, either."

She nodded, relaxing against him a bit when she realized he was probably right. But still, she worried. She'd feel much better if Gabriel was safe in her arms.

"We'll go as far as we can tonight." Concentrating, Michael peered through the snow-slicked windshield. Even with the wipers going full blast, he could barely see. "A friend of mine owns a cabin between the Illinois and Wisconsin border. I think we can make it up there before things get too bad. We'll spend the night, then take off first thing in the morning. Hopefully by then the snow will have stopped, or at the very least the roads will have been plowed."

She lifted her head from his shoulder, trying to stifle a yawn. Sitting so close to him, she could smell the wonderful masculine scent of him. Could feel the strong broadness of his shoulder, which somehow seemed meant as a resting place.

"Don't you have to call your friend to let him know we're coming?" She frowned as his mouth quirked in humor. "We certainly can't just show up unannounced and uninvited on his doorstep, especially three days before Christmas."

Michael laughed, shocking her. She'd never seen him laugh before. His whole face softened and his eyes danced wickedly. It was just another fascinating side of him.

"Trust me, this is one friend I don't have to call." At her curious look, he continued. "Ryce McCall is not just a friend, but my partner. We've worked homicide together for the past fifteen years. His cabin is sort of communal property. Ryce leaves a key hidden so that anyone who needs the cabin can use it." Michael's eyebrows drew together and he leaned forward trying to make out the signs on the expressway, but the snow was seriously impairing his vision. "We're less than an hour from there now. We get off at the next exit." His whole body was tense from trying to keep the car on the road, and see where he was going. His damn knee felt as if someone had been hammering on it. He didn't realize how tired he was until this moment.

Turning toward Alex, he frowned, not liking the paleness of her skin. She looked dead on her feet. He felt bad; she looked worse.

"When was the last time you had something to eat?"

Alex's smile was weary. "That depends. What day is it?" Running a hand through her tousled hair, she yawned again. "I've been so busy the past few days, I just haven't had time to eat, sleep or do much of anything." She snuggled closer to him. "I was really looking forward to having a few days off at Christmas. Sort of a minivacation at my folks'."

"I'm sorry this isn't the kind of vacation you had planned." There was genuine regret in his voice.

"It's really not your fault," she admitted, feeling guilty over her earlier accusations. "And keeping Gabriel safe is the most important thing right now. Nothing else matters." A sudden thought brought on a rush of panic. "Lord, Michael, what about my job?" She shook her head. "I've been so caught up in what's happened tonight I completely forgot about my other charges. What am I going to do? I can't just not show up. There's still three days before Christmas and I've got children to deal with." Lord, what was wrong with her? She'd never been so caught up in something that she'd forgotten her responsibilities. But then again, her son had never been in grave danger before. And Gabriel's welfare took precedence over everything, even her job.

Michael glanced at her. "Can't you call someone? A supervisor or someone and let them know that something's come up and you won't be in for a while?"

"A while?" she repeated in shock. She looked at him suspiciously. "I thought we were just going to get Gabriel."

"We are," Michael confirmed. "But once we pick him up, I'm going to have to take you and him to a safe house."

She bolted upright. "What do you mean, you're taking him and me to a safe house?" Confused, she shook her head. "What safe house? I have a perfectly good house that was perfectly safe until tonight," she added with a frown. She shook her head. "Michael, I don't understand. I think you'd better start explaining. Fast."

He almost grinned. She was back to being sassy again. "It's simple, Alex. Until Webster's trial, or until we can pick him and his goons up on something more substantial than scaring you or tailing us, you and Gabriel should consider yourselves in protective custody."

"What!" She stared at him in shock. "But I...I thought once we had Gabriel we could...could—"

"Could what, Alex?" He gave a derisive snort. "Go back to your nice, neat little condo? Go back to your job and your life?" Michael shook his head. "Not on a bad bet, Alex. If you weren't listening to me before, you'd better listen to me now. Until Webster is safely back in prison, both you and Gabriel are in danger."

"But—"

"But nothing, Alex. Listen to me." He shot her a look. "You are in *serious* danger. Do you understand what I'm telling you?" Her eyes widened in genuine fear. "Tonight they merely broke into your apartment, but what do you think will happen if Gabriel's there the next time?"

"Oh, my God!" Her hand went to her mouth. She'd never even thought about it. Her stomach lurched and she felt sick. Unable to bear the thought of anything happening to her son, Alex inched closer to Michael, wanting to feel some sense of safety once again.

"Precisely my point, Al. I told you these guys play for keeps. They intend to finish what they started, and that means finding Gabriel, and doing whatever is necessary to keep him from testifying again, and they'll use any means possible to do it. Do you understand what I'm telling you?"

His dark, penetrating gaze met hers and she slowly nodded her head, vividly aware that his words had caused a deep trembling within her.

"Which puts you and Gabriel in serious jeopardy. It's my job to see that nothing happens to either of you as long as Webster and his goons are out on the street. So as of this moment, Al, consider yourself in protective custody." He gave her a wicked grin. "Mine."

## Chapter Five

The roadside diner situated along the barren country road was a combination restaurant, mini food-mart and gas station. Still, Alex was delighted and surprised to find the coffee was good, hot and fresh. At the moment she probably would have been grateful for motor oil if it was hot and in a cup. She was so cold and tired, not to mention famished, she felt as if she'd collapse if she didn't get some food and coffee into her soon.

Nestled in a back booth away from any prying eyes, Alex carefully sipped her coffee, savoring the delicious brew while waiting for Michael to return. As soon as they'd ordered, he'd headed toward the rear of the diner to call and check in with his captain. Alex frowned over the rim of her cup. He'd been gone an awfully long time for only one phone call. A skitter of fear washed over her and she quickly brushed it aside. She was just tired, she assured herself. What more could possibly go wrong? She refused to entertain all the possibilities her imagination conjured up.

Turning toward the parking lot, her eyes scanned the stormy landscape. The neon sign that had guided them to the diner kept flashing its mixture of blues and greens. The country road was deserted except for a few straggling truckers who were creeping along at a snail's pace in deference to the weather. Snow was falling even harder and faster. The wind had picked up and now was blowing the falling snow into a virtual whirlwind, making it nearly impossible to see through.

It was beautiful, Alex thought with a weary sigh, taking another sip of her coffee, as long as you didn't have to drive in it. Or walk in it, she thought with a scowl, curling her toes in her now seriously damp boots. The snow was coming down so hard it was impossible to keep up with it. Crews had been plowing the parking lot even as she and Michael had alighted from the car, but she still had had to walk in ankle-deep snow. So in addition to everything else, she was now wet as well.

Shivering a bit, she stifled a yawn, then propped her elbows on the table, leaning her head on one hand, watching Mother Nature's fury. She was so unbearably tired; in spite of the strong shot of caffeine her eyes kept sliding closed.

"Alex?"

Michael's voice caused her to jump. Blinking, she realized she must have dozed for a moment. Embarrassed, she flashed him a sheepish smile.

"I'm sorry." She picked up her coffee and sipped, surprised to see her hand shaking.

Shrugging out of his leather jacket, Michael slid into the opposite side of the booth. He started to say something, but paused when the waitress came bustling over with their order.

"Steak and over-easy eggs," she said as she slid a plate in front of Michael. His stomach growled. He hadn't realized how hungry he was until he'd actually smelled and seen the food.

It had been a long day, and somehow he'd forgotten to eat. He glanced at Alex, feeling something tug at his heart.

The lady looked dead on her feet. Fatigue circled her eyes and she was seriously pale. Her hands were shaking as she brought her coffee cup to her lips. He was going to have to get her to the cabin and into bed—soon—before she collapsed on him.

"Steak and over medium for the lady." The waitress slid Alex's plate in front of her with a wide smile. "I'll get you a refill of coffee." Alex wasn't listening, she was watching Michael. He looked grim—more so than usual. Something was wrong. She could see it in the worry lines around his eyes, and in the harsh set of his mouth. Her heart began to beat faster.

"What's wrong now?" Her eyes searched his face, and he lifted a finger to his lips to caution her as the waitress returned to fill their cups. Smiling her thanks, Alex picked up her fork, then waited. "Well?" Her eyes searched his. She hated when he was noncommunicative. It usually meant something was wrong. But then again whenever Michael Tyler was around it almost *always* meant something was wrong, she thought with a frown. The man had an irritating habit of bringing trouble with him everywhere he went. She tried not to let her worry get the best of her.

As soon as the waitress left, Alex swallowed the fear in her throat. "Did you talk to your captain?"

"Yeah." Michael avoided her gaze, glancing down at his food.

"And?"

He sighed heavily, glanced out the window, then back at her, knowing she wasn't going to like what he had to say. Then again, she usually never did.

"And...it seems as if your apartment isn't the only place Webster and his men broke into tonight." His words were edged with sarcasm and just a hint of temper as he began eating his food.

Touching her throbbing forehead, Alex frowned in confusion. "Michael," she said with a weary sigh. "What are you talking about?" She was far too tired for riddles.

Michael's shoulders moved in an indulgent shrug. Picking up his coffee, he took a sip, letting the liquid sit in his mouth a moment before swallowing.

"Michael?" Impatient, she watched him. She knew him well enough to know when he had something to tell her—something he didn't want to tell her: he hemmed and hawed and stalled. And she was entirely out of patience tonight. Taking a deep breath for control, Alex let it out slowly. "All right, Lieutenant. Let's hear it." She pinned him with her gaze, which, in spite of her fatigue, was clear, strong and impossibly angry. *"All of it,"* she clarified, lest he decided to be cute and force her to drag bits and pieces out of him.

His mouth quirked in amusement and he almost smiled. Even though she looked ready to drop, and fragile enough at the moment to make him ache to put his arms around her in comfort, she still had that sass.

Running a hand through his hair, Michael released a long breath. "Someone broke into your office tonight."

"My office?" she repeated with a decided scowl. "Why would anyone break into my office?" She shook her head, trying to make sense of this. "What on earth could they want?" Her frown deepened. "There's nothing in there but a bunch of battered old office furniture, a couple of typewriters that have definitely seen better days, and a secondhand coffeemaker that makes barely passable coffee. Hardly the stuff for a good score."

Absently, Michael rubbed a hand over his chin. It was stubbly and scratchy, and he realized he wanted a bath and needed a shave. He hoped Ryce still kept a stash of supplies at the cabin since he hadn't bothered to stop at his apartment to get his shaving kit, a change of clothes, or anything else.

"I don't think they were looking to make a score, Alex." He was deliberately being evasive, trying not to scare her. He cut another piece of steak and slipped it into his mouth.

"Then what were they looking for?" Her eyes searched his.

"I'm not sure." Michael shrugged again, cutting another piece of meat. "But the captain said it didn't look like anything was taken. They merely went through the file cabinets. The one with the employment records, to be exact." He watched awareness skitter over her face. She raised a shaky hand to her forehead.

"Employment records," she repeated softly. Her eyes suddenly widened in comprehension. "Oh, my God! Michael, my employment records list my parents as my next of kin, complete with their address." At the flashed warning in his eyes, Alex leaned forward and lowered her voice. "Michael," she hissed, "they have my parents' address. I'm a single parent—where else would my kid be at Christmas but with my parents?" He didn't like the look on her face or the threadiness of her voice. Without thinking, he reached across the table and covered her hand with his.

"Alex, listen to me." His voice was calm and deliberately soothing as he curled his fingers over hers. Her hands were trembling and ice cold. "The break-in happened *after* your apartment was broken into, and *after* they put a tail on us, which means they didn't know where we were going, and they didn't get your parents' address until late tonight." Absently he stroked the soft skin of her hand, trying to inject some warmth into her. "Sometime within the past two hours. Even if they had the address, and put two and two together, there's no way they're going to make it up to your parents' house tonight." Michael glanced out the window, now suddenly grateful that the snow was still coming down, that a good old-fashioned blizzard held them in its grip.

"Not in this weather. I guarantee it. If we can't make it up there and we've got several hours' head start, they certainly can't." He squeezed her hand reassuringly.

She threaded her fingers through his and held on, grateful for his reassuring touch. It gave her that unexpected feeling of safety again—a feeling never experienced with any other man before; a feeling she'd never thought she needed before.

The realization startled her, knowing she was going to have to spend who knew how many days and nights with him. She couldn't help but wonder if she was going to be able to control her feelings and emotions. It was difficult where he was concerned on a good day, almost impossible on a day like today when she was frazzled and near the end of her rope with worry and fatigue and being with Michael seemed the only safe place in the world. She realized that at the moment she wanted nothing more than to bury her head in his shoulder and have him hold her until all the fear was gone.

Astonished by her own feelings, and chewing her bottom lip in worry, Alex glanced out the window again, hoping against hope that what Michael was telling her was the truth, hoping that maybe *this* time he was being totally honest with her, hoping against hope that the blasted snow kept up so that Webster and his men couldn't get to Gabriel—at least not before they did.

She looked up at him, her eyes wide, wary and more than a little frightened. Michael found to his dismay he was drawn to that as much as he was drawn to her sass and fire. Without thinking, he lifted his hand and touched her cheek. Her eyes widened a fraction, then slowly slid closed as she nestled her face against the warmth of his hand, enjoying his comfort, his touch, knowing she was once again playing with fire. But right now she was far too fatigued to worry about the consequences. She just accepted his comfort, his touch, because she desperately needed something safe and calm in the face of all the fear that had invaded her life. And Michael was the safest thing in her life right now.

"Alex?" His voice was very soft, and she slowly opened her eyes. He could see the trust in them again. It was the same way she had looked at him back in the apartment and it made something shift and soften inside. He wondered if she knew just how damn dangerous she was. Dealing with Webster was going to be a breeze compared to the kind of danger he felt at the moment, looking into those scared, wary eyes, knowing he was responsible, knowing she was somehow getting to him. He did not find the thought re-assuring.

"Please, don't worry." A ghost of a smile touched his lips. Two smiles in one day. He was *really* losing it! But something about this little spitfire made him want to smile.

"I've got everything handled. I already called the Lake Geneva police department." She looked suddenly hopeful, and he almost smiled again. The look of hope gave him a warm feeling inside, reminding him that she trusted him. "I've briefed them on the situation and they're going to stake out your parents' house tonight. And don't worry," he added at the look that crossed her features. "They won't do anything to alarm your parents. They'll be very dis-creet—your parents won't even know they're there. They'll just keep a squad close by to keep an eye on things until I can safely get up there and get Gabriel into my custody."

Michael's eyebrows drew together suddenly. "Al-though, it might not be a bad idea to call your parents and let them know what's going on. Don't alarm them," he advised seriously and Alex smiled. "What?" He scowled. "What's so amusing?" She shook her head, picking at her food, then pushed her plate away. She'd lost her appetite.

"Michael, you don't know my parents." She was sud-denly filled with a sense of warmth and love. Just thinking about her parents and her family and the love and security that had always been a part of her life made some of her fear soften. She raised her gaze to his.

"Michael, my parents are as protective of their grand-children as they were with their own children. When my parents find out someone is after Gabriel—" She shook her head, chuckling softly. "I hope for Webster's sake he has the good sense not to try anything at my parents' because he might get a lot more than he bargained for."

"Oh, Lord," Michael groaned, wondering if her par-ents were anything like her. No doubt. The thought made him scowl. Well, she had to inherit her grit and determi-nation from someone. He just hoped her parents weren't going to do anything stupid. "Do you think it would be better not to tell them?"

Alex shook her head. "No, they'd never forgive me if I did that." Her eyes met his. "We're a family, Michael. We stick together, especially in times of trouble." She watched him intently, and from the look on his face it was clear he didn't have a clue what she was talking about. Obviously Michael Tyler had no loving familial memories in his past, or ties in his present.

"Do you understand?" She saw his eyes darken and narrow, but not before she noticed the utter bleakness in them and instantly knew that not only didn't he understand, but whatever family memories he had were not pleasant or warm or loving. It made her tender heart ache just a bit more for him. Lord, the things this man was capable of doing to her heart.

Alex glanced away, trying to steel her emotional defenses. She'd never really thought about her own family ties simply because they were so much a part of her life, a part of *her*, that perhaps she'd never fully appreciated how much a part of who she was they were until now.

She couldn't even imagine not having the love and support of her family. Sure, at times they could be annoying and interfering, but their intentions were always honorable and well-meaning. There was no disguising the love and devotion they all had for one another. They were one extended unit connected by love.

She glanced at Michael. He had never said anything about his past or his parents; actually, he'd never said much about anything personal, so she couldn't help but wonder if his emotional barriers had something to do with his childhood. Thinking about what he'd said about Gabriel earlier this evening, she saw the pieces were beginning to make sense; but as curious as she was, she decided this wasn't the time or the place to ask about it. Not that she expected an answer anyway.

"Michael." Alex touched her forehead where an incessant throb had started. She wanted him to understand how important family was to her. "My parents are very protective." Her eyes lit with respect and laughter. "Just let them think that someone is hurting one of their loved ones, especially one of their kids, and all hell would break loose. We used to tease my mother because she's this tiny little thing, but boy, she's one lady you don't want to tangle with, especially when it comes to her family or someone she loves." Alex chuckled. "My mother gives the word *protective* a whole new meaning."

"Sort of like you with Gabriel?" Now he understood why she was so defensive and protective of her son and all her other helpless charges. She came by her love and sense of family honestly. It was what she knew; the *only* thing she knew.

Family.

They'd loved and protected her, and now she was doing the same with her own son. The thought brought on an unbearably heavy feeling in Michael's chest.

"Yes, Michael, just like me and Gabriel." She shrugged. "Our family sticks together in times of trouble. It's the only way we know how to do things." She frowned suddenly. "And if this isn't trouble," she added miserably, "boy, I don't know what is."

"You're right." Michael's mouth quirked. "I have a feeling I'm going to like your parents."

Her face softened. "You will, Michael. They're wonderful. They've always been there for us. No matter what the circumstances, no matter what the problem, we always knew we had their love and support." A soft smile curved her lips. "That didn't mean they always liked the things we did, but they always made sure we knew that their love and support was unwavering." Sipping her coffee, she dragged a hand through her hair. "It's just something I've never had to think about."

Pausing, Alex took a deep breath. "When I decided to adopt Gabriel, I talked at great length with my parents as well as my brothers and sisters.'' She hesitated a moment, glancing away. ''Since I was no longer married, adopting a child as a single parent was a very difficult decision. I wanted Gabriel to be in the best home possible, wanted him to have all the love and care I believe every child needs and deserves. It took a while before I realized that even single, I could give him all the things he needed, that I wanted to give him all of that, and in fact I needed him as much as he needed me.''

Shock flickered across Michael's features. She'd never mentioned that she'd been married, and it had never occurred to him simply because she seemed so devoted to her job and her charges. For some reason he just assumed she'd never had a special man in her life—by choice. She was a beautiful, giving woman, the kind of woman any man would want.

So what the hell happened to Mr. Kent? he suddenly wondered.

''Michael?'' She was looking at him curiously. She seemed to have lost him somewhere along the line. Blinking, he brought his attention back to her. ''Is something wrong?''

He shook his head, sipping his coffee, trying to get his emotions under control. ''No. Go on, what were you saying about adopting Gabriel?''

She spoke slowly, carefully. ''I loved Gabriel almost from the moment I laid eyes on him.'' Her face softened into a warm smile. ''Even though he was rough and ragged, there was just something about him, something very, very special.'' She shook her head. ''I can't really explain it,'' she added softly. Michael understood. He'd felt the same way about the kid himself. ''I knew it would be difficult, but I was certain I could handle him.''

''And you did,'' Michael said with admiration, watching her. Something was bothering her. He knew it as surely as he knew she was sitting in front of him. It was that invisible emotional connection rearing its ugly head again, that twining thread that ran between them, signaling what she was thinking or feeling without her ever saying a word. He wondered why it no longer seemed to annoy him. "What's wrong?"

Taking a deep breath, Alex licked her lips. "Do you remember during the trial, especially when Gabriel was testifying, how brave and full of macho bravado he seemed?" Michael nodded, wondering where she was going with this. "He acted so...so fearless," Alex added.

"It took a lot of guts to do what the kid did." Michael adjusted his long frame, trying to get comfortable and ease the ache in his knee.

"I know." Alex stared into her coffee cup for a moment. "I'd applied for temporary guardianship and by the time the trial was over Gabriel was living with me." She sighed heavily. "Anyway, after the trial was over, I was so relieved, I thought Gabriel's problems were behind him now and we could start to make a new life for ourselves."

A skitter of alarm washed over Michael. Instinctively, he laid his hand over hers again, knowing something was desperately wrong here.

"What happened, Alex?" His eyes searched hers and she avoided his gaze, not wanting him to see her pain. Her eyes swam with tears for a moment, but she stubbornly blinked them away.

"Gabriel started having nightmares," she said slowly. "Very bad nightmares. I thought...I thought they were just a result of the trial, and I thought they'd just go away eventually."

"But they didn't?" he asked softly and she shook her head.

"No. They got worse. He would wake up screaming. His whole body would shake." Her voice dropped to a hushed whisper. "He wouldn't let me near him, Michael." She paused to wipe her eyes. "He wouldn't let *anyone* near him. Gabriel was literally terrified of everything and everyone. He'd curl up in a corner somewhere and he just wouldn't move. He wouldn't talk, he'd just—shake and shake."

Michael's jaw clenched as her words registered. He didn't say a word but he looked as if someone had just yanked his heart out. He struggled to control his emotions. The thought of her and Gabriel going through this alone suddenly infuriated him. Anger he could handle right now; it allowed him to bury some of the other emotions swamping him.

"Damn it Alex! Why didn't you call me? Maybe I could have done something to help." He was in serious danger of losing what was left of his temper, but the pained look on her face caused his anger to wither.

"Call you?" Alex repeated, showing a little temper of her own. "Excuse me, Lieutenant, but if I recall, the day the trial was over you walked out of the courtroom and out of our lives without so much as a goodbye. And I didn't see you again until a few hours ago when you dropped into my life, once again bearing glad tidings." Swiping at her damp eyes, Alex glared at him. Call him, indeed!

There were quite a few things she'd like to call him at the moment, and none of them were pleasant. How dare he get angry over her actions! He was the one who'd just up and walked away without ever looking back.

Leaning forward in the booth, Alex lowered her voice, but it was still etched with anger. "And why would I even consider calling you?" she demanded, and he realized with a start that he'd hurt her somehow. He looked at her curiously, stunned. "I didn't even know how to find you," she accused, her eyes welling with tears again. "And somehow, storming into the police station with the news that I was looking for a wayward cop just didn't sit very well with me." Pride prevented it. She'd *never* chase a man, especially one who'd rejected her.

Astonished, Michael simply stared at her, wondering what the hell she was so angry about.

Could she have been hurt because of the way he'd just walked away from her two years ago?

At the time he hadn't been thinking of *her* feelings—just his own.

Was it possible she had been having trouble controlling her feelings and emotions for him, too?

The thought intrigued him. If so, that meant...she cared about him.

Stunned, Michael frowned. She had cared about him even two years ago. The thought brought a warm smile to his empty heart. No wonder she was so mad at him when he showed up tonight. Lord, the lady must think he was an insensitive brute. He almost grinned. He had a feeling that was *exactly* what she thought of him. But he realized now probably wasn't the time to go into the matter. There was something else far more important.

"Alex, what happened to Gabriel?" He watched her try to control the emotions that swept over her, but she couldn't seem to find the strength. Her eyes grew watery with tears and they slipped down her cheeks. Twice, she opened her mouth to try and speak, but simply couldn't manage it.

Worried, without a word, Michael slid out of the booth and in next to her, dropping an arm around her shoulder and pulling her close. It wasn't like her to cry and lament over things; she was more the "grab the problem and take charge" kind of lady, so this lapse alarmed him. Damn it! He wished he had known. Maybe he would have handled things differently. Then again, maybe not. Michael sighed wearily.

He'd laid a lot in her lap tonight. An awful lot. And from the sound of things, she'd already had more than enough to handle, but he had no doubt she would do what she always did—handle things—with or without his or anyone else's help. He cursed himself again for having to get her and Gabriel involved in this again.

Stroking her hair, he pressed her face against his shoulder, and felt the silent sobs shake her. Her hand snaked up and clutched at his shirt, clinging to him for comfort. He wanted to give her that comfort, yet knew how dangerous it was.

From the moment he'd laid eyes on her again tonight he'd been moving closer to her instead of away from her. He knew she was trouble—big trouble to him and his absent heart. Yet for some reason he couldn't seem to find it in him to hold her at bay. Or control his own emotions, which were seriously in jeopardy right now. Any other time he'd have run like hell, but he couldn't run; not this time. She and Gabriel needed him. So he had nowhere to go and nowhere to run.

He had no choice but to stay. And hope like hell he could handle it.

And her.

"It's all right." Stroking her hair, he tried to bank down his feelings at having her so close. Even though she was cold, wet and tired, not to mention emotionally drained, she still smelled like heaven.

"Take your time, Alex." He waited, letting her gather some strength from him. "Just take your time," he said quietly, glancing out the window in an effort to divert his attention from her scent and from her. He watched the snow blast down with a fury. It hadn't let up at all. It just kept blowing and accumulating.

Sniffling, Alex relaxed against him, wondering if anything ever shook the man. He was so calm all the time. It was as if *nothing* ever got to him. Maybe that's why he was so good at his job.

And so lousy at dealing with his emotions. You couldn't reach something you couldn't touch.

Swiping at her nose, she lifted her head, trying to control her resentment. Too many feelings and memories were engulfing her at the moment; she simply felt overloaded and she knew the man sitting next to her had a lot to do with what she was feeling.

Michael reached across the table and handed her a clean napkin to wipe her face. She did, then swiped at her nose again, taking a deep, calming breath.

"Alex," he said quietly. "What happened to Gabriel?"

She hesitated only a moment. "He . . . he had to be hospitalized."

Dragging a hand through his hair, Michael exhaled a long, deep breath. "Tell me about it, Alex." He prodded gently, wanting to hear all of it. "What happened?"

Alex sniffled, then swallowed hard. "Gabriel's nightmares kept getting worse. They didn't just happen at night. Suddenly, Gabriel was having some kind of episodes during the day." She rubbed a hand over her weary, watery eyes. "The doctor finally had to hospitalize him." Chewing her lower lip, she glanced up at Michael, realizing she had his absolute undivided attention. "Have you ever heard of post-traumatic stress disorder?" she asked quietly, and he nodded.

"Of course," he replied, grabbing another napkin and gently dabbing at her cheeks where she'd missed a few tears. The tender gesture had an unbelievable effect on her. She felt most of her resentment and anger vanish, to be replaced by something far more primitive. She wondered if he knew how wonderful he could be, how gentle, how tender, if he'd just let himself go, and stop controlling every damn emotion. "It happened to a lot of Vietnam vets." He tossed the crumpled napkin to the table.

She finally smiled. "Yes, I know, but it's not limited to veterans." Inhaling deeply, she wearily leaned against him, grateful once more that he was there and she was safe. At least for the moment. Her eyes slid closed and she took a long, deep breath, trying to gather her composure.

Leaning on Michael was becoming habit-forming, and she knew she couldn't afford *this* habit, at least not emotionally. And certainly not with him.

She had promised herself long ago that she'd never lean or depend on a man for anything ever again, and she especially couldn't afford to ever lean or depend on *this* man. It was a clear path to heartache. He hadn't returned to her life because of her, but because he *needed* something from her. Again. Just like the last time.

He'd used her once before and she had no doubt he would do it again if necessary.

It wasn't her he was interested in, but what she could *do* for him. She had to remember that. She would never allow herself to be used again, especially not when it concerned her son.

Leaning on Michael either physically or emotionally wasn't safe. She knew it, but for the moment, she decided to indulge herself. She was too drained to do anything else. Gathering her emotions around her like a cloak, she continued.

"Post-traumatic stress syndrome can happen to anyone, especially if they've had a very traumatic experience. Something happens in the brain when a person sees or experiences something so horrible that they simply can't cope with it. A part of your brain shuts down. It's almost as if your brain is protecting you from something you couldn't protect yourself from." Snuggling closer to his warmth, she sighed heavily. "It's a basic survival instinct."

"Paco's murder," Michael said tonelessly. Unconsciously, his jaw tightened. He knew all about basic survival instincts and what it took for a helpless kid to survive when faced with trauma and horror, pain and fear. A brief flash of pain—a memory—flittered through his consciousness. Defiantly, he fought it, tried to push it away and bury it where he'd buried it so many years—and tears—ago.

"Michael?" Concerned at the look on his face, Alex laid a hand on his arm. His eyes were dark, vacant, bleak, so bleak. Her heart constricted. "Are you all right?" she asked softly, and he nodded.

"Gabriel witnessed Paco's murder. That was his horror." He was aghast at how much he ached for Gabriel; how much he wished he could just take away the kid's memories and banish them to hell, never to return. He knew what memories could do, knew how they could hurt and torment.

Alex nodded. "Exactly. But for some reason, during the trial, Gabriel managed to pull off that false bravado baloney, or as I like to call it, his 'macho manly man' act. But after the trial, something happened, and we're still not sure what, but Gabriel became very, very ill." Her voice dropped to a hushed whisper again as her eyes met his. "He was only eight years old, Michael." Her eyes filled with tears again. "And eight-year-olds shouldn't have to go through what he did."

"Yeah, I know." Drawing her close, he sighed heavily. "I know." He just hugged her close for a moment, wanting to take away some of her pain. There were things neither kids nor adults should have to go through, but that didn't amount to a hill of beans when life and reality intruded. He stroked her hair. "How long was he in the hospital?"

"Almost four months," she whispered, remembering and shivering against him. Michael tightened his arm around her, feeling guilty that he hadn't been able to help them when they needed him, and feeling guilty and responsible for his part in the problem.

He brushed an errant strand of hair off her cheek, tucking it behind her ear. Feeling inadequate, he wasn't entirely certain what to say. He wasn't used to offering comfort, but he'd done it twice tonight. Or was it three times?

"It must have been tough, Al."

"It was, Michael. But I had my family, and they helped tremendously." She forced a smile she didn't feel. "For a while the doctors weren't sure if Gabriel would ever get well. I don't know what I would have done without my family or their help and support. I'd taken a leave of absence when Gabriel first got sick, but I had to go back to work, so my mom stayed with him during the day, and I stayed with him every night. On the weekends my dad and sisters and brothers all came down so someone was with him at all times. He was never alone." Licking her lips, she paused.

"It was very important that Gabriel bonded with the family, and even as sick as he was, even though we weren't sure he even realized we were all there, *we* knew it. Maybe it helped us more than him." She took a deep breath. "Slowly, he began to get better. By the time he was fully recovered he'd been with me almost six months, and he was no longer just the child I'd put in to adopt. By then, Gabriel was *my* son in every sense of the word. A couple of pieces of paperwork wouldn't make a difference, and in fact, weren't all that important to us. Do you understand what I mean?" Her eyes steadily searched his and she wasn't sure he understood. His negligent shrug said volumes. She took a deep breath and continued.

"One of the things to come out of Gabriel's illness was his...dependence on me. He was a child who had never had a family, or a parent whom he could depend or rely on. In his experience, both with his real family and his foster homes, family didn't stick around. They shipped him off somewhere, or sent him back to the agency whenever he got into trouble, or whenever things got too much for them."

Michael's face showed signs of strain. His body was rigid with suppressed anger. "No wonder the kid couldn't trust anyone," he said bitterly. "He'd never had anyone he could trust." He knew exactly how Gabriel felt; knew, too, what happened when you never allowed yourself to trust, to love, to care. He knew how empty it left you. Empty and desolate.

"Exactly, Michael." She looked at him, surprised to see so much emotion on his face. "But I didn't go away, and neither did my family. Not once during the entire time he was sick was Gabriel ever alone." She smiled softly, fiddling with the remains of a napkin. "For Gabriel, my being there meant more than anything. Of course, I didn't know that then, but by the time he was released from the hospital we had bonded in a way that he'd never been able to do with anyone else." She glanced up at him. "Michael, he actually allowed himself to start loving someone."

"You," Michael said in admiration, wondering why he wasn't in the least bit surprised. Proud, fierce and protective, this lady could probably get a rock to soften and love her.

"Yes," she admitted proudly. "Gabriel began to learn how to love. But more than that, Michael, he finally began to hope that he'd found the home and family he'd always wanted but never had, the one place he belonged. He'd never had that hope before. Do you have any idea how bleak life is for someone without hope?" From the look on his face she had a feeling he knew very well. It saddened her. "It's hard enough to handle that kind of cynicism as an adult, but for a child, it's even worse because it hardens their feelings and emotions, paralyzing them in a sort of emotional limbo. Sometimes they're never able to rekindle those feelings. They go through life without ever being able to trust anyone enough to love. They end up living in an emotional vacuum."

Uncomfortable, Michael shifted his frame. He knew she was talking about Gabriel, but he had a feeling she was also talking about him. Knew, too, how true what she was saying was. He knew all about paralyzed feelings and emotional vacuums. He'd spent his life living in a self-imposed vacuum, devoid of any ties, any emotions or any commitments.

"Gabriel finally had that hope, Michael, and something far more important—the love he'd never had before. He knew that I would never leave him, no matter what. Even though I had told him that a hundred times, trying to reassure him, I guess my actions when he was so sick spoke more than I could ever say." She paused for a moment, inhaling deeply. "I think that's when Gabriel's healing finally began. Within six months of his release from the hospital a great deal of the anger and resentment he'd carried around with him most of his life had been erased, replaced by something far more suitable to a little boy."

"Love," Michael said gruffly, wondering why the one word made him so decidedly uncomfortable. He was so happy and pleased for Gabriel, happy that he finally had all the things he should have had from the day of his birth.

Happy he'd found those things with the woman sitting next to him. Yet, discussing these feelings—feelings he'd never allowed himself to experience—made him decidedly uncomfortable.

"Yes, Michael. Love," Alex said, covering his hand with hers and watching him carefully. "Love really can work miracles. I've seen it in Gabriel. Gabriel's a completely different little boy from the one you knew. The Gabriel you knew was an old, bereft man in a child's body, unable to trust or give or receive love." Her face lit with pleasure. "*My* son Gabriel is a warm, loving, secure little boy. Now that he knows he finally has a family, a real family, and knows that we are never going to be separated, that we'll never go away, no matter what, I think it gave him the security he's been looking for his whole life. He knew that I would never, ever let anything happen to him, that I loved him, and would do my best to make him happy and protect him."

Squeezing his hand, she smiled up at him. For a long heartbeat their eyes met, held, clung, saying more than words could or would ever say. Finally, Alex dragged her eyes away, shaken to the core, but not certain why, knowing only that it had something to do with the man sitting next to her; a man she responded to on every level—physically, emotionally, spiritually.

What was it about him that called to all the primitive female feelings languishing inside her? Feelings she'd thought dead and buried when she buried her marriage. Only when she was with Michael did she realize that those feelings were very much alive. And so was she.

Uncomfortable, she realized she couldn't afford to have such feelings, not for him. It was too dangerous to her heart, and far too costly for her emotions. She couldn't forget he had used her once to further his own aims, and she knew he would do it again if need be.

She couldn't take that kind of betrayal again. Never again. And especially not from him.

"Gabriel is part of us now, part of our family, something no one can ever take away from him. He has just as much love and loyalty as any other member of the family." She paused, looking at him. "Now do you understand about family?"

"Yeah," he said grimly. "At least, your family."

"Michael, what about your fam—"

Instantly, he was on his feet. "We'd better get a move on," he said abruptly, cutting her off. He grabbed the check, deciding it was best to end this conversation now before things got too sticky. Lifting his jacket, Michael shrugged into it, aware she was carefully watching his every move. Draining the last of his coffee, which was now bitter and cold, Michael set the cup down harder than necessary.

"You'd better go phone your folks. Remember what I said, try not to alarm them." He'd deliberately changed the subject, not giving her a chance to speak. "While you're doing that, I'm going into the Mini Mart and get some supplies for the cabin. Ryce generally keeps it well stocked, but his wife is expecting and he hasn't been up in a while, so I don't know what's there. I want to lay in some things just in case." His eyes searched hers. She was still pale and still looked unbearably fatigued, not to mention a little annoyed. If he wasn't so tired it would have amused him. "I'll meet you back here in about ten minutes."

Realizing their conversation had come to an abrupt, and rather rude halt, Alex regretfully realized she'd hit a nerve with Michael. A very sore nerve. It wasn't one she intended to leave alone forever. It was something she intended to pursue—at the right time. She'd seen a miracle with Gabriel, and if he could overcome all the obstacles he'd had to face, surely there was hope that maybe Lieutenant Michael Tyler just might be able to overcome his emotional obstacles as well.

"Does this cabin have a phone?" Annoyed at being so rudely dismissed, she spoke more sharply than she'd intended. "I'd like to give my parents the number."

Wearily, Michael shook his head. "No, it doesn't and even if it did, I wouldn't let you give anyone the number. Calls are too easy to trace. You're supposed to be in protective custody, Alex, remember?" Impatience tinged his words. "Generally you don't go around broadcasting your whereabouts."

"Michael," she said stiffly, getting to her feet. "This is my family we're talking about. After all I've told you, do you honestly think they'd do anything to endanger me?"

"Of course not. At least, not intentionally. But lines can be tapped. There are a hundred ways to find out someone's location or whereabouts from a single call. It's much better if they don't know." His face was grim. "What they don't know they can't tell."

Alex pulled on her coat. It was still damp from the cold and snow. If Lieutenant Michael Tyler thought this conversation was finished, he had better think again. "Do you have any idea what time we'll get to my parents' house tomorrow?"

Michael glanced out the window again. "Depends on the weather. Probably before noon." Looking at his watch, he sighed. "We're about half an hour from the cabin now— that is, in good weather. In this weather, probably an hour to an hour and a half." He glanced at his watch again, obviously impatient. "Let's get a move on, Alex. It's too late and too dark to get stranded." He started toward the doorway leading to the Mini Mart. "I'll meet you here in ten minutes." With that he ambled off, leaving her staring after him.

## Chapter Six

Set back nearly a quarter of a mile from the road, the cabin could barely be seen through the snow. The road had miraculously been plowed, probably by one of Ryce's neighbors, Michael surmised, as he downshifted and eased the Camaro into the long, winding drive.

What should have taken half an hour had taken nearly two hours, and he was tense from the task of simply trying to keep the car on the road. He glanced at Alex. She hadn't said one word since they'd left the restaurant. He knew he'd been rude when he cut her off, but he couldn't help it; he wasn't up to taking a trek down memory lane. Especially not tonight, and not with her. Raking a hand through his hair, Michael sighed heavily. She made him feel things, think about things he knew he had no business thinking or feeling. And until he got a handle on himself and his emotions, he knew better than to play with fire.

As the cabin finally came into view, a small smile played along Michael's lips. Lights flickered somewhere inside and a puff of smoke ambled lazily from the chimney, welcoming them. It wasn't until Alex grabbed his arm that he realized she was anxious.

"What's wrong?" he asked with a frown, noting how rigid she was.

"Someone's here, Michael." Her voice was soft, but edged with tension.

He shook his head. "No, Alex, no one's here."

Her hand tightened on his arm. Even through the leather of his jacket he could feel her warmth. "But the lights, and the chimney..."

He maneuvered the car onto the widened pavement that served as a driveway and led to one of the outer buildings situated just to the right of the cabin itself. He shut the engine off, sighed in relief that their journey was over at least for this night, then turned to Alex.

"When I called the captain back at the restaurant, I also called Ryce to let him know we would be staying here for a few days. His neighbors keep an eye on things for him. Ryce said he'd call one of them and have them turn on some lights and start a fire." He nodded toward the drive. "They probably plowed the drive as well, knowing we'd never be able to get in here tonight if they hadn't." The snow was still coming down so hard, the tracks the tires had made were already disappearing in a haze of white.

Alex heaved a momentary sigh of relief, then another thought had her tensing. "But I thought you said the less people who know who we are, the better?"

"True, very true," he agreed. "But Ryce is my partner. In fact, we both worked the original Webster case. I have to keep him informed of what's going on and where I am." Just in case he needed backup, he thought but didn't add, not wanting to frighten her anymore. At least not tonight.

Ryce was the one person he trusted with his life. After fifteen years they were closer than brothers, and in fact, Ryce was the closest thing to family he'd ever had. Ryce was the one and only person he'd ever been able to count on, truly count on, in his whole life. There wasn't anything he wouldn't do for the man, and vice versa.

He glanced at Alex again. "What do you say we get this show on the road? It's late and you've got to be exhausted." Hungry too, he thought, since she'd done little but pick at her food. He planned to rectify that as soon as he got into some warm, dry clothes.

Alex opened her car door and stepped out, glancing around. The cabin was situated on a large plot of land dotted with huge evergreens and pines that were hung heavy with snow. The cabin itself was low and squat. Set so far back from the road, it would be impossible to see from there, giving her a momentary feeling of relief and safety. It would be difficult for anyone to find her here, unless of course they knew where the cabin was, which Michael had already pointed out was highly unlikely.

Alex heaved a sigh of relief. Wet snow pelted her already damp hair, and blew against her face. Now that she was actually within walking distance of a warm, safe place, she couldn't wait to get inside.

"Michael?" She glanced at him. He was already digging the box of supplies he'd bought out of the trunk. "What do you want me to take?"

"Just your suitcase and yourself." Slamming the trunk shut, he walked around the car. "I can handle everything else."

Nodding, she opened the back door of the car, retrieved the suitcase she'd hurriedly packed, then slammed the door shut and followed Michael up the walk. Balancing the box in one hand, he fished in a frozen planter for a moment.

"What are you doing?" Shivering, Alex stamped her feet against the cold.

"Looking for Ryce's spare key." He grunted, fishing in the frozen dirt some more. "He always leaves it in here." With a sigh of relief, he extracted the key, shook it off, then opened the door. A quick rush of warm air had Alex groaning in heartfelt relief.

"It's warm and dry in here," she said, following him through the doorway. The fire blazed a brilliant hue of orange, causing the snow accumulated on her coat to melt and drip to the floor. Too tired to care, she set down her suitcase and inhaled deeply, thrilled by the familiar scent that assaulted her nose. Her smile widened and she drew off her gloves and coat, rubbing her hands together as she glanced around the expansive room.

A small lamp was lit, casting a warm, hazy glow. The furniture was large, heavy on wood, and definitely man-size. Two brown-and-blue plaid couches dominated the middle of the room. In one corner was a worn recliner in a matching shade of blue. The floor was wood plank and bare. A large oval hand-hooked throw rug lay in the center. The windows were bare, allowing nature to form the pictures that adorned the room. There was a definite coziness to the cabin, as if it were a calm respite from life's chaos. Alex suddenly felt a peacefulness steal over her.

Smiling, she inhaled deeply again. Slipping off her shoes she wiggled her cold toes in relief. Someone must have used pine needles as a starter because the scent of pine emanating from the fire was strong and welcoming in the air.

"Michael?"

The wistful sound of her voice had him turning to glance at her as he tucked the key securely into his jeans pocket. "Yeah?"

Savoring the wonderful scent of the room, she felt her spirits lift. "It smells like Christmas in here."

Michael groaned in disgust, shaking his head. "Is that all you ever think about?" This woman had a one-track mind. He'd better not stand still too long or she might start stringing tinsel around him and hanging ornaments off him. Finish with a star sitting atop his head and she'd probably be thrilled. The mere thought made him scowl.

His humor was bad and getting worse by the minute. His knee was killing him and he was cold and just plain weary. His nerves were shot, and he wasn't exactly long on patience at the moment. It had been a long, aggravating day and he was just about depleted.

"Don't you ever think about it?" She watched him carefully. "Christmas, I mean." His face was etched with fatigue, and something else. Annoyance. She sighed. At least that was one emotion he allowed himself to feel, although she wondered if she should be insulted that she seemed to be the only thing he was ever annoyed at.

"Never," he growled with another shake of his head.

"Why?" Dropping her coat to the couch, she followed him through the living room that led directly into the kitchen. Apparently, there were only two large main rooms—a living room and a kitchen. She'd caught a glimpse of a bath down a long hallway, and guessed that's where the bedrooms were.

With a grunt, Michael set the large box of supplies down on a cozy wood plank table. The kitchen was decorated in soft shades of blue and peach. The wallpaper matched the chair cushions and touches of peach highlighted and dotted the rest of the room. Obviously a woman had had a hand in here.

Straightening, Michael looked at her, his jaw clenched with tension. "Al, do you think we could save the questions until later? *Much* later." He began unpacking the box of supplies, effectively dismissing her. "I think you'd better get into some warm dry clothes before you get sick. There's two bedrooms down the hall. One has a sofa sleeper and the other has a regular bed. Take whichever one you want—I'm not fussy."

No, just cranky, she thought, realizing he was in no mood to talk. Just mentioning Christmas had turned him into a bear. Again, she wondered why he had such an aversion to the day. With a sigh, Alex turned on her heel and went back into the living area to retrieve her suitcase, then headed off to search out the bedrooms.

The first one was rather small and compact, dominated by what was obviously a large, comfortable sleeper-sofa. Continuing down the hall, she found what was clearly the master bedroom. It was large, done in soft shades of green and pink, with a large four-poster bed set square in the middle of the room. Bureaus that looked like real antiques cradled the walls.

Dropping her suitcase, Alex slowly smiled, realizing this was the room she wanted. There was something in this room, she could feel it; something warm, wonderful and welcoming. Maybe it was the huge, inviting bed, or maybe it was the silver-framed family pictures that lined the walls and dotted the bureaus. Whatever it was, she wistfully acknowledge she wanted—no, needed—to enjoy this room if only for one night.

Moving to the photographs, she looked at them, touching the heavy silver frames, smiling at the images. A man and woman were prominent in each picture, and she could see the love and adoration between them. It was probably Michael's friend Ryce, she surmised, acknowledging that he was incredibly good-looking in a fierce, almost primitive way. The woman in the pictures with him was small and petite, and dwarfed by Ryce's incredible size. She was as light as he was dark. Frowning, Alex realized Ryce was probably as big as Michael. Possibly bigger. The mere thought of them as partners made her smile. She certainly wouldn't want to come face-to-face with the two of them in a dark alley—not unless they were on her side.

Feeling a little empty and lost and wondering why, she unpacked her suitcase, headed into the adjoining bath, and quickly ran a hot tub. Twenty minutes later she emerged from the steaming bathroom thoroughly clean, warm and totally exhausted, with her long, damp hair piled haphazardly atop her head, and dressed in a floor-length white flannel gown that fell to the tips of her toes, and rose to the top of her neck. A row of tiny buttons marched down the back of her gown.

Frowning, she struggled, reaching behind her to finish buttoning all the buttons. Her feet were still bare, but not nearly as cold as they'd been before her bath. She could hear Michael moving around in another part of the house.

Stifling a yawn, she followed her nose back to the kitchen where she could smell something familiar and heavenly. Coffee. Fresh coffee, and something else, something...edible. Her stomach began to growl impatiently.

At the restaurant she'd been too preoccupied to eat anything, and now that she was warm, safe and dry, she realized she was famished.

"Whatever you're cooking smells wonderful," she said, coming into the kitchen. Standing at the stove, Michael turned to her, coffeepot in his hand. His eyes quickly took her in from head to toe. He nearly dropped the coffeepot. Dressed in her business suits and heels, Ms. Alexandria Kent was a sight to reckon with, but barefoot, dressed in a feminine flannel nightgown that gently caressed her curves, she nearly took his breath away. She looked delicate and fragile and entirely too appealing for his peace of mind. Or for his poor, aching body.

She'd pulled her hair up, but a few loose tendrils had escaped and were now grazing her cheeks, which were flushed pink from the heat of her bath. Her face was scrubbed clean and devoid of makeup and he realized how really beautiful she was. Her lips were bare, and looked full and soft. An image of what those lips had tasted like suddenly flashed through his mind, and he gripped the handle of the pot harder, dragging his eyes from her mouth. The gown she wore would hardly be considered seductive, but on her, he realized probably anything would look attractive.

Michael swore softly under his breath as he crossed the room and poured her a cup of fresh coffee. As he stood beside her, her scent wafted up to him, enticing him, engulfing him. He hadn't prepared himself for being in such close, intimate quarters with her.

He'd never lived with a woman before. Oh, he'd spent the night with them—or rather a part of the night—but he'd never actually spent an *entire* night with a woman. When it was time to go, he left, anxious to put distance between them.

Realizing he was going to be spending a great deal, if not all his time with Alex for at least the foreseeable future made him realize how much on guard he had to be since he'd finally realized she was unlike any woman he'd ever met. Perhaps that was all part of her allure.

And her danger.

Swallowing hard, Michael turned back to the stove. "Pull up a chair," he ordered, clearing his throat and setting the coffeepot back down on the stove harder than necessary. "I made some soup and grilled ham-and-cheese sandwiches." He busied himself at the stove, trying to get some perspective and rein in his wayward emotions.

Pulling out a chair, Alex sank wearily into it, watching him. There was another bath off the kitchen and he'd showered and changed and now wore a pair of faded jeans and a flannel shirt that stretched wide across his broad shoulders. He'd taken his gun off, and it seemed strange to see him without it. He'd left the top two buttons of his shirt open and when he turned, she saw a faint dusting of dark hair curling upward. For an instant she curiously wondered how far down his body that dusting of hair went. Astonished at the train of her thoughts, she looked away from him.

She couldn't remember the last time she'd had such thoughts about a man; certainly not since her divorce four years ago. She suddenly realized she'd never had such thoughts about a man, not before *or* after her marriage. She'd dated, but not very often, especially now that she had Gabriel. He came first in her life. It had been an adjustment for him, just getting used to having a mother and being part of a family, and she certainly didn't want to introduce another person—specifically a male person—into Gabriel's life. Not unless that male person was going to become a permanent part of their lives.

She couldn't help but glance at Michael again. Michael Tyler wasn't a permanent man. She'd learned that the hard way two years ago, when he'd simply walked away from her without so much as a goodbye. She'd learned, too, how deeply it hurt to discover he'd used her just to get to Gabriel; merely used her to further his own gains.

No, Michael Tyler wasn't a permanent type of man, and she wasn't interested in any other kind. She realized once this situation with Gabriel was over and settled, Michael would no doubt disappear from her life again. The thought stung her, and she tried to fortify her defenses against him. She would never again let a man use her for his own purposes; especially now, especially if it involved her son. And there was nothing Michael Tyler could do this time to sway her or make her change her mind.

Suddenly nervous, she turned away from Michael, searching for something to do. The table was already set with paper plates, napkins, bowls and soupspoons, so there was really nothing left for her to do.

"What did your parents have to say?" Michael asked, trying to find a neutral subject as he carried the plate of sandwiches and the pot of soup to the table. He couldn't believe how nervous he was all of a sudden. It was probably just the close quarters, he decided.

His question brought on a shaky smile as Alex adjusted the trivets for him so he could set down the hot pot. "I spoke to my mother. I told her I'd be up to get Gabriel in the morning."

Pulling out his own chair, Michael sat down, reaching for a sandwich and dropping it onto his plate. Alex reached for a sandwich just as Michael reached for the soup. Their hands brushed and they both froze. Hesitantly, she lifted her gaze to his. It was dark, intense, and sent goose bumps racing up and down her spine. Alex tried to take a deep breath but found she couldn't; for some reason her lungs didn't seem to be working.

Anxious to break the hypnotic spell that was holding her in a death grip, Alex licked her dry lips.

"I—I also told them—" He was still looking at her in a way that was making her thoughts scramble. It was impossibly quiet in the kitchen. The only thing she could hear was the rapid pounding of her heart.

"What did you tell them?" Michael prompted softly, watching her, unable to look away from her, wondering what she was thinking. He knew what *he* was thinking, and knew he'd better get some new thoughts. Real quick.

Alex blinked, then broke the connection by averting her gaze in order to pull her thoughts together. "I...uh...told them not to mention anything to Gabriel—not even the fact that I was coming up there to get him."

Swallowing hard, she dared a glance at him. He was still looking at her with the fierce male intensity that made her body ache for things she knew better than to want. Or need.

No, she'd learned the hard way that wanting a man led to needing, and she could never need or depend on a man for anything. Ever again. Her miserable marriage had taught her that.

As had Michael's past behavior.

She could look and want, but nothing more. Not with him. Not now. Probably not ever. She wondered why the thought cut her to the bone, tearing away at her battered heart.

Alex stared morosely at the tablecloth, thought of sipping her coffee, but knew she might not be able to lift her cup without dropping it. Instead, she settled for taking a bite of her sandwich.

Michael couldn't seem to take his eyes off her. He watched the way her delicate lips closed around the sandwich and his own mouth went dry, remembering again how that mouth had heated under his. He suddenly wanted to do more than look. Much more. Realizing how dangerous his thoughts were, he deliberately rechanneled them.

Raking a hand through his black hair, he sighed. "I'm sure Gabriel would rather hear about this from you anyway." Her head had snapped up. She was merely staring at him, but all warmth was gone from her eyes. "You *are* going to be the one to tell about this, aren't you?"

She shook her head. "I'm not telling him anything about this, Michael." Her chin lifted stubbornly and she had that determined glint in her eyes again. Trouble, Michael realized immediately. That look was definitely trouble.

He frowned. "Why not?"

"Because he's not going to testify for you. Not now. Not ever. After what I told you happened to Gabriel after he testified the last time, I'm sure you can understand my position now. You'll just have to find some other way to put Webster away."

A look of disbelief or disapproval moved into his eyes. She wasn't sure which it was. "There is no other way, Alex," he said carefully. He knew how much he was putting Gabriel at risk, physically and emotionally, but he had no choice. The danger from Webster if he didn't testify was far greater.

"Find one." Her voice was as determined as his. She took a deep breath. "The only reason I agreed to tell you where Gabriel was, and to let you take us into protective custody, was to keep my son safe. That's all that matters to me. But don't think I've changed my mind, or will change my mind." Stubbornly, she shook her head. "Not about this."

"Alex, try to be reasonable here. You know I wouldn't ask if it wasn't absolutely necessary, especially knowing what I know." He studied her, holding her gaze. "We need Gabriel's testimony."

"Michael!" she cried in exasperation. "Would you please stop being a cop? This is my son we're talking about."

"I can't stop being a cop," he snapped. "That's what I am, what I've always been."

"But that's not the only thing you are," she retorted, her temper simmering.

"What are you talking about?" Scowling, he shook his head. "Speak English. It's too damn late and I'm too damn tired for riddles."

"You're a man as well as a cop," she said coldly, grabbing the ladle and helping herself to some hot soup. "At least, that's the way it's supposed to work."

His gaze flew to hers. "What is that supposed to mean?" he asked gruffly, not entirely certain she hadn't insulted him and questioned his manhood, as well.

Her gaze met his, the challenge bright and beckoning as she dropped the ladle back into the soup with a decided plop, sending the hot liquid cascading dangerously close to the rim.

"See, the way this is supposed to work is that even cops are supposed to be men, and men are supposed to have feelings and emotions, but I don't expect Michael Tyler, cop extraordinaire, to understand that, because Michael the cop doesn't allow himself to have feelings and emotions, because people just might think he's...human." She made a great effort of straightening the napkin on her lap in an attempt to do something with her hands rather than wrap them around his neck. "And you certainly couldn't have anyone thinking that you just might be human...and have, God forbid, feelings, now could you?" She snapped her napkin back on the table. "Why, Lieutenant Tyler, just think what that might do to your image."

Furious, he was instantly on his feet, sending his chair sprawling backward. His hands snaked out and he yanked her upward, hauling her close in one quick motion, so fast her feet actually left the floor.

Stunned and momentarily breathless, Alex tilted her head to look at him. She had an instantaneous sense of anticipation before his mouth swooped down and captured hers. There was no gentle subtlety to his kiss; it was pure male ruthlessness, as if branding her as his own. His mouth claimed and possessed hers, nudging it open. Sliding her arms up his chest and around his neck, she surrendered— completely. Her mouth opened under the assault of his, and she moaned softly when she felt the soft glide of his tongue against hers.

She couldn't remember ever experiencing such a hot rush of feelings before. They came quickly, erupting full force, making her ache for him. She moaned again, molding her entire body against his until she could feel the hard evidence of his arousal pressing against her.

Alex moaned as her fingers slid through the silky strands of his hair. It was softer than she'd ever imagined. Just like his kiss was sweeter than in her dreams, hotter than she'd ever imagined.

Michael heard her groan and wanted to drown in her. To bury himself deep and hard until the ache inside his heart was gone. He'd never felt this way with a woman. He'd wanted them, possessed them, but he'd never felt this... need, this... rightness, this intense, fierce desire to both claim and protect. The more of her he had, the more he wanted, until he knew he'd never get enough.

It scared the hell out of him.

Abruptly, he wrenched his mouth from hers and released her, setting her down gently on her feet. His arms were still around her, steadying her. She was so shaken she would have collapsed, had he released her.

"Don't ever say I don't have feelings," he growled, shaken to the core by the depth of his emotions and the seemingly insatiable desire storming through his already aching body. Dropping his arms, he turned and walked out of the room.

Still shaken, Alex stared after him. Absently, she touched her mouth with a shaky hand. She could still feel the warmth of Michael's mouth, could still taste his lips, could still feel her own need pulsing through her.

She'd hurt him with her words as surely as if she'd taken a knife and plunged it into his heart. The knowledge seared into her, shaming her, humbling her. She'd never meant to hurt him.

Slowly she walked into the living room. He was standing at the window, arms bracketed high on either side of the frame, his back to her. His stance seemed casual, yet she could see the tension in the long lines of his body.

"Michael?" Hesitantly, she came up behind him, but she didn't dare touch him; instead she crossed her arms across her breasts. "I'm sorry," she whispered. "I didn't mean—"

"Yes, you did," he said quietly, not bothering to turn around. A log jumped in the fireplace, sending a halo of orange sparks upward. There was a long pause and then he finally asked, "What happened to Mr. Kent?"

Alex blinked, not certain she'd heard him correctly. His question had come out of nowhere. The man had a habit of keeping her totally off base. "W-what?"

It had been eating away at him ever since they'd been in the restaurant and she'd mentioned she'd been married.

"Your husband," he repeated, his voice low and controlled. "What happened to him?"

Confused, she shook her head as she dared a step closer. "Nothing happened to him."

"Why isn't he your husband anymore?" He shifted his frame, easing the weight off of his aching knee.

Alex turned to stare into the fireplace. She rarely talked about her personal life with anyone; it was too painful, too humiliating—even now, after all these years. She considered it her own personal failure, and she didn't like to fail at anything.

But she'd had no choice, been given no choice.

"I divorced him," she said quietly; too quietly, Michael thought, wondering if Ms. Alexandria Kent had a few secrets of her own. He could hear the tension in her voice, but he couldn't turn to face her. Not yet. Not after his display of emotion in the kitchen, not until he got himself back under control. But he knew there was more here, more than she was telling; knew it as surely as he knew his name. Why hadn't he ever sensed it before? Maybe it was enough that he sensed it now.

"Why'd you divorce him?" There was a slight draft from the window, and Michael shifted out of its path, but continued staring at the drifting, swirling snow.

Alex was surprised by the emotion that suddenly clogged her throat. She'd been certain she'd buried all of that when she'd buried her marriage, and was surprised now to learn that she hadn't.

Her eyes burned for an instant, but she stubbornly held the tears back. She would *not* cry, not again, not ever over this.

"Alex?" he prompted softly, watching the snow blow and swirl around outside. He'd never merely stared at it before. It had a beautiful mystical quality to it.

Another log shifted and Alex jumped, her nerves taut. She took a deep breath, then glanced down at the floor, running her bare toe along the edge of the hand-hooked rug. Gathering her courage, she took a long, deep breath.

"I divorced my husband because...because he abandoned me."

## Chapter Seven

For the second time that night, he took her news the way a drunk takes a punch. Nausea rose and nearly choked him. Abruptly, Michael whirled around, his face a dark, dangerous mask. He didn't even notice his hands had balled into fists. Alex did. But she realized she had no fear—not of Michael, never of Michael. In spite of his size she'd always known it; maybe that's why there'd always been such a connection between them. In spite of his emotional coldness, in spite of the fact that he wouldn't let her or anyone else close to him, she knew in her heart, without question, without doubt, he was the kind of man who would always use his hands to *protect* her. *Never* to harm her.

Michael's jaw clenched. "He what?"

"He abandoned me," Alex repeated, her voice a whisper. She couldn't bear to look at him after her admission. Slowly, gently he lifted her chin until her gaze met his.

"Tell me about it," he encouraged quietly, his eyes tender, his voice concerned.

"There's really nothing to tell." She ran a hand through her hair, nervous, and needing to do something with her hands. "We were married about a year when we first started trying to have a child." She tried to smile against the pain that suddenly pierced through her, but simply couldn't manage it. "We'd both wanted children very badly." She glanced away. "I had a miscarriage. Then another and another." Taking a deep breath she laced her fingers together to stop their trembling.

Michael moved closer to her but saw her stiffen and backed away. He didn't want to spook her, especially now. Anxious to do something with his hands, he slid them into his jeans pockets, fearing he'd pull her close and hold her if he didn't.

"Go on, Alex."

"Finally, the doctors told me not to bother trying anymore." She dared a glance at him. "There was no way I would be able to carry a child to term." The emotion came stronger, faster, and this time she couldn't contain it. Her throat seemed to swell as well as her eyes. She turned away from him. "There would be no children for me. Not ever." The last words came out in a hushed whisper. "So he left me. Just walked out the door one day and never came back. No explanation. No fighting. Nothing. Just a set of divorce papers."

Shaking his head, Michael brought his hands to his face and scrubbed at it. He prayed her husband was dead. It would save him the trouble of killing him. How could anyone be so cold? So callous?

Carefully, he laid a hand on her shoulder but said nothing, letting her continue on at her own pace. She did after a few minutes.

"I had always wanted a family, a large family, but..." Biting her lip, she glanced away, trying to contain her tears. Unconsciously, she laid a hand across her barren stomach, and lifted stricken eyes to his. He suddenly felt as if someone had just squeezed his heart in a vise. And it hurt like hell.

FREE BOOKS!

FREE GIFT!

# PLAY THE "LUCKY 7" SLOT MACHINE GAME!

## AND YOU CAN GET FREE BOOKS PLUS A FREE GIFT!

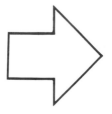

# NO COST! NO OBLIGATION TO BUY!
# NO PURCHASE NECESSARY!

## PLAY "LUCKY 7"
## AND GET FIVE FREE GIFTS!

# HOW TO PLAY:

1. With a coin, carefully scratch off the silver box at the right. Then check the claim chart to see what we have for you—FREE BOOKS and a gift—ALL YOURS! ALL FREE!

2. Send back this card and you'll receive brand-new Silhouette Special Edition® novels. These books have a cover price of $3.99 each, but they are yours to keep absolutely free.

3. There's no catch. You're under no obligation to buy anything. We charge nothing—ZERO—for your first shipment. And you don't have to make any minimum number of purchases—not even one!

4. The fact is thousands of readers enjoy receiving books by mail from the Silhouette Reader Service™ months before they're available in stores. They like the convenience of home delivery and they love our discount prices!

5. We hope that after receiving your free books you'll want to remain a subscriber. But the choice is yours—to continue or cancel, anytime at all! So why not take us up on our invitation, with no risk of any kind. You'll be glad you did!

© 1990 HARLEQUIN ENTERPRISES LIMITED

**NOT ACTUAL SIZE**

*This beautiful porcelain box is topped with a lovely bouquet of porcelain flowers, perfect for holding rings, pins or other precious trinkets — and is yours absolutely free when you accept our no risk offer!*

**DETACH AND MAIL CARD TODAY**

# PLAY "LUCKY 7"

**Just scratch off the silver box with a coin.
Then check below to see the gifts you get.**

**YES!** I have scratched off the silver box. Please send me all the gifts for which I qualify. I understand I am under no obligation to purchase any books, as explained on the back and on the opposite page.

235 CIS AX5X
(U-SIL-SE-02/96)

NAME

ADDRESS                                                      APT.

CITY                                          STATE            ZIP

| 7 7 7 | **WORTH FOUR FREE BOOKS PLUS A FREE PORCELAIN TRINKET BOX** |
| 🍒 🍒 🍒 | **WORTH THREE FREE BOOKS** |
| ● ● ● | **WORTH TWO FREE BOOKS** |
| 🔔 🔔 🍒 | **WORTH ONE FREE BOOK** |

Offer limited to one per household and not valid tc current Silhouette Special Edition® subscribers. All orders subject to approval.

© 1990 HARLEQUIN ENTERPRISES LIMITED          **PRINTED IN U.S.A.**

## THE SILHOUETTE READER SERVICE™: HERE'S HOW IT WORKS

Accepting free books places you under no obligation to buy anything. You may keep the books and gift and return the shipping statement marked "cancel". If you do not cancel, about a month later we'll send you 6 additional novels, and bill you just $3.12 each plus 25¢ delivery and applicable sales tax, if any.* That's the complete price, and—compared to cover prices of $3.99 each—quite a bargain! You may cancel at any time, but if you choose to continue, every month we'll send you 6 more books, which you may either purchase at the discount price…or return at our expense and cancel your subscription.

*Terms and prices subject to change without notice. Sales tax applicable in N.Y.

If offer card is missing, write to: Silhouette Reader Service, 3010 Walden Ave., P.O. Box 1867, Buffalo, NY 14269-1867

SILHOUETTE READER SERVICE
3010 WALDEN AVE
PO BOX 1867
BUFFALO NY 14240-9952

**BUSINESS REPLY MAIL**
FIRST CLASS MAIL    PERMIT NO. 717    BUFFALO, NY

POSTAGE WILL BE PAID BY ADDRESSEE

NO POSTAGE
NECESSARY
IF MAILED
IN THE
UNITED STATES

"Alex." He only whispered her name, then slipped his hands around her waist and slowly drew her close. He thought she'd resist, but she didn't. She came willingly, clutching his shirt and burrowing her head against his chest. Her eyes slid closed in relief. It had been so long since she'd talked about this with anyone, so long since she'd been able to; there were still the feelings of shame, of humiliation, of inadequacy. The feelings had faded with time and she'd gone on to build a happy, productive life for herself and Gabriel; but when she did talk about this, when she was reminded that at one time she wasn't so strong, so capable—that she had been vulnerable, needy, and devastated by the betrayal of a man she thought she'd loved.

So she rarely talked about it with anyone. But for some reason, she wanted to tell Michael about it. With a sigh, she clutched his shirt tighter. She wondered again why she felt so safe with him. Only him. Maybe because somewhere in that deep female instinct that every woman possessed, she knew she had nothing to fear from him. At least, not physically.

Emotionally... well, that was another story.

Resting his chin on the top of her silky head, Michael held her lightly. He'd always been aware of the differences in their sizes, even more so now that she was barefoot, and dressed in a barely there nightgown.

He couldn't help but smile. In spite of her size, or rather lack of it, she apparently had no fear. How many times did she go toe-to-toe with him, holding her own, cutting him and anyone else down to size with her sass and her spirit?

How had she recovered? he wondered, thinking about the hurt and loss she'd suffered.

How had she put herself back together again?

How did you get over a betrayal like that and go on to love again? And it was clear she loved, and loved well. All one had to do was hear her talk about Gabriel to know she loved him. Somehow, she'd managed to put her painful past behind and go on to build a happy life.

So why hadn't or couldn't he?

He pushed the thought away, unable to deal with it right now. They were two different people with two different kinds of pain, both wounded in their own way; and yet, she'd overcome it. She'd taken the risk, and succeeded.

So many risks, he reflected, tenderly caressing her back and still holding her loosely, not wanting to frighten her. He almost smiled again, remembering who he was talking about. He'd have bet money—big money—that nothing could ever frighten this lady. Now he knew differently. She had to have been frightened, probably terrified, and yet she'd somehow found the strength, the grit, the determination to get over it and go on.

He'd always known she had courage, but now, learning this, his admiration for her grew. It couldn't have been easy for her, not after what she'd been through. She'd have to have been left with some residual effects from her experiences. Not that anyone would know it.

Savoring her warmth, her scent, he closed his eyes and just held her, enjoying the feel of her soft curves pressed against him—a feeling that was quickly becoming hauntingly familiar. Now he remembered why he hadn't touched her before. Now he remembered why he'd deliberately kept his distance. Because he knew once he touched her, once he let her close, he might not ever be able to be free.

Rubbing her face against the soft flannel of his shirt, Alex took a deep breath, letting her body relax against his.

"Michael?"

"Uh-huh?"

"Did I ever tell you that I feel incredibly safe with you?" She slid her hands around his slender waist. "After my divorce, I went to stay with my parents for a while. I was so traumatized, I didn't think I'd ever get over it. I felt lost, abandoned, afraid of everything. I went into therapy. I needed to understand what had happened and why." She took another little breath. "I had to come to terms with what my life was going to be as opposed to what I had thought it was going to be."

"Alex." He lifted his head and glanced down at her, not knowing what to say. She went on.

"I guess I'd grown up with the idea of the fairy tale. You know, 'happily ever after'?" She smiled sadly. "My parents have such a happy marriage, I wanted the same thing. I thought when two people are in love, they're devoted to one another, each filling the empty spaces of the other. They're always there for each other, through good times and bad, unquestionably. I always thought that if two people loved one another, they could work out or overcome anything. But that was the key—both have to love enough and want it enough." She shrugged, realizing once again how poor her judgment about men had been. "I always thought a marriage should be two people who are like jagged puzzle pieces who found the right fit. The one place in the world they really belong." She shook her head sadly, not realizing that what she was talking about—one man, one woman, belonging together, fitting perfectly together like a puzzle—was something he'd never allowed himself to even think of, hope for. He knew what the world held for him, and belonging to someone like that wasn't in it. Not for him.

Alex swallowed, then continued. "I think I was mesmerized with the idea of marriage, rather than marriage itself. It took me a while to realize that one person doesn't make a marriage, and when only one person is trying, it won't work. It took me a long time to accept that I hadn't failed. That I was still a worthwhile person." She glanced up at him shyly. "And a woman." He held her tighter.

"You're not afraid anymore."

"No." With a relieved sigh, she laid her head back down on his chest. It felt so right, so...comfortable. So safe. "It took a lot of work and a lot of therapy to overcome my fears. But I was determined to go on, to build a new life for myself, to use my experience to help others. And I did. Maybe that's why I'm so protective of my charges. I know what it's like to be alone, afraid and abandoned." She swallowed hard. Michael's arms tightened protectively around her.

"I was afraid for a long time, Michael, especially of men. But the moment I met you, I knew you were someone I didn't have to be afraid of. I've always felt safe with you, even if you are the most unorthodox cop I've ever met in my life."

He chuckled. She could feel the sound rumbling in his chest and it made her smile. She couldn't remember him ever laughing or chuckling before. It made her heart soar and she looked up at him, loving the way his features had shifted and softened.

"Yeah," he admitted, touched beyond measure by her words. He'd make sure she always felt safe with him. You could bank on it. "I guess you're never gonna find my picture on the front of the Police Gazette." Drawing back, he looked at her. "But you don't ever have to be afraid of me. I'd never hurt you." Remembering the look on her face in the restaurant, he added. "Not intentionally."

"I know that," she said quietly. Lifting a hand, she touched his face, her eyes searching his. He'd shaved, and his face felt so soft. Strong, yet soft. Their eyes met. She felt as if she was drowning, as if she'd never want to look at anything or anyone else again.

A heartbeat passed, then two, three. Something in the air between them changed. It was still charged with electricity, but something more, much more. Alex caressed his cheek, loving the feel of him. She'd waited so long to touch him, to reach him.

"Michael, please, tell me about your family." Her words were slow, her voice soft. She knew she was treading on dangerous ground, but hoped she'd be able to reach him, to get him to open up; to trust her, at least a little.

For a moment he stiffened, and she thought he was going to turn away from her, shut her out. He didn't. He merely shrugged, but the veil in his eyes came slamming down again. "Nothing to tell."

"There must be something. Certainly you must have had parents." Mischief lit her eyes. "Unless, of course, you were hatched."

"Nope, not hatched." He shook his head, wondering why he suddenly *wanted* to talk to her. He wasn't a talking man. Maybe her own openness had softened something in him. But she'd trusted him with something he suspected she didn't divulge to everyone, and for the first time in his long, lonely life he felt a flickering moment of need to trust, to give, to open himself up. It came so quickly, he didn't have time to analyze it or be frightened by it.

"I had parents," he said quietly, raking a hand through his hair. "Never knew my old man. He took off when my mother got pregnant."

"I'm sorry, Michael." She touched his face again.

"Don't be." His voice had hardened a bit.

"Tell me about your mother."

He shrugged. "Not much to tell. I was born in a charity hospital on Christmas Day when she was seventeen years old." He heard her sharp intake of breath.

"Your birthday's on Christmas?" He nodded, wondering what she was smiling about. "Then that means your birthday is in... three days."

"Two," he corrected. "It's well after midnight, and let's not make a big deal about this birthday nonsense," he added with a scowl. He didn't want to be reminded about birthdays or Christmas. He'd done his best to forget them over the years.

Alex shifted in his arms, wanting to feel his warmth, and to give him some of hers to thaw some of the coldness emanating from him. So he hated birthdays as well as Christmas. Obviously he was an equal holiday-hater.

"What happened to your mother, Michael?" She felt him stiffen again until he was suddenly utterly still. Yet every muscle in his big body tensed, and his chest heaved as he took a deep, shaky breath.

Looking at him, Alex saw the raw, naked emotion in his eyes. It tugged at her heart. He tried to conceal it, to control it, but not quickly enough. She'd seen it all, and knew that whatever pain he felt went deep, very deep. Obviously she'd hit a nerve. A very sore nerve.

Alex stayed still, quiet, wanting to give him time. She had a feeling this was all very new to him; had a feeling, too, that this was something he'd probably never talked about—ever—with anyone.

"Michael?" she finally prompted softly.

His arms tightened around her. He felt as if someone had shoved a boulder down his throat. He'd always valued his control, but now, he felt it slowly ebbing away, out of his reach, and he didn't know what to do about it. He couldn't let out all those feelings he'd kept buried inside all these years; couldn't *feel* anything. He knew it, had known it his whole life; which was why he'd never allowed himself to feel anything for anybody. Feeling made you vulnerable; and if you were vulnerable you could be hurt. Viciously. Until the pain ripped away your insides and stripped away your dignity, your pride, your humanness. So he couldn't care about anyone. Ever.

But he'd cared once.

The flash of memory came, swiftly, so swiftly this time he didn't have a chance to banish it before it grabbed control of him. Michael's eyes slid closed as the memory curled and crawled through the recesses of his mind.

Even after all these years he could still smell her. *Baby powder.* He could never smell baby powder without thinking of her. She always used it after her bath, and the scent stayed, lingered, until it was the only scent he ever associated with her. He could smell it now, as if she were standing in front of him.

His throat burned and his guts began to churn. *Panic.* He felt it immediately, knew what it was. He'd felt it too many times before not to recognize it. He'd tried to hide from it, to run from it, but there was nowhere to go; the memory stayed, lingering, clawing at him. The panic seemed to grow, to intensify. His heart slammed against the wall of his ribs. He could feel the fine sheen of sweat course down his back.

He'd been almost five years old. He remembered it now as if it had happened yesterday. It had terrified him even then when he was so young, so vulnerable, unable to protect himself from grief, from the pain. Searing pain brought on by the fire. It was so hot. Even now he could hear the horrified screams echoing long into the cold night. It had been so cold that night; so very, very cold.

It was the day before Christmas, the day before his fifth birthday. They had finally scraped enough money together to get a tree. She'd been so happy that night—his mother—so very happy. They'd strung a set of old lights she'd found in the attic of the rooming house they lived in around the Christmas tree. They'd have a real Christmas this year, she'd promised. A real happy Christmas and a happy birthday, too.

She never lived to see Christmas or his birthday.

That night the lights caught fire. Before they even woke up the place was engulfed in flames. He remembered hearing her call for him, her voice high, frantic. He wanted to tell her not to cry, that he was fine. He'd climbed on his bed and opened the window to let in some fresh air. Smoke was everywhere. Hot. Suffocating. She called to him, told him to jump. He refused. He wouldn't leave her. Even at five there was a protectiveness about him, a strength of purpose. He knew if he jumped, he'd never see her again.

He hadn't.

She died, consumed by the fire. He'd been wrapped in a blanket by the firemen, but he couldn't stop shivering. He'd never cried. He sat there, watching the entire building go up in flames, knowing she was inside and there was nothing he or anyone could do. But he never cried. He couldn't. The part of him that allowed him to feel, to love, to care, went up in smoke that night, burned beyond recognition.

He'd never recovered; never forgot that caring that much meant you were vulnerable to hurt. He'd vowed never to ever care about anything or anyone ever again. He couldn't take the hurt, the betrayal; he knew how much caring and losing could cost you. Anger grew within him. Anger and resentment that she'd left him alone in a world he wasn't prepared for, where there was no place for him. No family. No one to belong to. No one to love or be loved by ever again. No bedtime stories. No birthday cakes. There was nothing left but the lingering memory of the scent of baby powder.

"Michael?" Alex touched his face. It was a fiery mask of emotion, but his eyes were vacant, staring straight ahead as if he were seeing images and pictures from far away.

"She died." He swallowed hard. The boulder seemed to be getting bigger. "My mother died. I spent most of my childhood being shunted from one unwelcoming foster home to another until I was sixteen and old enough to fend for myself." He couldn't elaborate, couldn't go on—not until he had the panic under control. He couldn't tell her how he'd felt all those years. Knowing he wasn't wanted, knowing there was no place for him, nowhere he belonged.

He was a scared, lost, lonely little boy, crying for love, dying with his memories. But there was no one there to care or to save him. So he'd learned the hard way to save himself. And he had, the only way he knew how. By not caring about anyone or anything. By not letting anything close enough to hurt him. It was the only way he knew to survive.

The panic intensified, stunning him. It had been years since he'd allowed it to consume him. Years since he'd lost his edge of control.

His gaze shifted to Alex and he wondered if she had something to do with his loss of control tonight. Probably. She tore at his insides, making him want and need things he knew he shouldn't want and could never have. He couldn't care about her, about anyone. *Too late,* his mind shrieked. He already cared—about her. And it scared the hell out of him.

He couldn't control the feelings racing through him, overwhelming him, frightening him. He wanted to run, to hide, but he couldn't—not this time—and he knew it.

Nearly desperate, he moved his hand to the silk of her hair, then drew her close until his mouth was hovering just above hers. He could smell her scent: soft, sweet, enticing.

"Michael?" She whispered his name, her head tilted, her eyes trusting, her mouth inviting. So inviting. He didn't answer her, couldn't answer her. He just wanted to ease the masculine ache ravaging his body, and the emotional ache ravaging his heart.

Sensing his need, Alex slid her hands up his chest, around his neck, drawing him the last few inches until their lips were almost touching.

A hairbreadth away was heaven, maybe hell. He no longer cared. He took her mouth with that same fierce possessiveness, wanting only to stop the pain, the memories.

Alex leaned into him, reveling in the intensity of his kiss. It didn't frighten her, only ignited the need and desire for him that she'd tried to keep banked. It erupted, engulfing her.

She knew she should probably stop him, pull away, but she couldn't. Her intellect deserted her and she reacted purely with her female heart. She wanted nothing more at this moment than to know what it felt like to have this man make love to her. She'd never wanted anything more in her life.

She stood on tiptoe to tighten her arms around him, to pull him closer, then closer still, pressing against him until there was not even air between them. She couldn't seem to get him close enough. She felt empty, so empty without him and consumed with need for him. She craved his touch, his mouth, his hands. She needed to be filled—by him. Only him.

He obliged.

He wanted to go slow, to touch, to savor, but too many emotions had built between them, connecting them . . . too many emotions denied, avoided. But he couldn't avoid this or deny this. Not now. Not any longer.

Desperate, he ran his hands over her, quickly yet gently, tracking the slender slope of her spine, the gentle curve of her hips, the roundness of her shoulders, as his mouth ravaged hers. Need and desire mixed, nearly consuming him. He had to have her—now.

He made a sound low in his throat. His heart slammed against his rib cage, his breath seemed to stick in his lungs. He pulled her closer, angling her hips against his hardness. It wasn't enough, not nearly enough. He pressed her closer, and heard her moan of arousal. It nearly sent him over the edge. He thought he'd frightened her with the intensity of his touch, his feelings, but her hands were as frantic as his.

Drawing him closer, she molded her softness against his hardness until he was certain he was going to go mad. His blood was pounding through his veins, pulsing in his head, throbbing in his loins.

She was so soft, so unbelievably soft. Her mouth, her lips, her breasts—everywhere he touched, he was drowning in her softness.

"Michael." Alex moaned his name as he shifted her back over his arms, and bent his head to her breasts. Her nipples were pouting, aching for him. When his mouth closed over one through the thin material of her gown, and slowly drew it into the warm cavern of his mouth, Alex moaned in utter, wanton pleasure, her hand going to the back of his head to press him closer. She felt the hot wetness of his mouth, his tongue, through the thin cotton and moaned again. The sound drove him crazy.

Her legs nearly buckled in pleasure. She'd never known that a man's mouth, his touch, could do this to her body. She'd never felt this before, never known that the power of desire could overwhelm her until nothing in the world existed except satisfying the man in her arms and the need in her body.

Hungrily, he moved to her other breast, drawing on the nipple, laving it with his tongue, circling it, tugging on it, teasing it. Her head lolled back and with another soft moan of pleasure, she threaded her fingers through the silk of his hair, offering him more.

Her actions, her giving nature touched him beyond measure, and drove the need higher. He drew the aching, distended nipple into his mouth to suckle gently.

Alex gasped softly as the hot pressure grew deep and low in her belly. Nearly desperate now, she moaned his name, half prayer, half plea as her knees gave way.

He moved quickly, scooping her into his arms and carrying her to the couch before gently setting her down. The hem of her gown rode up, almost to the tops of her thighs, revealing long, slender legs. He swallowed hard, his breathing shallow as he looked his fill before sliding down next to her. He said nothing, just looked at her, gently laying his hand on the creamy whiteness of her thigh. His hand was large, hot, but so unbearably gentle she wanted to weep.

With eyes clouded by passion, Alex looked at him and saw a moment of uncertainty. She smiled, then lifted a hand to draw his mouth down to hers.

"I'm not afraid of you, Michael," she whispered against his lips, knowing what he was thinking. And she wasn't afraid, not of him, not of this. Not with him.

Her eyes were full of trust, and something else—something he couldn't or wouldn't identify. It humbled him, and seemed to feed the hungry, lonely beast inside him.

Michael leaned over her, taking her mouth, taking what she offered, knowing it wasn't nearly enough. He'd never been afraid in his life, not with a woman; but he was afraid now, afraid of this with her. Afraid of not pleasing her, of frightening her, of disappointing her. Afraid that once he'd had her, he'd never want to let her go. He banished the thought before it could take hold.

Slowly, hesitantly, he slid his hand upward, pushing the gown out of his way until his hand rested on the curve of her hip. The gown bunched around her waist, exposing a thin wisp of white silk that was pretending to be panties. He lifted his head, and his gaze slowly caressed every inch of her.

Alex lay still, shivering under the intensity of his gaze. There was a franticness in his eyes, a desperation that made her quiver with a need so strong she ached to feel his touch every place on her body. No one had ever wanted her like this, no one had ever desired her like this. It was its own aphrodisiac, knowing she wanted and desired him in the same way.

"Michael." His name came out a husky whisper as she reached for him again.

His blood began to throb through his veins and he seemed to grow even hotter, harder until the ache seemed to pound through him as his gaze went over her again. He was drunk on the sight of her. She was as beautiful as he'd imagined. For two long years, the only thing that had filled his nights and his dreams was her.

Her legs were impossibly long and slender. Her hips were softly curved. Her skin was milky white and soft, so soft, like molten satin. He couldn't seem to get enough. His hand stroked her hip, her thigh, feeling her respond wildly to him.

Bending his head, he planted a string of kisses across her stomach, letting his mouth slide higher until he captured one nipple in his mouth, working it gently with his tongue, before drawing it into his mouth. Her eyes closed and her head fell back. She twisted against him, holding him close, mewing softly in pleasure.

She moaned again when he abandoned her nipple, then continued kissing her skin, going down her rib cage, lower still across her stomach, her hip, then sliding down to touch his tongue to the inside of her thigh. She groaned his name like a prayer. Her hips lifted and she arched back, her eyes gliding closed as his slick, wet tongue slid higher and higher up the inside of her thigh until she gasped as tiny shocks of pleasure overwhelmed her.

His tongue caressed her, tasted her, teased her until her nails were digging into his flesh, and she was arching against him, clutching at him wildly, moaning his name. The first wave came unexpectedly, catching her off guard. She cried out his name as ecstasy tossed and turned her.

The sound of his name, her pleasure nearly drove him over the edge, as she reached for him, bringing his mouth to hers until they were nearly fused together. Frantically, their tongues touched, tasted, explored, dueling in a frantic effort to assuage desire and give pleasure.

His mouth slid to the column of her throat, and he planted hot, fiery kisses there, inhaling her scent, branding it in his memory. He heard her soft whimpers, felt her body heat, then tremble as she rose to passion again. He'd never known a woman could be so responsive. Wherever he touched, she ignited. His tongue slowly caressed the length of her neck, gently pulling at the skin, tasting it, savoring it. She murmured his name, held him close, turned her head, giving him better access, allowing him to assuage his need. And hers.

Knowing he would never forget this—never forget her— only fed the fear and the franticness that drove him.

Pushing the gown up and over her breasts, his breath caught as she helped him slide it off and over her head, baring herself completely to him. She didn't flinch, but stayed perfectly still, her hands on his chest as he looked at her, his eyes sliding from her slender shoulders to her small feet, savoring her.

Her breasts were small, high, beautiful. So beautiful. He cupped each in his hands, his thumbs gently massaging the nipples until her eyes slid closed and she groaned again, reaching for him.

Her heart thundered wildly in her ear, the pulse a frantic beat that matched the raging desire growing inside her once again. His hands glided over her body, pressing here, pausing there until she was nearly wild, aching with the need to be filled.

"Michael, please?" Her breathless plea was his undoing.

At his muttered oath, the thin scrap of white silk gave way under a harsh tug. His hands slid over the flat of her stomach, then slid lower and lower, until she nearly cried out again.

With a soft sob, she tugged at the buttons of his shirt, until his chest was bare and she could run her fingers through the soft mat of dark hair she'd caught only a glimpse of earlier. Bending her head, she planted frantic kisses across his chest, running her hands over his shoulders, down his back, drawing him closer, wanting to feel flesh against heated flesh.

It was his turn to moan softly, pressing her head closer as her silken tongue snaked out and gently outlined the small male nipple hidden in the mat of hair. Her touch ignited him. Her small hands, so slender, gentle and soft, set his skin on fire. Everywhere she touched ignited. His blood pounded furiously and his hands shook as he unsnapped his jeans and quickly discarded them along with the last bit of his clothing. Turning back to her, his hard erection pressed against her. It wasn't enough. Not nearly enough.

She reached down and he felt the satin of her hands encircle him. He groaned softly, reaching for her hand, stopping her.

"I'll lose it if you touch me again." He looked tortured so she took pity on him and obeyed.

"Michael, please?" Her hips rose in welcome as he moved closer, gently turning her on her back. She twisted against him, toward him, just wanting to keep him close, to feel him inside her to assuage this wild wanting—a wanting she'd never felt before. Her arms went around his neck and she planted soft, loving kisses wherever her mouth could reach as he rose between her thighs, straining, then slid a hand beneath her buttocks to lift her. Their eyes met for a moment, a brief moment, then his open mouth came down, catching hers as he plunged forward and entered her.

A sound ripped from his throat. He shuddered against her, almost losing control. His eyes slid closed and he ground his teeth together, straining to slow down. Nothing had ever felt so good before. *No one* had ever felt so good before.

He moved slowly at first, trying to pace himself, trying to savor every moment. The aching pain that had assuaged him suddenly turned to pleasure—an incredible, unbelievable pleasure that surged within him, urging him on.

Clinging tightly to him, Alex moaned, then pressed her mouth to his heated skin. Anywhere. Everywhere. A thousand shock waves of delight assaulted her every time he moved and she arched against him, a soft cry escaping from her mouth into his. Pain and pleasure. So much pleasure. He was so big, so hard—impossibly hard—and he filled her completely.

It had been a long, long time—over four years—since she'd been with a man, but she knew she'd never *really* been with a man. Not like this. No man had ever made her feel this way. Wild. Insatiable. Desperate.

She gripped his shoulders as he moved against her, slowly at first, then more quickly. She kept up with him, anxious to satisfy the fire burning within her. Greedy for more, she lifted and tightened her legs around him, pulling him closer, wanting all of him, encouraging him, craving him the way a dying man craves another day. Her hands roamed his bare back, caressing him, loving him, urging him on as he blissfully moved inside her, filling her.

His mouth never left hers. A fury of emotion seemed to have caught him in its grip. Never before had he felt like this. Never before had a woman done this to him. He had nothing to give them, nothing to share. No tender words, no undying promises. All he had was an aching body and an empty heart. That's all he ever gave them, all he could or would ever give them.

*But Alex deserved more.*

He knew it, and knew he couldn't give it to her. But he wanted to. Wanted to give her everything she wanted, needed, deserved. But he couldn't. Couldn't open himself up. Couldn't lose his control. Especially with her. It was too dangerous. *She* was too dangerous.

He told himself to hurry, to outrun the demon.

Maybe now that they'd finally given in to their passion, he'd be able to get her out of his system, out of his mind. Maybe he'd be able to get back his control. The fear that he wouldn't—couldn't—drove him on.

Grunting softly, his body slick with sweat, he picked up the pace, wanting to hurry, yet not wanting this feeling to ever end.

She tightened her arms around him and held him close, her hips thrusting upward, accepting everything he had. Moaning, she moved under him, her hips rising in a rhythm to match his own. So good. She felt so good. Nothing, no one had ever felt this good before.

*Heaven.* Now he knew what it felt like. Now he knew the difference between sex, and making love. He wanted more of this, wanted more of her, wanted to make love to her again and again, but knew he'd be denied. He wasn't a man destined for heaven, he was more suited to hell. Suddenly, he felt as if he was drowning, and there was no one there to save him.

*She was there.*

*No!*

Not her. She made him want things he couldn't have, and feel things he couldn't deal with. She wanted it all—forever. Happily ever after. He wasn't a happily-ever-after kind of guy. Never had been. Never could be. She wanted—needed—things he couldn't give her, wasn't capable of giving her—or anyone else. But there'd never been anyone else, he realized. Not like this. There'd never been anyone like her.

He was buried deep in her body, but she was buried deep in his heart. He couldn't acknowledge it, couldn't accept it.

It scared him.

Too many risks.

Too painful.

She wanted too much.

He needed too little.

Sweat slicked, then ran down his back. He cradled her chin and angled her mouth, pressing it to his, needing to taste her, to remember. He thrust harder, deeper, faster. Waves of unbelievable, unbearable pleasure rolled over him. He groaned deep in his throat. So good. Too good.

It scared him.

He couldn't want or need anyone; couldn't care, not about her. Not about anyone. It was too painful, too hard, too costly. It meant giving up control. It meant allowing yourself to be vulnerable, to be hurt. He couldn't—wouldn't—do that for anyone. Not even for her, especially her.

"Please, Michael," she moaned, tightening her arms around him. "Please?" Her hips continued to thrust against his. She continued to hold him, her nails digging into his back. He heard her whimper his name, then cry her release into his mouth. The sound of her pleasure, the feel of her inner contractions drove him over the edge. He felt as if his head was going to explode.

Sliding his hands under her, he lifted her higher, drove himself harder, deeper, faster. Pleasure made him senseless, sightless. There was nothing but her, and him, and the feeling between them, connecting them, drawing them closer until the pleasure became unbearable. With a low growl, he exploded.

It was quiet for a long, silent moment. The only sound was their mingled breathing and the crackling of the fire in the now cooling room.

Alex stirred, snuggling closer to his warmth, sated beyond belief. The heated rush of desire had subsided, replaced by a satisfied peace she had never known, never even imagined. She kept her arms around him, luxuriating in the feel of him. She held on to him even when he tried to move away.

He lifted his head but didn't look at her, couldn't look at her, because if he did, he knew he'd lose the battle; the demon would win.

But he still wanted—oh, how he wanted. He wanted to smooth back the tousled hair from her face, kiss her eyes, which were sleepy and still hazy with passion; he wanted to taste her pouting mouth again, to feel it go soft and slack under his. He wanted to curve an arm around her and pull her on top of him, to fall asleep with her like that, warming him, holding him.

But he knew he couldn't.

He wanted to tell her all the things he'd felt, things he'd never felt before; he wanted to tell her all the things he'd always been afraid to say, to feel. But he couldn't. He'd never shared sleepy, satisfied love talk with a woman. It was far too intimate, far more intimate than having sex with them. Sex only required his body. Talking about what they'd shared required his emotions, his heart. They were off-limits. Always had been. Always would be.

He tried to roll off her, to break the connection, but she held on to him.

"I'm too heavy for you." It was an empty excuse and a poor one at that. He had to get away before she got a grip on him, before she crawled into his empty heart and carved a place for herself. There was no room at this inn.

The tone of his voice was unbearably cold. Turning her head, Alex looked at him in confusion.

"No, you're not." Kissing his shoulder, she chuckled softly, trailing a hand down his back. "And in any case it's a little late to think of that now, don't you think?"

He pulled away from her, stunning her, then reached down and scooped her gown up off the floor where it had been carelessly discarded. Shifting his weight off her, he handed it to her.

"You'd better put this on, it's getting cold." Turning his head away from her, he stared at the fire in the hearth. The embers were dying; it needed to be stoked.

"Michael?" Her voice was hurt, unsure, confused. It tore at his empty heart. Alex touched his shoulder, wondering what she'd done wrong. He hadn't said one word to her, not one during the entire time he was making love to her. She hadn't expected roses and candlelight, but she'd surely expected more than a cold dismissal and this... feeling of utter rejection.

Biting her lip, she blinked back tears. It was as if she'd imagined what had happened between them. He showed no evidence of even acknowledging it, or her, and she couldn't understand why. She suddenly felt this unbearable feeling of emptiness. Loneliness. It hit her like a brick, piercing her heart. She wasn't quite sure what to do, what to say. She'd never been in this position before. Other than her husband, she'd never been with another man, had never wanted to be with another man, not in all these years, until now.

Until Michael.

Swallowing her pride, she tried again, gentling her hand on his shoulder. "Michael?"

Shrugging off her hand, he rolled to a sitting position with his back to her. He scooped up his clothes and began dragging them on. Wearily, he raked a hand through his hair.

"I'm sorry, Alex. This shouldn't have happened—won't happen again." He took another breath. "I— Things just sort of got out of control."

*I'm sorry, Alex. This shouldn't have happened—won't happen again.*

Nothing he said could have hurt her more. He already regretted it. How could he regret something that was so beautiful, so right? Tears filled her eyes but she blinked them away, unwilling to let him see them. She couldn't understand why he was treating her like this, didn't understand why it hurt so much. But it did. Her heart ached in a way it never had.

"You're right," she said quietly, grabbing her nightgown and slipping it on. Even during the height of their intimacy she hadn't felt self-conscious or uncomfortable with him. She did now.

Scrambling over him, she climbed off the couch, and furiously turned to face him, her chin lifted, her eyes blazing. Female pride had chased away the discomfort, but not the hurt.

"This *was* a mistake, Michael, but you couldn't possibly be as sorry as I am." Tears threatened again, she blinked them back. Never before had anyone made her feel the way he just did. She'd always wondered about the difference between sex and making love. She'd been married, yes, but she'd only had sex; she'd never made love—until tonight.

Well, she'd *thought* he was making love to her. Now she realized making love was more than physical, it was much more. It involved more than the body. It was emotional, it was caring, it was tenderness; not physical caring and tenderness, but emotional caring and tenderness. She should have known he wasn't capable of anything remotely close to that. He wouldn't open up; wouldn't share that secret part of him where he kept all his emotions. She should have known. But she had thought what they'd shared was special; for her it was. It hurt to see how little it meant to him.

But she'd learned a long time ago not to take responsibility for other people's actions. If he wanted to behave like a jerk, that was his problem, and no reflection on her.

So then why did it hurt so much?

She swallowed hard, her chin lifted and her back straightened. Alex boldly met his gaze.

Michael nearly flinched at the look in her eyes. She was trying so hard to be brave, to be proud, to be strong, he'd expected nothing less. But he knew she was hurt—he'd hurt her deliberately, even after he'd promised himself he'd never hurt her. But it was for the best. She had to know the truth up front. He had nothing to offer her. It was time she learned that he was a man without a heart, without a soul. He was merely...lost.

So why did he ache to grab her to him and hold her, just hold her?

"And one more thing, Michael, you don't have to worry. This will *never* happen again. I make a habit of never repeating the same mistake twice."

With that, Alex turned on her heel and headed toward the bedroom, slamming the door shut soundly behind her.

She wasn't going to cry. She wasn't!

Leaning against the door, she did.

Michael sat on the couch long after Alex had gone. This was for the best, he decided. It was the safest thing he could do—for both of them. He wasn't the kind of man she needed, wanted. She wanted it all; she wanted the fairy tale.

Hell, no one had ever accused him of being a prince.

This really was for the best, he reasoned again, getting up to stoke the fire. He wasn't what she needed, and he couldn't want what she offered.

He stood there, staring at the fire, watching it, remembering another night, another fire. The memory came crawling back, inching its way into his mind until it was as vivid as yesterday.

Swearing softly, he ran a shaky hand over his face, trying to banish it. Too late, it had taken hold. He took a breath, waiting for the panic to come.

It didn't.

The panic didn't come.

A relieved breath sighed out of him. His shoulders slumped and he leaned his weary head against the mantel, thinking.

Was it possible the panic was gone? He didn't know, was afraid to hope. He'd never expected the panic to leave, or his memories.

But tonight they had.

He wondered why.

*Alex.*

Her face sifted through his mind. He could still smell her scent, feel her warmth, hear her cry out his name in pleasure.

One memory had just replaced another.

But this one, at least, he could handle, control.

Couldn't he?

Straightening, he lifted the poker and stoked the fire, sighing again. He'd done the right thing, the only thing he could have done under the circumstances. He couldn't afford to do anything else.

It *was* the right thing.

Wasn't it?

He glanced toward her closed bedroom door.

So why did he feel like such a bastard?

## Chapter Eight

Morning dawned cold, clear and dry. The snow had stopped sometime during the night, leaving the world looking much like a winter wonderland.

Alex hadn't slept much. She'd cried most of the night. Near dawn, she'd finally fallen into a restless sleep, only to be awakened a few hours later by the fragrant smell of coffee.

After showering and dressing, she headed into the kitchen, determined to be civil to Michael even if it killed her—although the thought of killing *him* was far more appealing.

She offered him a cool good-morning, then settled down to enjoy the breakfast he'd prepared. He must have been up for hours because he'd cleaned up the mess they'd left in the kitchen last night—the meal she'd never eaten.

But she had no intention of letting anything interfere with her appetite this morning. She was ravenous. She downed almost five pancakes and six strips of bacon before she finally began to feel human again.

When Michael rose to refill her coffee cup, she looked at him for the first time and felt her heart ache all over again. He looked like she felt. Lost. Hurt. Exhausted.

How on earth were they going to get through the next few days? They were going to have to come to some sort of peace agreement.

"Michael?" She laid a hand on his arm as he poured her coffee. Immediately, she knew it was a mistake. He jerked, almost spilling coffee all over the table. His scowling gaze flew to hers.

"I'm sorry," she said immediately, contritely. "I didn't mean to startle you." Touching him was obviously not the way to go—for either of their sakes. She took a deep breath and tried again. "I think we need to come to some sort of agreement." She didn't dare look at him. "We'll be picking up Gabriel this morning and this is going to be hard enough without having to worry about stepping on each other's toes as well." Taking a deep breath, she forced herself to look at him, and tried not to let the ache in her heart overwhelm her. "I think we have to put last night behind us."

He raked a hand through his hair, feeling like hell. "Alex, I'm sorry—"

"Yes, Michael," she said quietly. "You already told me how sorry you were, remember?" She couldn't prevent the bitterness from seeping into her voice. Swallowing hard, she tried to speak past the lump that had suddenly risen in her throat. He watched the emotions sweeping over her face and felt like a bastard again. "I haven't forgotten." Her words were very soft. "Won't forget. Don't worry, I heard you loud and clear."

No, she'd never forget his behavior or his words—words that she'd gone over a thousand times in her mind during the cold, dark night.

Alex swallowed hard again. "I think for both our sakes, as well as Gabriel's, we should just put this . . . incident behind us. I'm going to have enough to worry about when my son gets here. I don't need anything more." No, she didn't, but that didn't mean she wasn't going to worry. And wonder. Maybe if she understood why he behaved the way he had, she might not feel so hurt.

Michael turned and headed back toward the stove, putting the coffeepot down. When he said he was sorry, he hadn't meant he was sorry about last night, but sorry about his *behavior* last night.

He'd been up nearly all night thinking, feeling guilty, and he now knew he'd been wrong. He shouldn't have treated her like that. He should have just explained that he couldn't handle things, that things just sort of got out of hand, were too intense for him to deal with at the moment. He had a feeling she'd understand; but then again, maybe that was part of the problem— Alex seemed to instinctively understand so much about him. Always had. And that brought its own kind of fear.

He'd planned to explain this morning, not that it was an excuse for his behavior, but he thought he owed her an explanation as well as an apology.

But now she'd given him an excuse, an out, so that he didn't have to face up to what a bastard he'd been. Michael sighed, wearily rubbing a hand across his chest. He suddenly remembered the feel of her small, delicate hand doing the same thing last night. She wanted to forget last night. How could he forget, when all he'd done all night was remember?

Maybe this was for the best, he reasoned. Explaining might just open up another can of worms, and cause him to have to deal with something he wasn't sure he was capable of dealing with at the moment. He was too confused, too wrapped up in too many feelings, feelings he didn't know how to deal with.

He had a job to do, and he couldn't let his emotions interfere with his job. Funny, he'd never had this problem before—maybe because he'd never thought himself a feeling man.

Until now.

Until Alex.

Watching her, the proud way she held herself, the way she looked so fresh, so enticing, made the ache grow inside again. Damn! He wanted to haul her into the bedroom and stay there the rest of the day. To hold her until the hurt was gone from her eyes, replaced with something much more appropriate. Fat chance of that ever happening. Knowing her, after the way he'd treated her, and after her proclamation last night, he had a feeling he'd need a wish, a prayer, and probably three wise men if he ever wanted to touch her again. The thought made him infinitely sad. Touching her, holding her, making love to her had been one of the most pleasurable experiences in his long, lonely dismal life.

Sighing regretfully again, he took his seat at the table. "I agree, Alex," he said quietly, so quietly she glanced up at him in surprise. "I think we need to come to some sort of peace." Raking a hand through his hair, he toyed with the handle of his coffee cup to keep from reaching for her. Taking a sip of his coffee, he glanced at her. "Have you decided what you're going to tell Gabriel?" He held up his hand before she could open her mouth. He didn't have to hear the words to know they weren't going to be pleasant. "I know, I know. You're not going to tell him about testifying, but you're going to have to tell him something to explain my presence."

Her brows drew together in a frown as she poured cream in her coffee. "I know, Michael. I just haven't figured out what."

"Let me think about it. Maybe together we can come up with something plausible." He laid his hand over hers. He simply had to touch her. He thought she'd pull away; she surprised him when she didn't. "The last thing I want to do is frighten him."

"I know," she said with a sigh, grateful that he finally seemed to understand. His hand felt warm and comforting on hers. She wanted to pull away, but couldn't. She remembered the touch of that hand last night. So big, yet so very, very gentle. She dared a glance at him. "But I've always been honest with him. I don't believe in lying to children for any reason. I've taught Gabriel that being honest and honorable is one of the most important qualities a person can have and I certainly don't want to do anything to make him think that his own mother isn't honest or honorable."

"I know, Alex." His gaze met hers and she felt her heart tumble over. It always did when he looked at her like that. "But this is an exception, considering what happened after the last trial."

"Then you understand why I can't and won't let him testify again?"

"I understand," he said carefully. "But I don't agree. Testifying is the only way I can guarantee Gabriel's safety. Only when Webster is behind bars will I feel comfortable. And Gabriel's the only one who can make that happen."

"I know, but I can't put him at risk." Pressing her lips together, she shook her head. "I won't."

"I know." He stood. He kept hoping she'd change her mind, kept hoping he'd be able to change her mind, because if he couldn't he had no idea what he was going to do. He sure as hell didn't want to see Webster walk on this one, because if he did, Gabriel would never be safe. He'd always be a threat to Webster, and Webster would take care of him one way or another. And Michael had already promised he'd do whatever was necessary to keep Gabriel safe.

No matter how long it took.

Michael watched Alex for a moment, then laid a hand on her shoulder. The silk of her hair glided against his skin, reminding him again of how she had felt in his arms. It caused an ache in his gut. A deep, growing ache.

"Alex," he said quietly, causing her to hold her breath. His touch was making her heart thud wildly in her breast. "I think right now maybe we should forget whatever problems or differences we've had and work together on this thing with Gabriel. *For* Gabriel," he added softly. "I care about him too, you know." Had cared about him—perhaps too much—from the moment he'd laid eyes on him.

Michael almost frowned, surprised by his own admission. It was the first time he'd ever admitted his feeling to himself, let alone to someone else. But after last night, after Alex, he found some of his fear had diminished just a bit. Not a lot, but enough that he could express his feelings—at least for a little boy.

Surprised, Alex turned to look up at him. His words caused a warm ribbon of affection to wrap around her heart. Lifting her hand, she covered his. Their eyes met and a million shared memories traipsed through their minds.

He remembered the way she'd felt last night, the first time he'd pulled her into his arms. How warm, how soft, how welcoming.

She remembered the way he'd held her last night, at her apartment, when she'd been so scared. Furious at him, but scared nevertheless. Remembered, too, how safe he always made her feel, especially when she was wrapped in his arms.

He remembered the way she looked in the glow of the firelight last night, her skin so pearly white, so soft, so... welcoming. It made him want to haul her off her feet and into his arms in an effort to assuage this ravenous hunger that she'd ignited, and that he could no longer deny or ignore.

She remembered the touch of his hand—so big, yet so very, very gentle. Skimming over her body, bringing it to life in a way it had never been before. She remembered, too, how fragile her heart was, especially for him. Always for him. Only for him. It saddened her because she knew it didn't matter. He didn't want what she had to offer, and he couldn't offer what she wanted.

She looked so sad, he thought, brushing a strand of hair off her shoulder and wondering what she was thinking.

He looked so sad, she thought, curving her head toward his hand and wondering what he was thinking.

"I agree, Michael," she finally said softly. "We need to put Gabriel's needs and safety first. We'll just have to forget what happened...." She let her voice trail off, knowing she'd never be able to forget what had happened between them.

He nodded miserably, knowing he'd never be able to forget what had happened between them. Too much. Yet far too little.

He gave her shoulder a gentle squeeze. "Let's get going. I figure we can make the round-trip before dark." He picked up their plates and pushed in his chair. "I've got to stop and phone in before we get to your mother's, to let the captain know what's going on."

Draining her coffee cup, Alex carried it to the sink as he checked his holstered gun. It made her shiver, reminding her again just why they were together. She didn't know whether to curse Webster or to thank him.

After holstering his gun, Michael caught the look on her face. "Don't worry, Alex. I gave you my word nothing is going to happen to you or Gabriel." He caught her chin, and tilted it so he could look into her eyes. He saw fear, uncertainty, and something else, something he didn't dare hope to identify. "I always keep my promises," he said softly.

She stared after him as he sauntered into the living room, wondering how someone so intelligent could be so stupid. Didn't he know that something had *already* happened to her—last night?

"Alex, dear," her mother said as she shut the front door behind them and led them into the living room. "Why is Michael carrying a gun?"

"Because it was too heavy for me to carry." Kissing her mother's cheek, Alex grinned.

"Don't be cheeky, dear," her mother said with a smile, giving her a loving pat. "I was merely curious."

"Nosy, Mom," she said with a laugh, grabbing her mother in a hug and realizing how good it felt to be home again. "You know darn well you've always been nosy."

Her mother's delicate blond eyebrows drew into a slight frown and her hands worked at the ends of the apron tied at her waist. "Yes, dear, but I don't believe it's a capital offense. A mother's entitled to be nosy, especially when it comes to her children. Don't you agree, Michael?" She nodded her neatly coiffed head encouragingly, giving him a smile. He found himself smiling back at her. He'd liked this delicate woman immediately. She was still attractive, and he could easily see where Alex got her looks from. There was something warm and genuine about her mother, something that immediately put him at ease, and not many people had that ability.

"Absolutely," he agreed, earning a scowl from Alex. "Mothers are legally entitled to be nosy." Absently, he rubbed his chin as if deep in thought. "In fact, I believe it's covered in one of my books down at the precinct." His answer earned him another smile from Alex's mother.

"Whose side are you on?" Alex demanded, delighted that Michael seemed so at ease with her mother. She had expected him to be uncomfortable, but he wasn't. From the moment they'd walked through the front door he seemed perfectly relaxed. And utterly charming.

"May I remind you, dear," her mother said with an impish smile, "that I always taught you never to argue with a man with a gun?" Alex heard Michael's quick laugh, and impulsively hugged her mother for making him feel so much at home.

With her arms around her mother, Alex sighed in contented relief. She hadn't realized how much she needed one of her mother's hugs right now. She supposed no matter how old you got, when you were sick, hurt or scared you always wanted your mother.

The thought made her glance at Michael. She found him watching them intently, almost curiously. That warm curl of affection, deep and strong, wound itself around her battered heart. Remembering what he had told her last night about his own mother made her feel a profound sense of loss for him.

Who had he gone to when he needed a mother's love? Or a hug? Or reassurances?

The answer came quickly, stark and clear.

*No one.*

He'd never had any of the pleasures of knowing a mother's love or a family's security.

How sad. How terribly, utterly sad. The hurt she felt from last night began to fade under a barrage of other feelings and emotions. She mentally groaned, wondering why it hadn't occurred to her before now. Probably because her own pain had clouded her emotions. No wonder Michael couldn't and wouldn't deal with his emotions—he probably didn't have a clue how to do that. He'd locked them up inside him for so long, he probably didn't know what to do with them. They probably scared the devil out of him. The urge to grab him and hug him close came swiftly, and she fought it off, not knowing how he'd react.

Instead, she released her mother, then reached out her hand to him. He looked at her quizzically for a moment, wondering what had softened her eyes, then hesitantly took her hand, rubbing a finger up and down her thumb. No words passed between them; none were needed. The invisible emotional connection that bound them inexplicably together said more than mere words ever could.

Arranging herself on the couch, her mother beamed at them, pretending to be intensely engrossed in a dried floral arrangement that needed no further arranging.

Still holding Michael's hand, Alex turned to her mother. "Where's Gabriel?" Now that she was here, she couldn't wait to see her son. She'd missed him terribly.

"Your father took all the kids snowmobiling." She glanced at the grandfather clock that sat in one corner of the cluttered, homey living room. "I suspect they'll be back in about twenty minutes." She turned her smile to Michael. "With all the snow we've had the past two days, the kids have been anxious to get out in it."

"I'm sure." Michael fought back a frown. "Where... uh...exactly are they snowmobiling?" He should have in-

structed Alex to make sure her parents didn't let Gabriel out
of the house. Or their sight. Knowing that the Lake Geneva police had staked out the house made him feel a little
bit better. But not much.

Alex picked up the tension in his voice and found herself getting anxious. She laid a hand on his arm. "Michael, it's all right. They're just out back on my parents'
property. They have about ten acres, and there's a fence
around the whole place. This is a small town. Any strang-
ers would be noticed immediately, especially if they were on
our property."

He nodded, but she could tell he was not appeased.
"Alex, I want to try to reach my captain again. Do you
think I could use the phone?" Rubbing the weariness out
of the back of his neck, he shifted his weight off his aching
knee. "While I'm calling him maybe you could fill your
mom in?" His brow lifted in question and she nodded.

"Phone's in the kitchen." She pointed him in the right
direction, then lowered her voice. "I'll talk to my mom."

Nodding, Michael headed into the kitchen, found the
phone and quickly dialed the number. He called Ryce first
to give him a quick rundown, and get some information
he'd asked his partner for, then, still holding the phone, he
quickly dialed the precinct. Michael sighed, raking a weary
hand through his hair.

His nerves were humming and he didn't know why. From
the moment they'd pulled out of the driveway of the cabin
this morning, he'd had this . . . feeling. Nothing concrete,
nothing he could put his finger on; it was just there. And it
was driving him nuts.

He'd made sure they hadn't been followed, he'd checked
and double-checked the area around Ryce's cabin to make
sure they'd had no unexpected visitors during the night, but
still... Wearily, Michael rubbed the back of his neck again.
He'd already checked in with both the captain and Ryce
earlier this morning. The captain had nothing new to re-
port. Webster and his men were apparently keeping a low
profile. He had Ryce check out the plate number of the car

that had been tailing them last night, and as he suspected, the car had been stolen only a few hours earlier, and was found a few hours later, abandoned and wiped clean. So they didn't even have any prints, no hint of exactly who it was that was behind the wheel. He had no doubt it was one of Webster's men; he just wished he knew *which* one. He always liked to put a face on an opponent before going into battle, and from the way his nerves were jumping, the battle was close at hand.

Twisting the cord around, he turned, realizing he could see out the big picture window. The land seemed to go on forever. Snow was everywhere. It had blown and drifted into huge mounds.

In the distance, he could see the bright outline of gaily colored coats. It reminded him of the little tykes who'd been caroling outside the precinct yesterday. Was it just yesterday? he wondered, rubbing a hand over his forehead. It seemed like it was a hundred years ago, so much had happened.

Waiting for the captain, he kept watching out the window as the gaily colored coats came closer, accompanied by the shrieks and shouts of the kids.

The captain's gruff voice had him spinning around to concentrate. They spoke briefly. Michael listened, jotting notes down in the notebook he kept in the breast pocket of his leather coat. Satisfied that everything possible was being done, he told the captain his plans. At least for the next few days, he'd be at the cabin with Alex and Gabriel. Four days at the most. They couldn't risk staying much longer than that.

The key to a "safe house" was to keep moving so that it was almost impossible to be tracked or traced. Since only a few people knew about the cabin, and since there had been nothing to connect him to Alex or Gabriel for the past two years, he doubted that Webster's men would be able to figure out where he had them stashed. But still, he'd rather err on the side of caution. But right now he was anxious to get Gabriel back to the cabin. He'd feel much safer, once he had both Alex and Gabriel behind its doors.

The captain promised to find a new "safe house" before Christmas. Michael scowled at the mere thought of the holiday. He'd been hoping that this year, like all the rest, he'd be able to just ignore the holiday. In the past he volunteered to work every Christmas so the guys with families could have the day off. This year, with Alex around, forgetting Christmas was going to be impossible.

A great gust of cold air whooshed through the kitchen just as Michael hung up the phone. About six children in assorted sizes came laughing and barreling into the room, each with more snow on them than the other. None of them bothered to give him more than a cursory glance as they rushed into the living room except one little boy with huge brown eyes, who paused to stare at him.

Michael stared right back as the boy snatched his wool cap off his head and stuffed it into his pocket. Michael took a step closer, stunned nearly beyond comprehension.

"Gabriel?"

This couldn't possibly be the same little boy.

Could it?

He narrowed his gaze. The Gabriel he knew had a definite attitude, a street persona that emanated from him like a bad odor. It was a certain look that street kids had, a look developed over years for protection. Their clothing—their colors—were a badge of honor, as much a part of the identity as their attitude. Each street child, or gang member, proudly wore only certain colors that identified their gang affiliation. The Gabriel he'd known had been every bit a part of the streets. Bleak eyes, and a bleaker future.

*He'd been a child of midnight.*

But the little boy standing in front of him had no such attitude, nor was he dressed in the customary way. No colors to identify or distinguish him. No street tough persona. Nothing seemed to remain of the street-smart punk he remembered.

The little boy standing before him had on a bright blue ski parka and ski pants, with weather-repellent boots that came nearly to his knees. His cheeks were flushed and rosy from the cold. He'd grown, Michael realized, and filled out. He no longer had that pale, pasty look that came from not getting the proper nutrition. This child looked well-fed and well-nourished—physically and emotionally.

The wool hat Gabriel had snatched off his head revealed hair freshly washed and cut. A scarf that looked to be handmade was wound around his neck. The child of midnight he'd known was gone. This little boy looked just like what he was: a little boy.

The bleak emptiness in his huge dark eyes had been replaced by... warmth, happiness, love. Michael felt his throat close as he looked at the child. Maybe Alex was right; maybe hope and love could create miracles. Damn! She'd done it to him again! The next thing he knew, he'd be believing in Santa Claus!

"Gabriel," he said again, daring a step closer. "Is that you?"

Gabriel shifted his stance, snatching his gloves off. His eyes suddenly burned darkly bright. "Why are you here, Tyler?" Panic swept into those brown eyes. "My mother?" Gabriel's fists balled and his lower lip trembled. "Did something happen to my mother?" Frantic eyes searched his and Michael instinctively put his hands on the boy's shoulders in comfort.

"No, Gabriel. Your mother's fine. In fact, she's in the living room with your grandmother."

The child immediately relaxed, stuffing his gloves into his coat pocket. He grinned slowly. "So why you here, Tyler?"

Michael ruffled his dark hair. "I came to see you."

Gabriel laughed. "Yeah, right. Missed me, huh?"

Impulsively, Michael pulled him close for a quick hug. "Yeah, I did, kid." His arms tightened around the boy, as he remembered how many times in the past he'd tried to hug Gabriel only to be sidestepped or pushed away. "I really did, kid." Until this moment he hadn't realized how much.

Gabriel's arms slowly went around Michael and he felt a ghost of a smile curl his mouth and warm his heart. There'd been a time when Gabriel would have pushed him away, avoiding any physical contact. When you'd only known rejection you came to expect it. Evidently Gabriel's expectations had changed along with everything else.

"I missed you, too," Gabriel mumbled, so softly Michael almost didn't hear him. Abruptly, Gabriel pulled back, a knowing look in his eyes. Even though he might not be a child of midnight any longer, lessons learned were never forgotten. "So, how's Webster?"

Only a child could be so direct, so honest, Michael thought with a ragged sigh. He shrugged. "Probably the same," he hedged, wishing Alex were in here to help him deal with this. He knew how she felt about Gabriel knowing the truth, and about not telling him the truth. She'd sort of put him in a trick bag with this.

"Yeah, right." Gabriel faked a punch to Michael's stomach. "Don't mess with my head. You're here for a reason, and missing me ain't part of it."

Michael drew back, trying to look offended. "Are you saying you didn't miss me?" He tried to keep his tone light, tried to veer Gabriel off the subject at hand.

"Yeah, but that ain't what brought you up here." Gabriel's dark brown eyes, so huge, so bright, so *knowing,* pinned Michael's. He cocked his head, demanding honesty. "Tell me the truth, Tyler. What's going on?"

"Alex," Michael called, panicked. He wasn't doing this alone. No sirree. He was no fool; he knew better than to go looking for more trouble, especially from Alex. The last thing he needed was for her to be mad at him about something else. He was already in enough trouble with Ms. Alexandria Kent. He certainly didn't need any more.

"Alex," he called again, his voice rising. He knew the moment she swung into the room. He didn't have to turn to see her, didn't have to hear her; all he had to do was watch Gabriel's face. The kid beamed.

"Gabriel!" Laughing, Alex swept him into her arms for a hug, holding him close, reveling in his little-boy scent. Michael watched as Gabriel hugged her back, burrowing his face against her, wrapping his arms around her. Michael's heart seemed to stall somewhere in his chest. He'd never thought it was possible, never would have believed it if he hadn't seen it with his own eyes.

Alex heaved a sigh of relief, holding her son close. God, how she'd missed him. She drew back and looked at him, brushing his dark hair off his forehead. "Grandma said you went snowmobiling. Did you have a good time?"

Gabriel nodded. His face grew animated and his body bounced up and down in excitement. "Grandpa set up races. I was the leader of my team, 'cause I'm the oldest," he said proudly, all but puffing out his chest. "Carrie and Corey were my partners." Gabriel scratched his cold, dripping nose, swiping the back of his hand over it, then sniffled. "Carrie fell off and started to cry, but I just picked her up and helped her back on." He shuffled his feet nervously. "She was all wet and cold, but she didn't want to quit." He glanced down at the toe of his boot. Alex gently lifted his chin. Whenever he was unsure of himself, or insecure about something, he wouldn't meet her eyes, afraid of seeing disapproval or disappointment. She made sure he never found either.

When he'd first come to live with her, Alex had spent most of her time talking to the top of his head, but now, he rarely glanced away.

"We lost, Ma," he said, shuffling his feet again. "But I told Carrie it wasn't so important and it wasn't her fault." He frowned suddenly. "She's only five, Ma, and I don't think she really cares about winning. Just having fun." Gabriel hesitated for a moment. "Did I do the right thing?"

"Absolutely," Alex said with a smile, knowing how much Gabriel needed her approval, needed positive reinforcement. No matter what he did, she tried to find something positive in his actions, although it had taken some real ingenuity to come up with something positive when he'd come home with a *D* in math.

She herself was a math moron, she'd confided to him, earning a huge grin at the time. She felt it was important for him to know that not everyone was good at everything. Not even mothers. That didn't mean he wasn't supposed to try and do his best.

Alex ruffled his dark hair again. "That was a very nice thing to do, Gabriel. You helped Carrie feel better, and made sure she knew that her feelings were more important than winning." She hugged him again. "That was very wise. And I'm sure Carrie was just happy to be with her favorite cousin." As he shifted his weight uncomfortably, a tint of pink suffused Gabriel's face as he glanced at Michael, then his mother.

Corey and Carrie were her brother Jim's twins. From the moment Carrie had laid eyes on Gabriel she'd been smitten. The little girl squealed in delight every time she saw her cousin "Gabby." The two were almost inseparable, and it made Alex very proud to see the way her son interacted with his cousins, to know that he was kind and careful with even the youngest, littlest ones. He'd sort of set himself up as Carrie's protector, and to watch the loving relationships develop between Gabriel and all of his cousins warmed her heart.

Alex frowned suddenly, glancing over Gabriel's head and out the window. "By the way, where is your grandfather?"

"Grandpa's putting away the snowmobiles. He told me to come on in and get warm." Gabriel shifted his weight nervously again, his gaze going from Michael to his mother. "Ma?"

The tone of his voice, the look on his face had Alex tensing. She laid a hand on his arm. "What is it, son?"

He nodded toward Michael. "What's Tyler doing here?" He jammed his hands in his pockets, a knowing look in his eye. "He said it was 'cause he missed me, but I don't think so." He waited, watching his mother's face. He hoped she wasn't going to cry; he hated it when she cried, it made him feel all funny inside. And he didn't know what to do. He didn't even know *why* mothers cried. She'd said it was just a way to clean worry from her eyes, but he didn't believe it. Whenever she cried, he knew she was sad. She didn't look sad now, just worried, the same way she used to look when he was in the hospital. It scared him, but he tried not to show it. "Ma?" His eyes searched hers.

Alex looked helplessly at Michael, who merely shrugged his shoulders. He didn't know how to deal with this. He'd handle killers and psychos, but kids were definitely *her* department.

"It's got something to do with Webster, doesn't it?" Gabriel's gaze went from his mother to Michael, who noted Gabriel didn't seem to be frightened, merely curious.

For a fraction of a moment Alex thought of lying, of hedging, then realized she couldn't. It wouldn't be fair to Gabriel; and what would it tell her son about her sense of honesty? That it was subjective? Or only to be used when a lie wouldn't do? No, she couldn't. What kind of example would she set?

One of the biggest problems she'd had with Gabriel was trying to undo the damage that running wild and living by his wits had caused. And lying wasn't the only vice he'd acquired, she remembered, thinking about the time she'd found him locked in the bathroom, smoking. No, she'd worked too hard to instill values and morals in him to wreck it all now.

Alex sighed raggedly. She simply had to tell him the truth. She opened her mouth to say something, but Michael suddenly beat her to it.

"Gabriel, listen to me," he said, laying a gentle hand on the boy's shoulders. Alex tensed, staring at him in surprise. "It's nothing for you to worry about. I just thought I'd come up and spend a few days with you and your mom. You don't mind, do you?"

Gabriel was silent for a moment, those dark brown eyes boring into Michael's. He turned to his mother. "Ma? Could I talk to Tyler alone?"

Her forehead wrinkled in a brief frown, wondering what this was all about. Hesitantly, she glanced at Michael. He didn't have to say a word; she knew what he wanted her to do. She nodded slightly, not saying anything, but letting him know she understood.

Pushing the sleeves of her sweater up higher on her arms, Alex worried for a moment, then realized she was going to have to trust Michael. Again. She heaved a heavy sigh. She didn't have a choice. He knew how she felt about things, knew how she felt about Gabriel knowing what was going on, let alone testifying. She could only hope he'd honor her wishes. Or else. She wasn't putting Gabriel at risk, and she wasn't about to have him terrified again. Not for anyone.

Her wary gaze coasted to Michael's once again. His eyes softened. She was wringing out that invisible mop again. Her hands were working feverishly. It wrenched his heart.

*Trust me,* his eyes silently pleaded, and she hesitated a moment before nodding. She *had* trusted him. She *would* trust him. Even if she had a choice in the matter, she probably still would have trusted him. He'd already told her he'd never deliberately hurt her, and she believed him. There was something about the man. Even though he absolutely drove her insane at times, she had to face the fact that she did trust him. And they had agreed to put Gabriel's needs and safety ahead of everything.

Trying not to let her worry show, she smiled at her son. "Sure, Gabriel. If you need to talk to Michael, that's fine." With a warning glance at Michael, she went back into the living room, but not before she threw a "Behave yourself" over her shoulder, leaving them both wondering exactly which one she was talking to.

Michael was silent, knowing something was on Gabriel's mind. He'd give the kid the time he needed to gather the courage to tell him.

"Hey, Tyler?"

"Yeah, Gabriel?"

"You'd better not make her cry this time."

Michael's startled gaze flew to Gabriel's and he shook his head, totally confused. "What are you talking about?" Whatever it was had nothing to do with Webster. Maybe he should be grateful. He wasn't.

Gabriel's gaze hardened, and Michael caught a glimpse of the little boy he'd been. There was a dangerous glint in his eyes that almost looked ridiculous on a kid, until he remembered where Gabriel had been and what he'd been through.

"Remember the last time you showed up, Tyler?" Gabriel's eyes never left Michael's. His fists were balled in his jacket pockets. "You just took off after the trial. You made her cry."

"Your mother?" Michael asked, still a bit confused.

"Yeah," Gabriel grunted. "My mother." He absently glanced through the doorway, just checking to make sure she was still there.

*His* mother.

It had taken some getting used to, realizing he had a real home just like every other kid. And a real mother. Just like every other kid. But she wasn't just like every other mother. He was almost positive of it. He didn't know much about mothers—only the foster mothers he'd been forced upon. At first he thought Alex was going to be just like them. But she wasn't. She was nice; she never hit him, not even when he got sick or spilled something. She cared about him. *Loved him.*

He was finally starting to believe it, even if she did make him do disgusting things like brush his teeth *twice* a day. She'd made him quit smoking, too, and eating all the good stuff he loved like Twinkies and pizza and jelly beans. She cooked *real* food for dinner—meat and *green* vegetables— and then she made sure he ate it. The only pills he was allowed to take were wimpy vitamins, the kind with cartoon animals on them. The first time he saw them he almost laughed, until he saw the look on her face. He took the vitamins.

She also bought him new clothes. No more "colors," no more guns, drugs, cigarettes, no more scams, shell games, no more *nothing*. She wouldn't let him do *anything*. But he didn't mind so much.

Now, he was just like a regular kid from a regular family. For some reason the thought made him grin. Who'd have thought he'd be smiling about going to school and doing other things he'd always thought were stupid? They were stupid only because he didn't think he'd ever have them—not a kid like him. But he did, 'cause of her.

No, he was certain she wasn't like other mothers.

He thought for sure she'd change her mind about adopting him, seeing how he'd gotten sick and been so much trouble. He'd never told her how scared he was in the hospital; not scared of dying, but scared of her not being his mother.

But she didn't care how much trouble he was, didn't care that he'd gotten sick, and that sometimes he got clumsy and spilled stuff; she only cared about him and adopting him. He glanced at Michael. And he didn't want no one hurting her or making her sad.

"I made her cry?" Michael asked again, realizing he sounded incredibly stupid. Not to mention surprised. He'd expected Gabriel to say something about Webster, to demand to know what was going on. Instead, the kid was giving him a lecture about making his mother cry!

Michael couldn't help but smile. Gabriel really had changed. And so, obviously, had his priorities. Gabriel didn't appear to be the least bit worried about Webster; he only seemed concerned with the fact that Michael had made Alex cry.

A brief flash of memory skittered through Michael's mind. Quickly, so quickly, it had barely taken hold before a forgotten feeling registered. He'd forgotten how protective little boys could be about their mothers. He'd been protective, too, he remembered, not fighting the memory, but letting it come. There was something about single mothers and their sons.

He glanced at Gabriel, and felt his frozen heart thaw just a little bit more. The kid loved Alex. Genuinely loved her. Looking at the child standing before him, Michael realized they really were a family in the true sense of the word, maybe not by birth or blood, but Alex and Gabriel were connected by something far stronger: love. Michael's smile came full-blown this time.

"It's not funny," Gabriel said sternly, taking a step closer and trying to look menacing, but it was a little hard to pull off with a drippy nose and rosy cheeks. He swiped at his nose again.

Michael immediately schooled his features into a serious expression. "You're right, Gabriel. I'm sorry. It's not funny." He hesitated for a moment, the impact of what Gabriel said finally hitting him. "I made her cry?" he asked, scratching one eyebrow in surprise. "Really?"

"Yeah, really," Gabriel all but growled, making a fist and raising it toward Michael. "Don't do it again, Tyler, or you'll have me to answer to."

"I won't, Gabriel," Michael said, surprising himself by grabbing Gabriel in a hug again. "I promise."

"Better not," the little boy grumbled, his face pressed against Michael's midsection.

"I promised, Gabriel," Michael said, drawing back to look at him. "And you know I never break my promises." Michael's eyes, serious and soulful, searched Gabriel's. "You do remember that, don't you?"

Gabriel shrugged, then grinned. "Yeah, sure. I know. But I just . . . worry."

Michael draped an arm around the boy's shoulders. "Yeah, I know, kid. It's tough taking care of mothers," he teased. "Especially when they do all that girl stuff."

"Aw, she's not so bad." Loyal to the end, Gabriel instantly jumped to his mother's defense. Suddenly he shook his head. "But you don't want to make her mad, and you don't want to make her cry." He kept shaking his head, and Michael couldn't help the chuckle that escaped.

"Gabriel," he said wearily. "I know what you mean." At the look on the boy's face, he quickly added, "I might... uh... have made her mad a few times."

Gabriel's grin was quick and huge. He shook his head again. "Even *I* know better than that. And I'm just a kid."

"True. But I'm learning."

"You'd better learn fast," Gabriel advised, trying not to grin.

"Say, Gabriel, how'd you like to spend a few days up at my friend's cabin?"

"What about Christmas?" Hesitantly, Gabriel glanced around the warm, decorated kitchen. "Grandma and Grandpa were kind of expecting us to be here."

"I know," Michael said carefully, draping an arm around Gabriel. "But I thought it might be fun for you and me and your mother to spend Christmas together."

"It might," Gabriel said hesitantly. He'd learned how to read cops a long time ago; it was the only way to survive on the streets. Cocking his head, he looked at Michael carefully. "She know about Webster?" He was no dummy. He didn't need the details to know Tyler wouldn't be here if something wasn't going on with Webster.

Michael frowned. "Does she know *what* about Webster?" He tried to make his tone noncommittal. Gabriel sighed, shaking his head.

"Tyler, you're a cop, and I can see right through you. Your being here is because of Webster, right?"

Michael remembered what Alex had said about lying to him. He sighed heavily, dragging a hand through his hair. "You're right, Gabriel."

The boy nodded toward the living room. "Does she know?" He knew how upset his mother got about what had happened.

"She knows," Michael answered wearily, realizing *she* was going to kill him.

"Is she scared?" Gabriel shifted, unzipping his coat. "Is that why you're here, so she doesn't get scared?"

"Yeah, Gabriel, that's part of the reason."

"I don't want her to get scared or worried." Frowning, Gabriel began to do a little worrying of his own. His mother wasn't used to the things he was; she'd never lived on the streets, never dealt directly with the Websters of this world. He had.

And he didn't want to be any more trouble or have his mother worrying about him anymore. He glanced at Tyler, now feeling grateful he was here. Even if Tyler was a cop, he was cool.

"Is that why we're going to this cabin? So she won't be scared or worried?"

"Yeah," Michael grunted, wondering when and how this became *his* department.

"All right, let's go, then." Gabriel zipped up his jacket, and started toward the living room and his mother. He stopped and turned to Michael, who was still watching him, dumbfounded. "Are you coming, Tyler, or what?"

"Or what, I guess," Michael mumbled, following him, and wondering why he felt like he'd just been bush-whacked by a kid.

## Chapter Nine

"So what happened?" Alex whispered, mindful of Gabriel in the back seat.

Flipping his directional signal on, Michael glanced in the rearview mirror. That uneasy feeling was still trailing him. He just couldn't shake it. Satisfied that no one was following them, he turned his attention back to the road.

"Michael?" Alex nudged him. She'd scooted closer to him so she could talk without being overheard. From the moment he and Gabriel had come out of the kitchen, neither one had said a word to her about what had transpired.

"Nothing happened." Impulsively, without thinking, Michael dropped a hand over hers. Remembering what Gabriel had said about not wanting her to worry, Michael had done his best to tease her out of her nervousness.

She wasn't having any of it.

But then he should have known; Alex was not just stubborn, but determined, as well. He'd enjoyed teasing her. Enjoyed, too, the feel of her hand under his. Absently, he rubbed a thumb over the delicate bones in her hand. So fragile, he thought fleetingly, just as he felt a punch in the arm.

"Ouch!" He darted a glance at her, his eyes full of mischief. "What did you do that for?"

"Michael Tyler," she hissed through clenched teeth, trying desperately to keep her voice down so Gabriel wouldn't hear her. He was engrossed in a ragged comic book Michael had dislodged from that tomb in his car he called a trunk. "From the moment we left Lake Geneva you've been nothing but evasive. Now I want to know exactly what you said to Gabriel and vice versa. Does he know about Webster? What did you tell him about spending Christmas at the cabin? And what about what you're doing here?"

"Don't you know it's illegal to assault a police officer?" Rubbing his arm, he was desperately trying to keep a straight face at her outrage. He glanced at her, and realized maybe the time had come to come clean. "All right, Alex, I'll tell you what happened." He glanced in the rearview mirror again just as he guided the car up the ramp of the highway. "Gabriel asked me why I was there, and if it had something to do with Webster."

"And?"

Michael shrugged. "And I said yes."

"Oh, Lord," she moaned, and he flashed her a quick grin.

"Now, Al, it's not that bad," he assured her, squeezing her hand. "He didn't specifically ask me *what* it had to do with Webster, so I didn't have to lie to him."

"Michael, I don't understand." Frowning, she dragged a free hand through her hair. "If he didn't ask you specifically what your presence had to do with Webster, then what did he ask you?" She should have known she was going to have to drag this out in bits and pieces. Nothing was ever easy where Michael Tyler was concerned.

"He specifically asked me if you knew that I was there because of Webster."

"If *I* knew?" Alex frowned, confused. "And what did you tell him?" Tension laced her words as she waited, her mind racing, wondering what, if any, damage had been done. She glanced back at Gabriel. He had removed his jacket and his hat and was sprawled out on his tummy in the back seat, reading. He didn't look upset, she thought with a little frown. He just looked . . . preoccupied.

"I told him yes, you knew."

She sighed, wishing she had a set of prompter cards so they could just get this over with. She could flash a card at Michael and then he could give her the correct answer. Or at least she could *hope* he'd give her the correct answer.

"And?"

"And all he said was that he didn't want you worried or scared. He asked me if I had shown up so you wouldn't worry or be scared and I said yes, that was part of the reason. He lost interest in Webster or his whereabouts about that time. The only thing he cared about was that you not get scared or worried, which is why he agreed to go to the cabin without much of a fuss or more of an explanation."

"Oh, Michael." Touched, her hand went to her mouth and tears filled her eyes. She should have known that Gabriel would be more concerned about her reaction than he would be about any danger to himself. He still had some of that "macho man" act in him. She supposed it was something that might never leave him, considering that the man sitting next to her still had some of it in him as well.

"Oh, Lord, Alex, don't cry," Michael ordered, remembering Gabriel's warning. "Whatever you do—don't cry!"

Wiping her eyes, Alex sniffled. "For goodness' sake, why?"

"Because," Michael began, then lowered his voice. In the rearview mirror he suddenly saw Gabriel's head pop up and a frown claim his brow. "Because Gabriel also said I wasn't to make you cry," he whispered. "Or make you mad. Or else."

The direeness of his tone struck her as funny, and she couldn't help it, she started laughing. "Too late." She wiped her eyes again.

"Yeah, I know." He glanced at her for a moment, his gaze holding hers. "Alex, did I really make you cry two years ago?" The teasing glint was gone from his eyes, and she shifted uncomfortably under his searching gaze.

"I don't remember," she said, hedging.

"Thought you said you taught Gabriel never to lie?" He wiggled his eyebrows at her, infuriating her because she knew he knew she'd just told a fib. Couldn't she even tell one little fib and not get caught? This was totally disgusting.

"I...uh...did...uh...say that I taught Gabriel never to lie," she admitted stiffly, straightening her back, mortally embarrassed that *she'd* been caught in a lie.

"Thought you also said *you* never lied?" He was grinning, enjoying the flush that crept up her pale cheeks.

"Well..." She whacked him on the arm again. "Michael, that's not fair," she cried. "You're asking me about something I feel uncomfortable answering." That, at least, was the truth. She was afraid to let him know how she really felt about him, afraid that he'd run as far and as fast as his long legs would carry him and never look back. She knew he wasn't a permanent kind of man; knew, too, that as soon as this case was over, he'd move on.

And once again she'd be left with an aching heart and a gaping hole inside her.

But this time was worse than the last time—far worse. Because whether she liked it or not, she had to admit that *this* time, she'd fallen over the cliff she usually stood on so cautiously, and had landed flat on her face—hopelessly in love with him.

She knew it was futile and she wanted to cry again.

Michael wasn't a man who wanted to be loved, or who wanted all the things she had to offer. He was a loner, isolated on his island of loneliness, and apparently quite happy there.

"Why did I make you cry, Alex?" he asked softly. His gaze—warm, tender, and achingly sincere—found hers again. She glanced away.

"Probably because you were being a jerk." It was the only thing she could think of to say. She certainly couldn't admit the truth. Not now. She'd been humiliated enough last night. Last night she had thought she'd finally broken through that veil of emotional barriers. She'd thought she'd seen genuine caring and concern in his eyes. She'd obviously been wrong. And it hurt. Deeply. Perhaps if she'd had more experience with men she would have been better able to judge the situation. But she hadn't.

"You cried because I was being a jerk?" His grin was back. "But I'm usually a jerk," he explained, quite reasonably, he thought.

"True," Alex agreed with a sigh. "But maybe back then you were more of one than usual."

"So then you *did* cry?" She wished he wouldn't look so decidedly pleased. Heaving a sigh of exasperation, Alex nodded.

"Yes, Michael, I cried. Now are you happy?" she asked crabbily, wishing they could get off this subject before she died of mortification.

Her admission touched something inside him; called to something deep within on that lonely perch where he'd deliberately exiled himself. It was a moment before Michael spoke as he tried to control his emotions. It was getting harder and harder around her. He kept waiting for the panic to seize him and bury him, but so far it hadn't. Not in the past twenty-four hours. That gave him courage, if only for a brief moment.

"Alex?"

His tone caused her to turn and look at him. His voice, always so calm, seemed shaky. "What, Michael?"

Swallowing hard, he glanced in the rearview mirror again, at the side mirror, and would have glanced at the roof mirror had there been one—anything to avoid looking at her at the moment, when his emotions felt so close and so raw.

"Maybe...uh...I...uh...cried a little, too." He looked quickly at her, then just as quickly looked away. "In my own way, of course," he added. It was as close to an explanation as he could get. As close as he could get to admitting the real reason he ran, and the impact that both she and his own actions had had on him. He couldn't say any more. Didn't even try.

"Oh, Michael." Tears welled in her eyes again as she covered his hand with hers. He looked at her, their gazes colliding and holding, speaking in a language only they could hear.

"Hey, Ma?" Gabriel's voice shattered the moment. Michael's gaze captured Gabriel's, sitting up, hunched over the seat, looking like the gloom of doom, and glaring—at him.

"Don't cry," Michael hissed, shaking his head. "Lord, Alex, whatever you do, stop crying!" He was a cop giving orders. He was back on firm footing. Michael let out a breath he hadn't realized he'd been holding.

"Yes, Gabriel?" She wiped her eyes, then turned to look at her son, who eyed her curiously.

"What's wrong?" Gabriel's eyes went from his mother to the back of Michael's head. Michael was still watching him in the rearview mirror. He nudged Alex.

"You're going to get me in trouble," he whispered.

"You're already in trouble, Lieutenant," she retorted with a laugh, nudging him back.

"I know." His voice was suddenly serious, too serious. "That's exactly what I'm afraid of."

*Afraid.* He'd never said it aloud, never even said it to himself. He *couldn't* be afraid. He was a cop, for Pete's sake! He dealt with dangerous desperados most of his life and he'd never, ever been afraid. Never had one moment of fear.

He'd gone charging into buildings where hostages were being held. He'd had a loaded, lethal semiautomatic pointed at his head. Once, he'd even been hung upside down from the roof of a building by a drug dealer who'd gotten annoyed merely because he'd stolen his stash. Not once had he ever flinched, or even felt the tiniest bit of fear.

But this petite, blond dynamo sitting next to him had scared the daylights out of him more in the past twenty-four hours than anyone else had in the past twenty-four years.

Maybe she should have been the one out fighting the bad guys. The thought made Michael grin again, as he realized his money would be on *her*, and his sympathy with the bad guys. Definitely with the bad guys.

"Hey, Ma? I'm hungry." Squinting, Gabriel rubbed his nose. "What's for dinner?"

"Dinner?" Alex repeated weakly. So much had happened in the past twenty-four hours that she'd almost forgotten motherhood didn't take a hiatus. No matter what happened, kids were always hungry and they had to be fed.

"I...uh...haven't even thought about dinner," she admitted weakly, realizing she didn't even have a clue what, if any, food was in the cabin, or what Michael had stocked.

"I'm starving, Ma," Gabriel complained, still watching her.

"Not to worry, Gabriel," Michael piped in. "I've got the matter safely in hand."

"You do?" Alex's surprised relief quickly turned into suspicion at the mischievous look in Michael's eyes.

Michael's gaze met Gabriel's in the rearview mirror. "What do you say to frozen pizza, a couple of sodas, and for dessert, Twinkies?"

Appalled, Alex wanted to whack him again. "Michael!"

"All right!" Obviously thrilled at the prospect of this culinary disaster, Gabriel slapped the hand Michael held high in the air, sealing their culinary comrade-in-arms pact. "Now I'm *really* starving." He couldn't remember the last time he'd had anything *really* good to eat. He liked his mother's cooking and all, but she wasn't big on letting him eat the good stuff. He was really glad Tyler was here. He was going to help keep his mother from worrying and being scared. Gabriel's grin widened. And *he* was going to get some good food.

Daring a glance at Alex, Michael tried not to grin at the harassed expression on her face. "I saved the best for last."

"Oh, Lord," she moaned, wondering what else Michael had up his sleeve. She tried not to smile, realizing she couldn't really get too mad at him, not looking at the pure delight on her son's face.

"Now stop complaining, Alex," Michael scolded. "We'll let you have some pizza, and if you behave, maybe even some Twinkies. Won't we, Gabe?"

"Sure. Don't worry, Ma, we'll share," Gabriel piped in, poking Michael's shoulder and grinning, knowing his mother would never, ever eat any good stuff. She never even ate *candy*.

"I'm...delighted," Alex said, trying not to groan at the thought of "sharing" Michael and Gabriel's food fiasco.

"So what else have you got?" Excited, Gabriel was bouncing up and down in the seat. Alex wasn't certain who looked more thrilled, Michael or her son.

Michael's grin seemed permanently etched, Alex realized with a start. He'd seemed happier and more at ease since they'd picked up Gabriel. She realized she loved seeing him smiling, happy. At least he appeared so on the surface. She'd forgotten how much he enjoyed Gabriel, and how much they enjoyed each other and their male bantering. It was something Gabriel didn't have in his life, not since Michael had left, and something that he apparently missed and needed, judging from the impish grin and wicked gleam in her son's eye.

She'd been able to provide Gabriel with everything a child needed: love, affection, attention, security. But the one thing she hadn't and couldn't provide was a positive male role model, someone for Gabriel to admire and emulate. They had her father, of course, and he filled the bill completely, but with him living in Wisconsin, he wasn't a part of Gabriel's daily life, and Alex suddenly realized maybe Gabriel needed that constant male presence. She glanced at Michael wistfully, yearning for something she knew could never be.

Michael was still grinning at Gabriel. "In the trunk of this very car, I do believe I have some of the very original 'creature features.'"

"Creature features," Alex and Gabriel caroled in unison—Alex in dismay, Gabriel in question.

"What's a creature feature?" Gabriel asked with a frown, realizing it had to be something *really* good—judging by the look on his mother's face.

"Gabriel, you don't know what a creature feature is?" Shaking his head, Michael turned to Alex. "This child's education has been sorely lacking."

"Something you intend to rectify, right?" The smile that warmed her heart, now warmed her eyes.

"Definitely." Clearing his throat in a manner that indicated he was about to make a grand pronouncement, Michael began, "Gabriel, creature features are the very original monster movies."

"Monster movies?" Gabriel repeated suspiciously, not certain if he liked the sound of this. Sometimes those kinds of movies scared him, gave him nightmares—not that he'd ever admit it. His mother would start worrying again.

"Not scary monster movies," Michael quickly clarified, seeing the flash of fear and uncertainty sweep through Gabriel's eyes. "These are . . . campy."

"Monsters go to camp?" Gabriel was really frowning now, and Michael laughed.

"No, no, no, Gabriel. Monsters don't go to camp. The movies are campy," he clarified, realizing he was only confusing Gabriel more. He'd better get a handle on his explaining faculties since this apparently *was* his department. "These movies are funny. Silly. You know...sort of like a movie that's trying to be serious, but they do so many stupid things, you end up laughing."

"Oh, I get it now." Back to bouncing in his seat, Gabriel nodded his head. "You mean like...like Frankenstein meets the Three Stooges?"

"Exactly," Michael said with a grin. "And that's one of my all-time favorite movies."

"Mine, too." Gabriel rolled his eyes. "I loved it. The Three Stooges are so funny, they're always doing something stupid." He darted a quick glance at his mother. "They remind me of three kids in school."

"So what do you say, Gabe? Is it a food feast and then movies, or what?"

"Food feast and movies." Gabriel grinned. "Definitely." His grin faded. "But how much longer until we get there?" He gripped his stomach as if he hadn't eaten in aeons, instead of hours. "I'm really starving," he said with another dramatic roll of his eyes, indicating he was fading fast.

"Soon, Gabriel," Michael replied, checking the rearview mirror again, relieved to find no one was behind them. He wished he could shake this feeling, but it just wouldn't go away. At least he'd been able to successfully hide it from Alex. She'd been too concerned with Gabriel to notice his tenseness or his worry. "Soon." Michael glanced at Alex, then flashed her a wink.

She couldn't help smiling at him. He was infuriating, maddening, impossible, and at the moment, absolutely, totally endearing. She'd forgotten how good he was with kids—Gabriel in particular. She'd forgotten, too, how much Gabriel seemed to glow when Michael was around. Gabriel, with a child's candor, had trusted Michael instinctively, without a second's hesitation from the moment he'd met him. It was so natural, so much a part of Michael that she wondered why he couldn't share or show his emotions about anyone else.

Why was he so open with his feelings and emotions with kids?

And then it hit her.

She suddenly remembered what he'd said about his mother last night, remembered, too, how haunting his voice had become, how tightly clenched his muscles, his features had been. And she knew. She *knew*.

Michael understood these kids, cared about them and took care of them because *he'd* been one of them.

*Michael Tyler had been a child of the night.*

The thought left her heart aching to the point of breaking, and her insides twisting as if someone had coiled them into knots. Fighting back tears for the little boy Michael had been, the little boy no one had wanted or cared about, Alex found fury quickly replacing her tears. Fury at the system. A system that allowed helpless children to become victims and pawns of political idiots who cared only about how good they looked on the evening news, rather than whether the system was working correctly or if the charges in their care were being treated properly.

She'd had years of frustration fighting the system, trying to work within the system to save as many children as she could. No wonder Michael worked *around* the system; he'd been a victim of it and knew how little it actually worked, and how damaging it could be to a child who fell between the cracks.

Michael hadn't fallen—he'd been pushed through the cracks and there'd been no one or no way to save him. He'd simply been a lost, lonely little boy, left on his own, knowing that no one cared, trying to care for himself, by himself.

She glanced at his profile and the ache in her heart deepened.

Michael was still lost.

Still lonely.

He was still caring for himself by himself.

And he was still alone.

Not because he didn't care, but because he *did* care— probably so much it scared him. But he was too afraid to admit he cared, not just to himself but to anyone else.

Now she understood why he guarded his emotions. Now she understood why that veil kept snapping down on her and everyone else. It wasn't keeping the world at bay, but protecting *him* from the world.

Because if he cared, then he was vulnerable, and being vulnerable meant he could be hurt.

Remembering what she had told him last night in the diner, about a child without love or security losing hope, becoming cynical, and having their emotions frozen in a sort of vacuum, Alex realized that's exactly what had happened to Michael as a boy. But he'd never recovered, so Michael the adult was still frozen in limbo, stuck in that cynical emotional vacuum where he allowed no one and nothing to penetrate.

So many things made sense now. No wonder he'd looked so uncomfortable last night and had ended their conversation so abruptly.

She'd hit home.

Another thought nudged her consciousness. If what she suspected was true, then . . . then . . . Alex turned to look at Michael, endless hope in her heart and in her eyes. Then that meant that maybe she *hadn't* misread him last night. Or two years ago, for that matter. If what she suspected was true, Michael *did* care about her. Probably so much it scared the heck out of him.

That was why he ran two years ago.

And that was exactly what he'd done last night after they'd made love . . . run. Not physically, but emotionally. He'd let that veil come crashing down, pushing her out, keeping her at bay so that he couldn't be hurt. Now she understood that he'd never intended to hurt *her* by his actions, but had merely sought to protect himself.

He'd been doing it so long, he didn't know how to do anything else.

Still looking at him, Alex felt the hope in her heart blossom, wondering why it had taken her so long to understand.

After his mother's death, like Gabriel, Michael had never had anyone he could trust, depend on, care about. No one had cared about him. Hadn't he said he was shuffled from one unwelcome foster home to another, until he was old enough to fend for himself?

He, too, had found that no one cared enough to stay around.

As a result, all hope he had had been snuffed out, until only that bleak emptiness remained.

Now she understood. The bleak emptiness wasn't just in his eyes, but in his heart, as well.

The thought made her own heart ache again.

How was she ever going to convince him that she would never hurt him or leave him? How was she ever going to convince him to trust her? How could she ever convince him that her love and support were unconditional?

Chewing her lip, Alex glanced away, watching the landscape speed by. She didn't know. She simply didn't know. But her heart and her very life were counting on her finding a way.

Somehow, some way, she was going to find a way to let Michael know how much she cared about him, loved him, needed him. Needed his strength, his calm, his caring, his love. Needed him to fill all the empty spaces in her life, just as she would fill all the empty spaces in his.

Determination lit her eyes and her chin lifted stubbornly as she turned to face him.

"What?" Michael asked, glancing at her in worry. He recognized that look on her face; it was the one that said she was about to go toe-to-toe with him about something. And it usually meant he was about to come out on the short end. Michael sighed wearily. For some reason he no longer seemed to mind. "What's wrong?" He smiled. "Or should I ask what have I done *this* time?"

"Absolutely nothing," she said mysteriously, suddenly feeling a flare of hope fuel her determination. "It's what *I'm* about to do."

"Uh-oh." The tone of her voice made Michael groan. "I think I'm in trouble."

It was her turn to grin as she covered his hand and squeezed. "Definitely, Michael. Most definitely."

Michael scowled. Why did he have a feeling "trouble" was about to have a whole new meaning, especially when Alex was concerned?

Some time after two frozen pizzas, a six-pack of soda, two hilariously funny creature features, it had started snowing again, and Gabriel had fallen asleep.

Nestled on the big plaid couch between his mother and Michael, Gabriel's head was tucked against his mother's shoulder, his legs sprawled across Michael's lap. Still engrossed in the movie, head back, his own body sprawled comfortably, Michael seemed totally relaxed and completely oblivious to everything but the movie.

A fire was going strong in the fireplace, and the movie droned on as Alex watched the new snow fall. She'd been keeping an eagle eye on Gabriel all night, waiting, watching for any sign of stress or worry, but he'd seemed perfectly calm, and totally oblivious to anything out of the ordinary. He just seemed totally at ease with her, and with Michael, and from the way her son had been acting all night, she had a feeling he was totally delighted with this "adventure" Michael had conjured up.

She had to admit, Michael had a great deal to do with Gabriel's disposition. He had kept up a running patter of dialogue and teasing—of which she was the victim, much to her pretended chagrin and Gabriel's obvious delight.

Michael had even conned her into trying a piece of his frozen pizza, but only after she had peeled off an assortment of . . . things he'd loaded on top of it. She refused his offer to identify each and every one, glad only that he assured her there weren't any critters on it. Well, he'd amended, wiggling his eyebrows and making Gabriel giggle, there *probably* weren't any critters. She'd watched Gabriel's joy as she settled down in front of the TV with a

paper plate, a piece of mangled pizza, and a can of soda—
something in a sickeningly sweet grape flavor that Michael
and Gabriel seemed to favor, even if it did turn their
tongues and teeth purple. When she'd finished her "treat,"
she had to admit it wasn't so bad, as long as it wasn't a daily
habit. Finally worn-out, Gabriel had snuggled between
them, and promptly fallen asleep.

Shifting her weight a bit to get more comfortable, yet not
disturb or dislodge Gabriel, Alex continued to watch the
falling snow. An idea had begun to form in her mind tonight, an idea she hoped would work. Turning her head,
she glanced at Michael again. It had to work. It just had to.

For she had no idea what she was going to do if it didn't.

She wasn't a woman prone to acting foolish, or to failing. She was usually very methodical about things, which
was why she usually got her own way. It was difficult to argue with reason, and she was a disgustingly reasonable, not
to mention an incredibly reliable woman.

But she had a feeling reason and reliability weren't going to help her in this situation, not with Michael. No, she
had to do something totally unreasonable, maybe even un-
reliable; something he would never expect from her if she
was ever going to get through to him and finally break
through that emotional veil once and for all.

The idea began forming and growing and a smile slowly
claimed her mouth. This might work. It just might work.
But she'd need a little time.

What did she have to lose?

She glanced at Michael and her heart ached with love for
him.

Everything. Dear Lord, she had everything to lose.

"Michael?"

Turning his head, he stifled a yawn. The food, the fire,
and the company had relaxed him more than he'd been in
a long time. "What, Alex?" he murmured, not bothering
to lift his head from the couch.

"How long do you think we'll have to be in protective custody?" She spoke softly, brushing a hand across her son's sleeping head.

Rubbing his chin, Michael was thoughtful. He'd tried to keep the atmosphere light, to make it seem like it was just an adventuresome weekend in an isolated cabin. It had worked with Gabriel, but he should have known Alex wouldn't fall for it. She was far too aware of the danger they faced.

"I'm not sure, Alex. It just depends on how things go down." He tried to stifle another yawn. "Until we get a handle on Webster's whereabouts, you and Gabriel have to stay put."

She glanced around. "Will we stay here?"

Michael shook his head. "Only for a few more days. It's not safe for you to be in one place for too long." He tried to soften his words so as not to alarm her further.

"Has your captain learned anything more?" Her eyes searched his in question and Michael wanted to groan aloud.

Damn! Did she always have to ask the right questions? Dragging a hand through his hair, Michael sighed deeply, then passed his hand in front of his eyes. He was so tired. Two nights of little sleep had left their mark on his mind and his body. He was trying to stall, to come up with something he could tell her that wouldn't scare her, and yet not lie to her.

He'd talked to the captain and Ryce at least four times today simply because that nagging feeling wouldn't leave him. If nothing else, it had merely gotten stronger as the day and evening wore on. But he had nothing concrete to pin it on, nothing new to go on.

He darted a glance at Alex. He'd even wondered if maybe his own emotions had been clouding his judgment, making him see and sense something that wasn't there. It was a possibility. He'd allowed more emotion to escape in the past twenty-four hours than he cared to even think about.

He knew what happened when a cop let emotion cloud his judgment: he lost his objectivity. He also lost his edge, and the ability to act and react naturally, the way he'd been trained. When a cop started thinking instead of reacting, it was a good way to get himself, or someone else killed. The thought did not please him and he scowled.

"What is it, Michael?" Alex asked softly, touching his hand over the back of the couch. "What's wrong?"

"Nothing," he answered with a weary sigh. "The captain merely wants us to stay put here until they get a line on Webster. They think he was spotted at a club in downtown Chicago sometime this afternoon. One of his old stomping grounds."

She grinned, delighted. "Then that means he doesn't know where we are. If he did, he surely wouldn't be hanging around a club in another state."

Her logic was reasonable, if not just a bit faulty. He didn't want to tell her that men like Webster rarely did their own dirty work. Just because Webster was in Chicago, didn't mean either she or Gabriel were safe. Webster had a lot of contacts, he didn't need to be in the same state to be a threat. Another thought quickly filled his mind and he frowned. "Alex, don't go getting any bright ideas."

She tried to look innocent. "What do you mean?"

He laughed. "Nice try. I know how your mind works. Tomorrow is Christmas Eve and I have a feeling you're going to try to con me into letting you and Gabriel go back home for Christmas." Michael shook his head, holding up his hand so she couldn't even voice an objection. "It's completely and totally out of the question, Alex. Don't even think about it, let alone say it. You have to stay put. You can't go back to your parents, and you can't go back to your condo. This is one Christmas that will have to do without Ms. Alexandria Kent. You're stuck here—with me—like it or not."

Like it?

*She loved it.*

"All right, Michael," she said serenely, too serenely. It made him even more suspicious.

"That's it? Just all right?" Tilting his head, his gaze searched her face. Something was going on. Feeling as she did about Christmas, she should be screaming the roof down right about now, knowing they were going to be stuck in a barren cabin on the outskirts of nowhere, with not an ornament in sight. "What have you got up your sleeve?" he asked curiously.

She merely grinned, and it made him all the more nervous. "Why, absolutely nothing, Lieutenant." She touched his hand. "Would this face lie?" She desperately tried to look innocent, but succeeded only in making him laugh—nervously.

"Do I have to answer that?" he asked with another laugh.

Shifting her weight, Alex glanced lovingly at Gabriel. "I think I'd better put him to bed. He's out like a light." She started to lift Gabriel, but Michael stopped her.

"I'll do it." Effortlessly, he swung to his feet, lifting Gabriel up and cradling him in his arms. Gabriel sleepily lifted his head.

"What about my Twinkies?" he mumbled, briefly opening his eyes to look at Michael.

"We've got to save something for breakfast," Michael answered, ignoring Alex's groan and heading toward the bedroom. He was going to give Gabriel his room, and sack out on the couch tonight. Breathing heavily, Michael shook his head at Alex. "Your kid weighs a ton, lady."

She laughed. "I know."

She scooted ahead of Michael, turned on the light, and pulled the covers down. Luckily she'd already made Gabriel put his pajamas on so they wouldn't have to wrestle with him. She watched Michael gently lay Gabriel down, tuck the covers over him, then gently brush his hand across the boy's forehead, pushing his hair off his face. Alex had the strangest feeling Michael wanted to kiss Gabriel goodnight, but he didn't.

"We'd better get some sleep, too," Michael said, following her from the room and flipping out the light. The hallway was bathed in semi-shadowy darkness. The only light filtering in was from the living room. They stood awkwardly in the hallway together for a moment.

"Alex?"

"Michael?"

Nervous at being alone together again, Michael dragged a hand through his hair. "You go first, Alex. What were you going to say?"

She smiled, tucking her hands in the pockets of her slacks. "Do we have any popcorn?"

He looked so startled she almost laughed. This was clearly not what he expected. "Popcorn?" He glanced at his watch. "Alex, it's almost one in the morning and you want popcorn?"

She shook her head. "No, Lieutenant, I don't *want* popcorn. I just asked if we had any."

He was back to looking at her suspiciously again. Thoughtful for a moment, Michael finally nodded. "Yeah, I think we have some popcorn. It's in one of the cabinets in the kitchen." Tilting his head, he looked at her carefully. "Why?"

She merely shrugged. "No reason."

"Fess up, Alex," he urged, leaning against the wall with a faint smile. "What do you want popcorn for?"

She took a step closer to him, making his eyes narrow for a moment. She saw his body tense, and ignored it. Standing on tiptoe, she laid her hands on his shoulders, then lightly brushed her mouth against his. He tasted faintly of something sweet and grape, and she'd never tasted anything more heavenly. Deliberately, she kept the kiss light. It was the first time she'd touched him since this morning. The first time she'd kissed him since last night. It astounded her how much she missed his kiss, needed it.

"Good night, Michael," she whispered against his astonished mouth. She turned and headed toward her bedroom. He was still standing against the wall, staring at her, stunned by her actions and the impact of one kiss.

"Wait a minute." He caught her arm just as she reached the doorway of the bedroom. "What was that?"

"That was a kiss good-night." She grinned at him. "Do you have a problem with that, officer?"

Still holding her arm, he grinned right back, resisting the urge to lift a hand and stroke that silky hair. He wanted to feel her skin, her hair beneath his hands. Had fought the need all day, knowing he'd only hurt her. But now, she'd made the first move; she'd come to him and he wanted his turn. His turn to try to diminish the burning need and desire for her raging inside him. "No, I don't have a problem with that," he agreed amiably. "But if you get a kiss good-night, then I want one."

He didn't give her a chance to protest, he merely hauled her into his arms and covered her mouth with his. Alex's breath withered somewhere in her throat as the force of his desire nearly swept her off her feet. With a low moan, she wound her arms around his neck, and sagged against him, letting his mouth take her to the edge of reason.

Regretfully, Michael finally released her, gently lowering her to her feet, knowing if he didn't do it right now, he'd follow her into her bedroom and climb into that bed with her, and then they might never come out. Seeing the cloud of passion in her eyes, and the thrust of her slightly swollen lower lip, he gently caressed it with his thumb.

"Good night, Alex," he whispered, leaning his forehead against hers and trying not to smile at the look on her face. She looked a little befuddled, and incredibly intoxicating. He smiled when she laid a shaky hand on his chest.

"Michael?" Her voice was still breathless.

"Yeah?"

"Let me give you a clue about something."

Still smiling, he laid his hand over hers. "Sure."

She lifted her gaze to his, then blinked through the haze of desire his kiss had ignited. "Next time you give someone a kiss good-night, specifically *this* someone, do you think you could try to remember that I'm going to have to try and sleep afterward?''

His smile widened and his eyes glinted mischievously. "Are you saying you didn't like my good-night kiss?''

"Oh, no,'' she hurried to assure him. "It's not that I didn't like your good-night kiss, it's just that I don't think I'm going to be able to sleep after your good-night kiss.'' How was she supposed to walk into that bedroom, close the door, and fall into a peaceful sleep, when he'd just kissed her nearly senseless, leaving her body and her heart aching for him?

He wiggled his eyebrows. "Want me to come tell you a bedtime story? I'm a great storyteller. It might help you sleep.''

"No doubt,'' she agreed with a laugh, glancing at Gabriel's closed door. "But I'll take a rain check.'' Reluctantly, she stepped away from him, wanting nothing more than to hurl herself into his arms and stay there. Forever. "Good night, Michael.''

"Good night, Alex.'' He pulled himself away from the wall and ambled down the hallway toward the living room. He turned back to her just as she was about to enter the bedroom. "Hey, Alex?''

Still a little dazed, she turned to look at him. "What, Michael, what?''

"What's with the popcorn?''

She just smiled at him. "You'll find out. Tomorrow.'' Walking into the bedroom, she closed the door softly behind her, leaving Michael scratching his head, wondering what on earth she had on her mind and what tomorrow would bring.

Trouble, no doubt.

## Chapter Ten

He found out first thing the next morning. Leaning against the stove, wearing an apron and brandishing a pancake flipper, Michael let loose his temper.

"Alex," he thundered. "Are you out of your mind?"

"Probably," she agreed, reaching behind him and sneaking a piece of bacon from the platter. She shrugged. "But that's nothing unusual." Popping the bacon into her mouth, she merely grinned at him.

"Alex," he growled, wondering how he could get her to listen to reason. "It's not a distinct possibility. It's not even a possibility."

"It's a definite possibility," she countered. Undeterred by his stubbornness or his anger, she stood toe-to-toe with him, knowing she was going to have a go-around with him about this. She'd made up her mind and he was simply going to have to go along with it, whether he liked it or not. Judging by the dark look on his face, she suspected he didn't like it—at all. Well, he'd get over it.

Unable to believe what she'd just proposed, Michael shook his head, although the temptation to shake *her* was becoming more appealing by the moment.

"It's out of the question, Al." He wasn't backing down on this, no matter what she said, what she did.

Placing her hands on her hips, Alex merely leveled him with a glare. "I don't believe I asked a question," she corrected reasonably, snatching another piece of bacon. "I stopped asking permission for things when I became an adult." She popped the bacon into her mouth. "I merely made an announcement."

"Stop eating all the bacon," he scolded, slapping away her hand. "That's for your breakfast." Shaking his head, Michael tried to find a way to get through to her, to make her understand, she'd really gone overboard this time. Way overboard. "This announcement of yours as you called it is not even up for consideration." He cast a glance at Gabriel, who was sitting at the table, happily eating his way through his second batch of pancakes and bacon. Michael didn't want to be overheard.

Without a word, Michael grabbed Alex's arm and dragged her into the living room, determined to get her to listen to reason. Then again, maybe he should try logic. He turned her to face him, still holding on to her elbow, fearing she'd bolt if he didn't.

"Listen to me, Al, be reasonable. I can't let you go into town. You're in protective custody, remember?"

"I know," she said softly. "But Michael, it's Christmas Eve."

"Oh, Lord," he moaned, shaking his head. "You're not going to start that nonsense again, are you?" His eyes darkened and his jaw tightened. "Didn't we already have this conversation a few days ago standing in the frigid cold outside your apartment? And do I need to remind you what protective custody means?" Furious, he pressed his face close to hers and spoke directly into her startled face. "Alex, I told you, crime and criminals don't take the day off because of a stupid holiday."

"It's not stupid, Michael," she scolded, wishing she could make him see her point and agree willingly to let her go. "And neither am I, so stop glowering at me."

She was going into town—whether he agreed or not. Tomorrow was not just Christmas, but Michael's birthday. And she was determined to show him what a real Christmas and a real birthday could be like, to show him what it was like to be loved, to belong, to be part of a family. *Her family.* It was her last hope; her last chance to reach him, to get through to and break down that emotional veil once and for all. And she wasn't about to be dissuaded. She knew the miracles love could produce if given a chance. Now, if Michael would just listen to reason, just maybe she'd be able to have that chance—a chance they all needed.

She tugged on the front of his shirt. "Listen to me, Michael. Just for a minute try to be reasonable." Maybe if he wasn't wearing an apron and brandishing a pancake flipper she could take his glowering and his anger a little more seriously. But at the moment, he looked like a gentle endearing giant.

"Me, reasonable?" he thundered again. "Lady, you're the one who sounds like you have a few screws loose."

"Come on, Michael, just try to listen to me for a minute and you'll see that what I'm saying makes sense." She leaned closer until the intoxicating scent of her infiltrated his breathing space. He wasn't going to weaken, not on this. He wasn't. "Michael, you said last night that Webster was spotted in one of his old haunts in Chicago. That means he probably still doesn't know where Gabriel is. If he did, I don't think he'd be idling away his time in a bar somewhere, in another state. And besides, I'm not the one he's after," she whispered, making sure her voice didn't travel into the kitchen and Gabriel's ears. "We don't even know for sure that Webster knows I've adopted Gabriel, now do we?"

She had him there. Exasperated, Michael rubbed his forehead. He hated it when she tried to use logic and reason on him. "Alex—"

"Answer my question, Michael. Do you know for a fact that Webster is aware that I've adopted Gabriel?"

"No," he admitted reluctantly. "But that doesn't mean—"

She couldn't help smiling. "What it means, Lieutenant, is that you're probably behaving like an overprotective grandmother for nothing."

"Probably isn't going to cut it, Alex." He shook his head. "I can't take a chance on 'probably'."

"I'm not asking *you* to take any chances, Michael. I'm the one who wants to go into town." She tugged on his shirt again. "Let's look at the facts," she suggested, hoping he'd see the logic in her argument and give in. "First of all, there has been nothing to connect you and I or you and Gabriel for the past two years, isn't that correct?"

Reluctantly, Michael nodded, wondering where she was going with this.

"All right." On a roll, she took a deep breath. "Webster's been out of prison, what? Two days?"

Reluctantly, Michael nodded again. He had a sinking feeling he was losing the battle.

"What are the chances he even knows about Ryce's cabin?"

Michael scowled. "No one knows about this cabin except for about five people." This was Ryce's secret hideaway. The place he used to get away from everything when things were coming down around him. Other than him and the captain and a few other close police friends of Ryce's, no one knew about the cabin or even where it was located.

"So you see, Michael. Let's just say for argument's sake Webster does know I've adopted Gabriel. I'll give you that one."

"Well, thank you," he snapped sarcastically, making her smile again.

"Don't be crabby, Michael. Now, even if Webster does know I've adopted Gabriel, and let's say when he broke into my office he was able to get my parents' address. What good will it do him since we're not even there? We're here.

But he doesn't even know about this cabin, and since there's nothing to connect you, Gabriel or I in the past two years, what do you think the chances are that he's going to know about a cabin that belongs to a friend of yours that only five other people in the whole world know about?" She shook her head at the scowl that hardened his features. "Be reasonable, Michael. Webster will never be able to find us, or connect us to Ryce's cabin, especially if he's idling his time away in some bar in Chicago."

"Alex, please listen to—"

"No, Michael, *you* listen. I'm not deliberately trying to aggravate you—"

"You could have fooled me," he grumbled wearily, wishing he'd had the good sense to bring some rope along. At the moment, he would gladly have hog-tied her.

Her back went up and he watched a stubborn glint light up her eyes. He sighed again, knowing he was fighting a losing battle.

"Michael, it's not like I'm asking you to let me go sauntering down Michigan Avenue in the buff—"

"You'd better not," he growled, realizing the thought of her sauntering *anywhere* in the buff made him incredibly jealous. She read it in his eyes, and laughed happily, tugging on his shirt again.

"All I'm asking for is an hour, just sixty little minutes. What on earth could happen in sixty minutes?" He opened his mouth to say something, but she pressed her fingers against his lips. "Don't say it," she warned, ignoring the way he shaped his mouth to her fingers and kissed them. She felt the tingle all the way to her toes. Did he have to get romantic on her now, when she was trying so hard to be reasonable? How was she supposed to think clearly? "Just don't say it," she pleaded, not willing to give in on this point.

She had to do this—for him, and for Gabriel as well as for herself. It was about time Michael Tyler knew that she loved him, that she needed him, and that she wasn't going anywhere. Ever. And she didn't know how else to show him, except to give him all the things he'd never had, the most important of which was love, unconditional love, *her* love. To give him what he'd never had, a place where he belonged. And he belonged with her. She knew it, had known it for two years. He was the other half of her puzzle; the one that fit all her jagged edges, the way she fit his. Now, if she could just get it through one cranky cop's thick head, they just might get somewhere.

Trying to ignore his kiss and the tingle it sent through her, Alex continued. "All I want is just time enough to get a tree, maybe a few decorations and some gifts for Gabriel." Her eyes softened. "He's still a little boy, Michael, and as much as he says he doesn't care about missing Christmas at his grandma's this year, he does. I know my son, know how much this day means to him." Her eyes hopefully searched his. "Michael, could you stop being a cop just for sixty minutes in order to make a little boy happy? Please?"

He wasn't sure if it was the softness in her eyes, the hopefulness in her plea, or her comment about him being a cop; it reminded him of her accusation the other night that he didn't have any feelings. If he refused to let her go, then it would just indicate he didn't have any feelings, especially for Gabriel, and that wasn't true, had never been true. He'd always cared about the kid; probably more than she'd ever know, more than he could ever tell her. And he sure as hell didn't want to be responsible for ruining another Christmas for Gabriel; the kid had suffered enough rotten days, Christmas included, in his young life.

Realizing he'd lost the battle, a battle he never had a fair chance at winning anyway, not in light of Alex's determination, Michael gave in. "One hour," he warned finally, shaking a finger at her. "Sixty minutes, and not a minute more. Understand?"

"I understand." Laughing, she launched herself at him, planting soft little kisses all over his face in spite of his muttered grumbling. "Thank you, Michael. Thank you." His arms automatically went around her, holding her close, enjoying her sudden display of affection. A smile snuck up on him. He couldn't remember ever seeing her this happy. Maybe he hadn't realized how much this meant to her.

"And," he continued, setting her on her feet but keeping his arms around her, "try to stay out of trouble." He looked at her warily for a moment. Why did trouble and Alex always seem to go hand in hand? "Do you need any money?" he asked abruptly, startling her. When he'd hustled her out of her apartment, he hadn't given her much time to think or to gather too many things. He had no idea how she was set financially, at least right now. This certainly wasn't the Christmas she'd planned on.

Touched by his concern, she lifted a hand to his cheek. "Thank you, Michael, but I don't need any money. I have my checkbook, but I do need your car keys." He was shaking his head, scowling again.

"Alex," he said in exasperation, already regretting his decision to let her go. His fists clenched unconsciously at his sides. He'd prefer it if he could keep her locked up in her bedroom, without the key, until this thing was over. "You can't write checks up here. No one is supposed to know you're up here, remember? Let's not advertise your whereabouts or your identity."

"Oops, sorry, I didn't think about that." She chewed her lip, thinking. "Guess that means I can't use credit cards, either?"

"Nope." He shook his head. "No credit cards, either." Hopeful he had her now, and she'd give up this crazy idea, he smiled.

"What about cash? Is cash acceptable to you, Lieutenant?" she teased. "Or are you worried that someone might be able to pick up my prints off the bills?" She tilted her head, and there was a light of mischief in her eyes. It only made his scowl deepen.

"Alex, you're not taking this seriously."

Immediately, she sobered. "Yes, I am, Michael. I'm just trying to get you to lighten up and stop worrying." She touched his cheek again. "It's not good for you to worry so much. You know my reasoning is right. I promise to be good and careful. I promise not to write checks or use credit cards. I'll even wear a disguise if that will help." She struggled to contain her grin. "Although I think bouncing metal eyes and a fake bulbous nose might draw some unwanted attention, I'd be more than happy to do it if it will make you happy."

"Keeping you here in this cabin until this thing is over is the only thing that will make me happy."

"The *only* thing?" she asked softly. The words hung in the air between them, thick, heavy. Unanswered. Her eyes bore into his, waiting. Wanting.

Uncomfortable, Michael glanced away, wishing he could tell her that the past forty-eight hours with her had been the happiest forty-eight hours he could remember in a long time. Probably his happiest ever. But he couldn't find the words to tell her, couldn't even admit that being with her always made him happy. Instead, he gently laid his hands on her shoulders.

"Just be careful, please?"

"I promise," she said with a nod, realizing it was the closest he'd come to even admitting he had feelings about her. It gave the hope in her heart a lift. She struggled with the urge to smile, determined to tease the worry from his face. "Aren't you going to tell me to dress warm and wear my mittens?"

"That, too," he added, shaking his finger at her again. "And if anything out of the ordinary happens—anything," he stressed, squeezing her shoulders gently, "you get your butt back here on the double. You got it?"

"Butt back here on the double," she said with a nod and a salute. "Got it."

"I don't want you taking any chances."

"I won't, Michael," she said softly. "I'm not stupid. Nothing is going to happen. Remember, I'm not the one Webster wants. I'm absolutely no good to Webster." She sighed. "But I promise I'll be very careful. Now stop worrying." She held out her hand. He just looked at it, then at her, his eyebrows raised in question.

"What?"

"Your car keys, Michael."

"You want to drive my car, too?" He tried to look alarmed at the prospect, but couldn't quite pull it off.

"Trust me, Lieutenant, on my worst day my driving would put yours to shame."

"That's not saying much," he said with a laugh, digging in his jeans pocket for his keys. He dropped them in her hand, wishing he felt better about this. She was totally unfamiliar with the area, and the idea of her wandering around for an hour by herself made him incredibly nervous.

"Hey, Tyler," Gabriel said from the doorway, breaking Michael's train of thought. Gabriel licked his lips, but didn't succeed in dislodging the mustache of milk circling his mouth. "Got any more pancakes?"

Turning toward him, Michael laughed. "Kid, have you got a hollow leg?"

Confused, Gabriel glanced down at his legs with a frown. "I don't know." He looked at Alex. "Ma? Do I?"

Laughing, she shook her head. "Gabriel, don't worry, your legs are fine. Michael's just making a joke."

"Jokes are supposed to be funny, Tyler." Gabriel's glance went from Michael to his mother. "What's going on?"

"I'm going into town for a little while, Gabriel, to get some things for Christmas."

Gabriel's face lit up. "Can I come?"

"No," Alex said with a shake of her head.

"Aw, come on, Ma," Gabriel whined, shuffling his feet. "Tomorrow's Christmas and I didn't get to go shopping with Grandma."

"You don't need to go shopping, Gabriel," she assured him, only making him scowl more.

"Then how come you do?" he asked with a typical child's logic. "Come on, Ma," he wheedled. "It's Christmas Eve and we don't even got a tree."

"Have a tree, Gabriel," she corrected. "*Have* a tree."

"Yeah, well we don't got or have a tree," Gabriel complained, his eyes clear and direct on her. "Why can't I come?"

Why, indeed? She didn't know what to tell him. Certainly not the truth. There was no explanation she could give him that would make any sense to him, and if she tried, she knew he'd just see through it, and then he'd really become alarmed. She didn't want that to happen. Helplessly, she glanced at Michael, who merely shrugged as if to say this wasn't *his* department.

"We could drive you into the town and just stay in the car," he offered softly, trying to be helpful, yet couching his words so that Gabriel didn't understand exactly what they were talking about. "I'd be with him every moment. It would be no different from being here in the cabin with him."

"Come on, Ma, even Tyler wants to go. Please? Oh, please? I'll behave."

Alex sighed. If she didn't let Gabriel go with her, she'd have to give him a reason he could understand, and she didn't have one. Not letting him go just might make him more suspicious and even alarm him. She didn't want to risk that.

They'd successfully managed to keep the true and alarming details of what was going on from him, but if she made too big a deal about him staying here, she wasn't certain she'd be able to do that any longer. And more than anything else, she did not want to frighten Gabriel, or do anything to shake his sense of security.

"I know you'll behave, son." She glanced at Michael again and he gave her hand a reassuring squeeze.

"You can always cancel your trip," Michael said hopefully, but she shook her head. She couldn't expect him to understand when he had no idea what she was planning or how important this was to her. And to him.

Besides, if she decided not to go, Gabriel would assume she simply didn't want him with her, and he'd be hurt. She knew her son, knew how fragile his sense of belonging and acceptance was, knew how sensitive he was to rejection. She'd been very, very careful these past two years to make certain by her words and actions that Gabriel knew he was always wanted, always loved. She never wanted to give him a reason to feel otherwise.

But if she canceled her trip simply because she didn't want him to come, he would immediately sense it. He might not know or understand the real reasons, but the reasons really wouldn't matter. The only thing that mattered was that Gabriel would know that she didn't want him with her, and he'd take it as another rejection. She couldn't do that to him.

"No, Michael," she said with a sigh. "I don't want to cancel my trip." She glanced at Gabriel, who was still standing in the doorway, looking at her hopefully.

"All right," she finally said in exasperation. "But you stay with Michael and do everything he says. Do you understand me, young man?"

Grinning, Gabriel crossed his fingers over his heart—his idea of a solemn oath. "Promise."

"Go get dressed," she ordered softly. With a fretful sigh, Alex handed Michael back his keys. "I didn't have much choice," she complained, and he nodded.

"I know. You were kinda between a rock and a hard place." His mouth curled into a soft, comforting smile. "Don't worry, Alex. I promise he'll be perfectly safe. We won't even leave the car." He squeezed her shoulders, not liking the frown furrowing her brow. "Now, don't you worry."

"I won't." She smiled. "I trust you, Michael, and I know you'd never let anything happen to Gabriel."

"Not ever," he confirmed, his determined voice low and gravelly. "Or to you." He tilted her chin up, glad that she wasn't going to be parading around town alone. At least if he was nearby, he'd feel he could protect her. "I'd never let anything happen to either of you. Remember that."

* * *

Sneaking another glance at his watch, Michael sighed, staring silently out the windshield. Alex had been gone almost forty-five minutes and his heart had been pounding in triple time every moment. He'd parked right in front of the one and only department store on the main street so she could just climb out and walk right in.

"Hey, Tyler?"

"What, Gabriel?" He glanced in the back seat.

"I gotta go to the john."

Michael glanced at his watch again. "Your mother will be back in less than fifteen minutes."

"Tyler, I gotta go *now!*"

Sighing, Michael glanced at his watch again. "Gabriel, can't it wait just a few minutes? I'm sure—"

"Tyler, this ain't gonna wait." Gabriel threw open the back door and started to climb out. Michael grabbed his arm.

"Hold it." He jumped out of the car and quickly came around to Gabriel's side. He checked the street up and down, both sides. Seeing nothing out of the ordinary or unusual, he checked again. The streets were teeming with Christmas shoppers doing their last-minute shopping; hopefully they'd just get swallowed up in the crowd.

"Tyler," Gabriel complained, wondering why he was getting so upset about going to the john. "What are ya doing? I gotta go."

"All right," Michael said, unzipping his jacket so he'd have easier access to his gun as Gabriel scrambled out of the back seat. "But you stick close to me, you got it?"

"I got it, I got it."

Michael dropped an arm around Gabriel's shoulder, holding him close enough so that nothing or no one could get between them.

"Jeez, man, you take your baby-sitting chores seriously," Gabriel complained as Michael led him into the crowded store. Michael's eyes swept the area like a camera. He led Gabriel to the men's room, sticking to him like glue. The washroom was surprisingly empty, despite the crowds, much to Michael's relief. By the time they were ready to leave, several others had entered the small area, making Michael tense, but they got out of the store and back to the car without a hitch.

"Hey, Tyler, you got a ticket." Laughing, Gabriel leaned forward and snatched the paper from underneath the windshield wiper before Michael had a chance. Suddenly, Gabriel's face leeched of all color and he raised horrified eyes to Michael's.

"What's wrong?" Michael asked quickly, tightening his hold on Gabriel's shoulder. The hair on the back of his head suddenly stood on end, and every nerve began to scream in silent alarm. Instinctively, he reached for his gun. "Gabriel, what is it?" His voice was filled with urgency.

"They've got her, Tyler." Gabriel's voice was a trembling whisper as his huge brown eyes filled with tears. "They got my mother."

She had no idea what time it was. But she knew it was way past the time she should have met Michael and Gabriel back at the car. By now Michael would know what had happened and he'd be furious. Struggling against the ropes that bound her wrists and ankles, Alex tried to keep her panic down.

She'd never even seen them. One minute, arms loaded with packages, she was happily humming Christmas carols as she waited for the elevator to take her back to the second-floor men's department, and the next thing she knew, someone had pushed something horrible smelling over her mouth and nose.

She'd struggled briefly, dropping her packages and letting elbows and feet fly at whoever was holding her. She'd heard a few grunts, felt her head jerked back, and then everything went black. When she came to, she found herself with an incredible headache, locked in this dark, dank closet with her hands and feet bound.

Everything hurt. Her wrists and ankles burned from the rope, which they'd tied far too tight. It was cutting into her tender skin and probably cutting off her circulation, since her feet were cold and tingly with numbness. Her neck and head were pounding incessantly, probably from when she struggled with them and they'd yanked on her hair, jerking her head back and nearly off her body. Her shoulders were throbbing from the unnatural position they were in. The air in here was close and musty, making it hard to breathe. All in all, she was utterly miserable.

And scared.

So scared.

Trying to stay calm was a losing effort and Alex finally let the tears of frustration, fear and anger come. Dropping her head to her raised knees, she sobbed quietly.

When Michael found out what had happened he was going to kill them.

Then he was probably going to kill her, too, she thought miserably, for talking him into letting her go shopping.

Nudging her tears away with her knee, she sniffled, wishing she had a tissue. Her nose was dripping, she was cold and scared, but feeling sorry for herself wasn't going to help. She had to do something.

She'd overheard them talking. They were going to try to get Michael to exchange her for Gabriel. For a brief moment she'd felt a thread of panic wind through her, nearly making her nauseous. They were bartering lives like used-car salesmen negotiating a car deal.

But nothing could erase the fact that they wanted Gabriel.

Her tears came in earnest now.

Trying to stem her panic and fear, Alex tried to think logically. Michael would never ever let anything happen to her son, no matter what the circumstances. He'd given her his word. He'd promised her that nothing would happen to him. She couldn't even imagine him entertaining the idea of giving Gabriel to them. The mere thought made her shudder uncontrollably.

But that was before she'd put him in a compromising position.

Sniffling, she scooted back against the wall, trying to get warm and stop crying. It was so cold in this place. Cold and dark, but her fear was making her colder.

She heard footsteps and scooted even farther back against the wall, trying to appear smaller. The handle turned, the door creaked and light suddenly flooded the little closet. Her eyes hurt, and she blinked against the harsh brightness.

"Just a couple more hours, little lady, and we'll let you go." The large figure looming over her stepped closer, bending down to peer into her stricken face. He smelled of alcohol and sweat. It made her nauseous. "Once we get the kid, you're free." Laughing, he rubbed his jaw. "You sure pack a wallop for such a little bitty thing."

Furious, she lashed out at him. "Untie me you creep, and I'll give you a wallop you'll never forget." She thrust out her bound feet, aiming for his bony shins, but he sidestepped her, and laughed again, shutting the door firmly behind him, leaving her in darkness.

Still sniffling, Alex's fear slowly turned to fury. She couldn't and wouldn't just sit by and let them do this.

She had to do *something*.

But what?

Stretching her legs to ease a cramp, she swiped at her tears with her hunched shoulder and forced herself to think clearly. She knew they were going to try to make an exchange. That meant they'd have to take her out of here. Once she was out, maybe, just maybe, she might be able to get free, might be able to do something.

Her thoughts turning to Michael, she wondered what he was doing, thinking, planning. She knew it had to be something. Michael wouldn't just sit around and do nothing, just waiting to hand Gabriel over. Feeling overwhelmed, Alex wished with all her heart that Michael was here with her, holding her, making her feel safe with his own brand of craziness.

She wondered if she'd ever feel safe again.

*Oh, Michael.*

She'd never even had the chance to tell him all the things in her heart. Now, she might never get the chance. Alex sniffled again. Earlier today she'd believed love created miracles. She sure hoped she was right, because right now, they sorely needed a miracle.

It wasn't miracles on Michael's mind, but murder. Pure, unadulterated murder. If they'd harmed one hair on her head, if they so much as scared her, or looked at her the wrong way, he had every intention of sending Webster and his men to hell via the fastest route possible, and then, he'd gladly join them.

Fueled by scalding white fury, Michael had hustled Gabriel back into the car, then roared out of town, stopping at a gas station to make one phone call.

One call was all he needed.

*No emotion,* he kept telling himself as he flew down the barren streets, anxious to get Gabriel back into the safety of the cabin.

He couldn't afford to feel anything right now. Right now, he had to act purely on instinct, relying solely on his training and experience. But that didn't stop the panic and helplessness that had infiltrated his entire body the moment he'd read the note. Everything inside him had grown icy cold. Now he knew why he couldn't shake the feeling that something wasn't right yesterday. Someone *had* been following them. It was the only way they could have known about the cabin. He thought again about what Alex had said this morning as she'd cajoled him into letting her go. He cursed himself every which way. He should have known better. But he'd let emotion blind and bind his instincts. And he'd put Alex at risk.

The thought of anything happening to her terrified him more than anything else in his life ever had.

Damn! Why had he let her talk him into going shopping?

He knew how Webster worked; knew how dangerous he could be, how deadly. Knew, too, how stubborn Alex could be. He hoped like hell she had kept her head and her temper. If not, there was no predicting what might have happened.

He didn't even know if she was still alive. The idea brought on such a bout of fear he couldn't bear to think about it, couldn't even imagine it. He forced the thought from his mind.

*No emotion,* he kept telling himself as he pulled the car right up to the front door and nearly dragged Gabriel inside.

"They're gonna kill her, aren't they, Tyler?" Looking lost and forlorn, Gabriel stood there looking at him, tears threatening, his chin trembling. It was the first time he'd spoken since he'd found the note.

"No!" The word exploded from Michael's mouth and he went down on his knees and hauled Gabriel to him. Sobs shook the child's body and Michael held him closer, feeling his own eyes burn. "Gabriel, shh, shh, don't cry. I promise they won't hurt her. I won't let them. I wouldn't let anyone hurt you or your mom. We're going to get your mother back safe and sound. I promise." Feeling completely helpless, Michael stroked the back of the sobbing child's head. Gabriel's slender arms slowly crawled around him, and the gesture almost broke Michael's heart.

He knew how the kid felt.

Alex was everything to Gabriel.

Michael's eyes slid closed and his throat felt as if he'd had a boulder lodged in it.

Oh, God.

He didn't realize it until now; she was everything to *him.*

He couldn't even begin to imagine life without her, couldn't bear to go back to that lonely, isolated island he'd banished himself to. With a ragged sigh, he adjusted Gabriel in his arms, trying to keep his emotions under control.

He'd never felt so lost or alone in his life. He'd spent a lifetime alone. Deliberately. It had been his choice. But he'd never *felt* lonely or alone—until now, until he'd learned Alex was gone. Now he felt utterly, undeniably, unbearably alone.

Somehow, when he wasn't looking, the little spitfire had crawled into his heart and carved a place for herself.

And now, they'd taken her away from him.

His jaw tightened, his teeth clenched as he held Gabriel tighter. There was no way they were going to let Alex go. None. They'd never leave another witness alive. They'd never leave him alive, either. He didn't care about himself; it was Alex and Gabriel that mattered.

Damn!

Carefully, deliberately he banked down all the feelings that had erupted, slowly coming to life. He couldn't deal with them now. Now, he had to keep a clear head and heart in order to focus on what had to be done. It was the only chance Alex had.

The exchange was supposed to take place in less than three hours. He knew he'd have one chance, that was it, and he couldn't afford to let emotion cloud his instincts. He had to keep cool and calm. Alex's life depended on it. He'd let her down once; he'd never do it again.

"Don't cry, Gabriel," he whispered, blinking against the burning pain in his own eyes. Helplessness washed over him again as his body absorbed Gabriel's sobs.

"Tyler?" Gabriel drew back to look at him. His eyes were dark, bleak. "They're gonna...kill...her... And it's all my...fault." Gabriel's lower lip trembled and big fat tears rolled down his cheeks and dripped from his jaw.

"Oh, God, Gabriel. No, it's not. It's not your fault." Michael hauled him close again, feeling sick. He couldn't worry about his own feelings right now; he had to take care of Gabriel.

He remembered what Alex had told him about families. They loved, supported and protected one another. He had never understood it, experienced it until now. Gabriel needed all of that from him now—needed his love, his support and his protection—and somehow he was going to have to find the strength to give it to him. It was what Alex would have wanted.

"Don't even think like that, son. They're not going to kill her." Drawing back, he looked at Gabriel, wiping away his tears. "We have to think positively. I'm going to get your mother back, Gabriel. I promise." For the boy's sake he forced a smile he didn't feel.

Sniffling, Gabriel looked at him solemnly for a moment. "Tyler?"

"What, son?"

"I'm scared." He flung himself against Michael again, his skinny arms looping around Michael's neck as sobs racked his little body again. "Real scared."

The sound of Gabriel's voice, so soft, so terrified, coupled with the haunted, bleak look in his eyes caused a pain deep in Michael's aching heart.

"I know, Gabriel. I know." Michael heaved a ragged sigh. "So am I, son. So am I."

In the quiet of the cabin, bound by love and fear, they just held each other.


It was getting colder.

Shivering in earnest, Alex tried to curl tighter into a ball to keep herself warm. They'd taken her jacket, leaving her dressed in her turtleneck and her jeans which weren't protection enough against this cold.

She wished she'd remembered to buy a battery for her watch. She had no idea what time it was, or how long she'd been here. Her stomach growled, reminding her she hadn't eaten. She almost smiled. Waking up to find Michael cooking breakfast for Gabriel had been such a wonderful sight. She wished now she'd taken the time to eat, as Michael had insisted, but as usual, she was stubborn and had refused.

She'd kill right now for one of Michael's home-cooked pancakes. Or even one of his disgusting frozen pizzas with all those little things on top. Her stomach rumbled again and she realized she had to stop thinking about food.

Or disgusting grape soda.

She was so thirsty. Her lips were chapped, her mouth parched. She'd gladly drink a case of sickeningly sweet soda right now and not utter a word of complaint.

Shifting, she tried to tuck her legs under her but just couldn't manage. Tears were threatening again, so she took several deep breaths, determined to stop feeling sorry for herself.

She'd think of something pleasant.

Gabriel.

Michael.

She smiled through her tears. She hoped they were all right. She hoped they weren't worried. She hoped they understood.

Her eyes slid closed.

More than anything else, she hoped Michael and Gabriel were taking care of each other. The last thought had her gulping air, her heart pounding in fear.

Laying her head back down on her knees, Alex closed her eyes and waited.

"Tyler, you sure this is gonna work?" Gabriel watched as Michael checked and double-checked his gun before holstering it.

"It's going to work, Gabriel." He glanced at him, forcing another smile and ruffling Gabriel's hair. "Trust me. I'm one of the good guys and the good guys always win." This *had* to work. Michael couldn't even think of anything else.

Bending down, Michael checked his ankle holster where a small .38 caliber was snugly tucked. If they checked him for weapons, they'd never think to check his ankles. "Are you sure you remember what you're supposed to do?"

Gabriel nervously shifted his weight. "I remember," he said with a sigh. His head was hurting from crying and he was tired. He just wanted to see his mother.

"Want to go over it again?" Michael asked, straightening and pulling on his leather jacket and slowly zipping it.

"Naw, I remember."

"You're sure?" Michael laid a hand on Gabriel's shoulder when he nodded. "This is a very brave thing you're doing, Gabriel. I couldn't do this without your help. Your mother will be very proud of you." Squeezing the child's shoulder, Michael glanced around the cabin one more time. "Are you ready?"

Gabriel nodded. He'd been real scared before, but Tyler had made him feel better. He'd explained everything to him. He wasn't so scared now. "I'm ready."

"Let's go, then." When Gabriel hesitated, Michael waited, holding his breath. He'd had no choice but to explain his plan to Gabriel because he needed Gabriel's cooperation in order to make it work. In order to save Alex. Gabriel had taken it much better than he'd anticipated. In fact, knowing he was going to be doing something to help his mother seemed to ease some of Gabriel's fears.

"Tyler?"

"What, son?"

"Do you suppose they made her mad?" Gabriel watched Michael steadily.

A ghost of a smile touched Michael's lips and he sighed wearily. "Knowing your mother? No doubt."

For the first time in hours, Gabriel smiled. "Fools."

Chuckling softly, Michael checked his gun again, then said a silent prayer as he led Gabriel out the door.

And to Webster.

## Chapter Eleven

The exchange was to take place at an isolated and unoccupied cabin on the other side of the lake. A long, narrow winding road led to the front of the cabin, while the back faced the frozen lake.

Michael had been instructed to come alone, unarmed, and with Gabriel. Once they were certain he had Gabriel with him, they'd release Alex.

Right.

And he was Santa Claus.

Deliberately, Michael arrived at the meeting place early. He needed a chance to scope out the area. With Gabriel safely hidden in the back seat, Michael checked his watch again. His nerves were shot, his hands shaking. His professional wits had deserted him. This wasn't professional now; when they'd snatched Alex they'd made it personal, *very* personal.

"Here they come," he whispered to Gabriel, watching the dark green sedan rumble slowly along the narrow drive leading to the front of the cabin. "Now, no matter what happens, Gabriel, remember what I told you. Don't get out of the car.'' Michael checked his watch again. ''When I signal you, I just want you to sit up so they can see you, but don't get out of the car. You got it?''

''I got it, Tyler,'' Gabriel snapped. ''I got it.''

''And stay down until I give you the signal.'' He didn't want Gabriel to become a target. ''Whatever you do, just don't get out of the car.''

Narrowing his gaze, Michael watched the car approach. His eyes darkened. Webster was in the back seat with Alex, and he could see the shiny glint of metal in the sunlight. He had a gun pointed at Alex's head. Michael's fists clenched, but he forced himself to stay calm. Not just for Alex's sake, but for Gabriel's, as well.

''Can you see her yet?'' Gabriel whispered. ''Is she all right?''

Michael let out a long, weary breath, his sights on the two goons in the front seat. ''Yes, Gabriel.'' Gabriel's head almost popped up, until he remembered what Tyler had said. ''I can see her.'' Michael dragged a shaky hand through his hair. ''She looks fine.''

Michael waited until the car came to a complete stop directly in front of the cabin, then slid his gun out of the shoulder holster and laid it on the front seat, before slowly getting out of his car. He stood there, waiting, watching. Everything stilled until he was barely breathing. Instinct took over as he watched Webster drag Alex out of the back seat by her hair. Michael's fists clenched tighter. He could see the pain etched on her delicate features. Could see, too, a faint hint of bruising along her cheekbone. If he could, he'd kill Webster with his bare hands, and consider it too good for him.

Deliberately, Michael avoided Alex's terrified gaze, hoping she'd understand. He couldn't look at her—not yet. If he did, he wouldn't be able to block out his feelings, his emotions; and now, he couldn't afford to allow anything to distract him.

"Webster." Nodding gravely, Michael moved a few steps closer as the other two goons got out of the car, positioning themselves a little behind Webster, one on either side. Their guns were still holstered, he noted, as he moved another step closer, then another. He knew he'd only have one chance and he had to get close enough to make the best of it.

"Hold it right there, Tyler." Webster had one hand tangled in Alex's hair—tightly. Michael could see the tension in her face, the terror in her eyes. He banked down his own terror as he watched Webster carefully. Webster's other hand held the gun, still pointed at Alex's temple. "Open your coat, Tyler. Let me see your holster." Michael did as he was told, holding his jacket open wide so they could see his empty holster. He released the edges of his jacket slowly. Webster's gaze turned to the car. "Where's the kid?"

"In the car." Michael shifted his weight. In the distance, behind Webster, he caught sight of movement, then slowly let out a deep breath of relief. "Sleeping."

"Wake the kid up." Webster laughed crudely. "Tell him he's got a visitor. And don't try anything funny." He yanked on Alex's hair until her feet nearly left the ground. Michael's fists clenched, as did his gut.

The urge to wipe that smile off Webster's face—permanently—came swiftly, but Michael banked it down. Slowly, his gaze shifted to Alex. For a fraction of a second, he saw the panic in her eyes, on her face. He looked at her for a long, long moment, willing her to understand the message he was trying to send her. Her eyes suddenly cleared, and he knew she understood. He'd never really appreciated that strange emotional connection they'd had between them—until now. He had no doubt she knew exactly what he was trying to communicate to her without him having to say a word, in the same way he knew her thoughts without her opening her mouth.

*I'll be careful, Alex,* he silently promised. *Don't worry. Just stay calm. I told you I'd never let anything happen to you or Gabriel. Trust me.*

Slowly, his heart thudding wildly against his chest, he shifted his gaze back to Webster, then walked backward toward the passenger door, never taking his eyes off the other man.

He didn't need to turn his head or look up, didn't need to *see* Ryce to know he was there, in position, against the back wall of the cabin just as they'd planned. After fifteen years of working together, they could sense one another.

Shifting his gaze to Alex, Michael slowly opened the door with one hand, and reached down for his ankle gun with the other. "Stay down, Gabriel," he hissed, a moment before he rose and whirled, firing.

He caught Webster right in the chest, watched the slash of red spread outward with vicious satisfaction. Webster was stunned, his face slowly contorting in surprise. He was still holding on to Alex.

"Alex!" Michael yelled. "Get down." He watched her try to get free, but Webster still held her by her hair. Other shots rang out. The goons had managed to unholster their guns.

"Get down, Alex," he cried as he watched her lurch forward, freeing herself from Webster's grasp. She slid to the ground. Michael kept firing until Webster slumped forward to his knees, clutching his chest with both hands. He saw Ryce running toward them as both goons hit the ground almost at the same time.

"Check Gabriel," Michael called to Ryce. "Alex?" Holstering his gun on the run, Michael went down on his knees next to her. She was too still. "Alex?"

He turned her over. His eyes widened in horror and he touched a hand to her chest. Blood. Oh, God, she'd been shot.

"No, no, no," Michael cried, cradling her limp body close against him and rocking back and forth. "Oh, my God, Alex. Alex!" Terror edged in, gripping him. He held her closer, rocking. "God, Alex," he cried. "Please, don't do this to me. Don't leave me." He wanted to shake life into her—his life—wanted to give her his very breath. He'd give her anything and everything if she'd just open her eyes and talk to him. If she'd just come back to him.

God, she couldn't leave him. Not now.

He'd thought they would have forever; thought there'd be time to tell her all the things he'd never had the courage to tell her before, time to tell her all the things he'd held hidden in his lonely, aching heart.

For her.

Only for her.

Why hadn't he told her?

He'd been afraid; afraid to hope, afraid to love, afraid to take a chance.

Fear. A futile emotion. He knew that now. Nothing in his life had scared him as much as the thought of living without her. He couldn't live—wouldn't live—without her.

He'd been isolated on his lonely island for so many years—by choice—but it wasn't until she'd barged into his life, turning it upside down and inside out, that he realized he no longer wanted to be alone. He wanted, needed her like he'd never needed anyone before.

And now she was going to leave him.

"Dear God, no! Alex, open your eyes. Please, look at me," he pleaded, desperately trying to will life into her. He traced the outline of her lips. They were cool and dry to his touch. It wasn't until this moment that he realized how much he needed her, loved her.

*Loved her.*

God, how he loved her.

He'd never even had a chance to tell her.

Desolation, desperation were in his touch as he traced her lips again. He could feel her slipping away from him. In the distance, he could hear the wail of sirens, could see the flashing lights.

"Say something, damn it!" He shook her, then grabbed her tighter, holding her close. "Alex! Hold on, just hold on."

Her breath rasped out unevenly and her eyes briefly fluttered open. She tried to smile but simply couldn't manage it, not even for him.

"Michael?" she whispered, barely able to get the word out. Something hard and heavy was pressing against her chest. She tried to lick her dry lips. The thought of something cool and grape flittered through her mind and she wondered why it made her want to smile.

"Gabriel," she finally managed, reaching out a hand to touch Michael. He grabbed her hand, kissed it, cradling it against his chest. She was so cold, so damn cold.

"Alex, please, don't leave me." Anguish ripped through him. He pressed his lips to her hair. Like silk. So much like silk. He'd never forget it, never forget her scent. Never forget her. He cradled her body close to his. The metallic scent of blood filled the air, fouled his nostrils. "Please, Alex, don't leave me. I need you. I love you." He shook her gently. "I love you, damn it!"

She clung to him, her fist curling gently against his jacket. "Take...care...of...Gabriel." Her eyes slowly slid closed and her hand went limp.

"A-lex!" Michael's anguished cry could be heard long into the cold, dark night, hours after the rescue team had arrived and nearly pried her limp body out of his arms.

Alex spent Christmas Eve and Christmas Day hovering just on the edge of consciousness.

Michael spent Christmas Eve and Christmas Day pacing the hospital corridor like a caged animal. When the doctor first came out and announced it would be touch and go for the first twenty-four hours, Michael promised to shoot him if he let Alex die.

Gabriel spent Christmas Eve and Christmas Day at the cabin, with Ryce. With Webster dead, Gabriel was finally out of danger. He didn't know his mother had been shot. Ryce explained in his calm, no-nonsense way that after what had happened, Michael had wanted Alex to be looked at by a doctor, and they'd decided to keep her for a few days. Assured that there was really nothing wrong with his mother, and that she'd be home soon, Gabriel allowed Ryce to con him into teaching him how to play poker.

By the third day, Alex was out of danger. The bullet had grazed her breastbone. The wound was not as serious as it looked, but she'd lost a great deal of blood and had gone into shock. When she fell to the ground, she'd hit her head, which had caused a severe concussion and an even severer headache.

By the third day Michael was nearly out of his mind, certain the doctor was deliberately trying to provoke him. When the doctor announced that Alex was out of danger and would probably be well enough to leave the hospital in a few days, provided she had complete bed rest, Michael lifted the doctor off his feet and twirled him around in the hallway in gratitude.

Stunned, the doctor suggested Michael might want to see a colleague of his—a very prominent psychiatrist. He was quite certain the wrong patient had been hospitalized.

By the third day, Gabriel was tired of playing poker and tired of eating Ryce's idea of dinner, which was frozen TV dinners. Anxious for some real food, Gabriel decided he would gladly have eaten every bit of his mother's green vegetables and meat if she would just come and cook for him.

On the fourth day Alex woke up, wondering if anyone had caught the name of the guy who had obviously whacked her in the head with a baseball bat. It took her a few moments to get her bearings, but then she realized she was in a hospital.

She had no idea why, or how she'd gotten there. Until she tried to sit up. Pain radiated from every nerve ending and she fell back against the bed with a groan. Then she remembered. Webster. Michael. The shooting. Webster was dead; she remembered that, which meant Gabriel was finally safe. Relieved, she tried to take a deep breath, only to have pain slice up and around her chest. She moaned softly, clutching at the wad of bandages someone had wrapped around her.

"Alex?"

The gravelly male voice had her trying to lift her head. It seemed to weigh too much for her wobbly neck and she just couldn't manage it. The throbbing that had started when she tried didn't let up any so she merely kept her head flat on the pillow and took slow, little breaths, trying not to move as she stared at the ceiling.

"Michael?"

Her heart lifted and her hopes soared. She'd been dreaming of him for what seemed like days, dreaming of his touch, his arms, his *love*.

And grape soda.

She wished she could lift her head to see him, wished he would move closer so that she could get a look at him. A few days ago she didn't think she'd ever see his beloved face again.

"Michael?" she softly repeated, reaching out a hand to him. At least her hands still worked.

"No, Alex." The figure moved closer so that she could make out his features. Dark, and a bit forbidding, he was as big as Michael yet he wasn't Michael. She knew it instantly. "It's...uh...Ryce McCall..." He shifted his weight, obviously uncomfortable. "Michael had to..." His voice trailed off and she felt a pain even deeper in her chest, and knew this pain wasn't from her wounds but from her breaking heart. "Michael had to...uh..." Obviously uncomfortable, he glanced away.

"I understand," she said quietly, biting her lip and refusing to cry.

*Michael was gone.*

The thought edged into her mind, settling there, increasing the pain; but this pain radiated in her heart, in her soul. She tried not to cry, tried not to embarrass herself in front of Michael's friend. Slowly, carefully, she turned her head toward the window, not wanting him to see the hot, salty tears she could no longer control.

Michael was gone.

She had to face reality.

Tears slipped unheeded down her cheeks. She didn't even have the energy to wipe them away.

She'd known it was going to happen, known that he'd take off again once all of this was settled.

So why did it still hurt so much?

Because she'd allowed herself to hope, to hope that maybe once and for all she'd be able to break down that self-imposed emotional veil Michael hid behind. She'd hoped that maybe her love would be enough to make him realize what they could have together, be together, if only he'd trust her, and love her in return.

She'd thought, hoped and believed that love could create miracles.

Now she knew she'd been wrong.

Because Michael was gone.

She wouldn't cry anymore. It wouldn't help. It only made her head hurt, and made her feel even more miserable. Licking away a tear, she sniffled, and slowly turned her head back to face Ryce.

"Gabriel?" She swallowed, licking her parched lips. She was still so thirsty. "How's my son?"

Ryce's harsh features softened into a smile. "That is one helluva kid."

"He's all right then?" she asked in relief and Ryce smiled again, nodding his dark head.

"He's fine, but dying to see you." He glanced behind him. "In fact, he's in the hallway. Been driving the nurses crazy with his incessant questions." Ryce laughed. "He's been pacing off the linoleum, too, waiting for you to wake up." Ryce went to the door. "Hey, kid? She's awake." He turned back to her, gesturing toward the sheet. "You might want to...uh...pull that up. I didn't tell him you'd been shot."

Understanding, Alex lifted the sheet, shielding the large white bandage covering part of her shoulder and chest, noting that Ryce had said *he* hadn't told Gabriel she had been shot. She wondered how long Michael had been gone.

"Ma?" Gabriel came bounding into the room, almost knocking Ryce over in his hurry to get to Alex. Relieved to see him safe and sound, she tried to hold out her arms to him, but winced as pain shot through her left side.

"Easy, tiger." Ryce caught Gabriel around the waist and lifted him off the floor in order to halt his forward propulsion. "No jumping on her. She's got a headache." He lowered Gabriel to the ground, and kept an eagle eye on him while he slowly edged closer to the bed.

"Ma?" Gabriel hesitantly took a step forward, reaching out a hand to touch Alex's arm. When he saw the large bandages and all the tubes hooked up to her he paled. The look on his face almost broke her heart. "Are you... all right?" His worried eyes searched hers and she smiled, wishing she could hug him tightly and never let him go. She was eternally sorry she'd put that anxious look in her son's eyes again. No doubt there'd be some fallout from this, but whatever it was, she was sure her son was going to be just fine.

But what about her?

She forced a smile for him, reaching out to catch his hand and hold it.

"I'm fine, Gabriel. I was grazed by a bullet. Just grazed," she went on quickly at the horrified look on his face. "And the doctor says I'm going to be just fine." She gave his hand a gentle squeeze, relieved to feel him squeeze back. It was their own private signal, the one they used to let the other know that they were worried or scared. If the other person squeezed back, it let them know it was all right. They understood. And you were going to be all right.

When Gabriel had first come to live with her, when he still had trouble voicing his feelings and emotions, she had devised this nonverbal message as a way for him to communicate his feelings to her.

In the beginning, he had reached for her hand, gently squeezing it several times a day whenever he felt scared, worried or anxious. He knew if she squeezed back that she understood, and that he was not to worry, that she was there, would be there, and he'd be all right. It had been her own little way of giving Gabriel a security blanket without causing him any embarrassment. She was relieved to see he still remembered.

"I'm sorry you were worried," she said quietly, wishing she could lift her other hand and brush the hair out of his eyes.

"I wasn't." He glanced at her sheepishly. "Much." Shuffling his feet, he eyed the open box of candy on the night table. "When you coming home?"

Following his gaze, Alex smiled. "Are you hungry, Gabriel?" She had no idea who had brought her candy, but apparently someone had.

"Starved," Gabriel admitted, reaching across her to grab a piece and stuff it into his mouth. "Ryce ain't exactly a great cook," he whispered around a mouthful of candy. "Tyler's much better." He chewed noisily. "Much."

"I'm sure," Alex said with a sad smile, realizing Michael must have been gone for a while if Ryce had been taking care of Gabriel. Michael hadn't even bothered to say goodbye, at least not to her. But he hadn't the last time, either, so why was she surprised? "I'm sure you appreciate Ryce taking care of you while I've been here."

Gabriel's mouth stopped working when his mother nudged him. He looked at her in confusion for a moment. She glanced pointedly at Ryce, who was still hovering close to the bed.

"Oh, yeah, sure." Gabriel turned his head. "Thanks, Ryce." Gabriel reached for another candy. It wasn't often his mother let him eat it, and he intended to have as many as he could before she realized what he was doing. He'd had it with Ryce's idea of cooking.

Amused, Ryce scratched one eyebrow. "Sure, tiger. Any time." His gaze shifted to Alex. "Doc says you can go home tomorrow." He looked decidedly uncomfortable, she realized, understanding he probably was anxious to get out of there. This wouldn't have been easy for him, either. How dare Michael leave this to Ryce! He could at least have had the courtesy to tie up the loose ends himself, instead of dragging Ryce in to do his dirty work.

Ryce shifted again, absently rubbing his jaw. "I... uh...thought I'd bring Gabriel by in the morning and then drive you home."

"Thank you." She fiddled with the edge of the sheet. "I appreciate that, and everything you've done. I know that we would never have been rescued from that madman if it hadn't been for you and Mich—Lieutenant Tyler." It hurt just to say his name.

"No problem." Ryce shoved his hands in his pockets. "That's our job."

"I know," Alex murmured, realizing she'd been right all along. It only made the pain intensify. She'd been nothing more than part of a job to Michael. A means to an end. Just like last time. He'd used her to get his own way, to get what he needed done. Now that Webster was dead, and there was no need for Gabriel to testify, Michael had no need for her. She wished the truth didn't hurt so much. But it did. And this time she wasn't certain she'd ever recover.

Ryce slid a piece of gum into his mouth, curling the wrapper into a ball and shooting it at the garbage can. He missed. "If you don't mind, I think I'll take Gabriel home so you can rest."

"Thank you." She managed a weak smile before slowly turning toward her son, who looked like a chipmunk; a chocolate chipmunk. Her smile widened. "Gabriel, stop eating candy and give me a kiss."

Wiping his mouth with the back of his hand, Gabriel grinned sheepishly. "Sorry, Ma." Bending over her carefully, he kissed her cheek, then impulsively kissed her again, happy now that he'd actually had a chance to see her and see that Ryce hadn't lied to him; she was all right, except for the bandage she was trying to hide from him.

"See you in the morning," Ryce said, as he corralled Gabriel out the door.

Lifting her hand to wave goodbye, Alex waited until the door closed before she allowed the tears to come.

## Chapter Twelve

"You missed Christmas," Gabriel said, as Ryce maneuvered his Jeep through the sleepy town toward the cabin. The doctor had refused to allow her to be driven all the way back to Chicago. He wanted her to have at least three or four days of bed rest up here before tackling the long drive back. She'd had no choice but to agree, since he'd threatened to keep her in the hospital if she didn't cooperate.

She was anxious to get back to her own home, and her life—a life she knew she was going to have to live and face without Michael. She'd thought of nothing else all night. She didn't know how she was going to do it. How could she go back to her little world as if nothing had happened? As if Michael had never happened?

She'd forced herself to do it once before, but she didn't think she could do it again. Not now. Not when she knew she was hopelessly in love with him.

But it didn't matter.

Not to him.

And she knew it.

Her mind might be fooled into forgetting him, but her heart never would be. He had a permanent place there.

Unfortunately, she'd never had a chance to tell him, would probably never get a chance to tell him now. And she deeply regretted that he'd never know just how important, how *necessary* he was to her. It would be easier to stop breathing, than to stop loving him.

How could she go home and just pretend none of this had happened?

She couldn't.

So maybe being forced to spend a few days up here was for the best. Maybe it would help her adjust to what her life was going to be like now, or rather, how *empty* her life was going to be now.

"I'm sorry, Gabriel." She touched a hand to her head, which had begun to throb again. "I never meant to miss Christmas," she said softly, turning her head just as the department store whizzed by. She felt a sudden chill, remembering what had happened there less than a week ago. Wondered, too, what had happened to all the packages she'd dropped when they'd grabbed her.

She couldn't bear to think about it; couldn't bear to think about being bound and locked in that dank, dark little closet, scared out of her mind, wanting nothing more than to feel Michael's arms around her so she'd once again feel safe.

She wondered again if she'd ever again feel safe.

Not without Michael.

"I know you didn't mean to miss Christmas, Ma." Gabriel shrugged. "It's no big deal."

She looked at him carefully. He was taking all that had happened awfully well. She'd expected him to have some sort of reaction. It wasn't every day that a killer was after you, or that you missed Christmas because your mother had been kidnapped and shot, but apparently Gabriel was beginning to feel more secure than she realized. And if he did have any problems dealing with all that had happened, she was certain therapy would once again help him over it.

But what, she wondered, was going to help *her* get over *her* pain? The pain that filled her heart and touched her soul?

"We're here," Ryce announced, pulling into the driveway. "Alex, let me help you out first, get you out of the cold, then Gabriel and I will come back for your bags."

Nodding, and mindful of her still-bandaged shoulder, she gingerly slid to a sitting position with Gabriel's help, wincing softly.

Ryce killed the engine, then jumped out of the car to help her out. "Take it easy, now," he cautioned. "You're still kinda shaky." Holding her arm, he led her to the front door. "Gabe, take your mom in while I get the bags."

On shaky legs, Alex walked into the cabin, holding Gabriel with one hand and her chest with the other. She inhaled deeply and tears filled her eyes. Ryce must have lit a fire, using pinecones as a starter. The cabin smelled exactly as it had the first night she and Michael had arrived.

"Merry Christmas."

The deep, masculine voice had her lifting her head. She winced in pain, then froze as her watery eyes drank him in. Michael was standing in the middle of the living room, dressed in faded jeans and a flannel shirt, wearing that ridiculous apron again, and a grin that was entirely too mischievous for her peace of mind, and looking better than any man had a right to look.

She didn't know whether to hug him.

Or hit him.

"Michael." His name whispered through her lips. She was so stunned, she almost fainted. "What...what...are you doing here?" she stammered, clutching her chest tighter. Her heart was beating in double time, and she was certain if she didn't sit down, she was going to fall down.

"Waiting for you." Michael's gaze caressed her. She was looking pale and wan, but he'd never seen a more welcome sight in his life. He wanted to haul her against him and never let her go, never let her out of his sight. But he couldn't, not yet. He had some explaining to do, and they had some talking to do.

That was if she didn't kill him first.

Noting the color, or rather lack of it in her face, without another word, Michael crossed the room in two large steps and swept her into his arms. She didn't protest when he gently laid her down on the couch, then lifted a blanket to cover her, protectively tucking it under her chin like she was a two-year-old. It almost made her smile.

Too afraid to hope, too afraid to let her aching heart soar, Alex merely stared at him.

"Michael, what are you doing here?" she asked again. "I thought . . . I thought . . ." She glanced down, unable to stop the tears from threatening.

"You thought I was gone?" He brushed a strand of hair from her cheek. She was far too pale for his peace of mind. Always slight, now she didn't look small, she just looked fragile. It scared the hell out of him.

She couldn't answer him. Biting her lip, she merely nodded, praying she wouldn't start crying.

He sat down on the couch next to her, taking her hand in his, wondering when her sass and spit were going to kick in. "How could I leave you and Gabriel alone on Christmas?"

She blinked at him in confusion. "Michael, I know you don't pay attention to these things, but Christmas was almost a week ago."

"Guess that depends on whose calendar you use." With his eyes twinkling mischievously, he grinned at her, making her suspicious. Another thought crowded her mind and her hand flew to her mouth in horror.

"Your birthday, Michael. I missed your birthday." Impulsively, instinctively, her hand reached for him, clutching his shirt in her hands. "I'm sorry, Michael." This time the threat of tears came stronger. She wasn't going to hope; she'd done that before, knew how much it hurt when he dashed all hope.

Laughing, he lifted her hand and kissed it, tickled at how dismayed she was. "Could we take one holiday at a time? I'm sorta new at this." His eyes met hers, and hope slowly flickered to life. "Look around, Alex," he said softly, "and I think you'll see Christmas hasn't even arrived yet. At least, not at this house."

Her eyes widened in amazement as she glanced around. When she'd walked in, she'd only seen him. Now, her gaze coasted around the room and her heart slowly began to thud.

"Oh, Michael." Her hand went to her mouth again. There was a huge Christmas tree nestled in one corner. It was beautifully decorated with ornaments, tinsel and lights. Underneath it were stacks and stacks of gaily wrapped presents. And a train choo-chooing slowly round a track.

Everywhere she looked, every place her eyes landed on looked like...Christmas. The windows were frosted with fake snow and a wobbly snowman she suspected Gabriel had drawn. Two huge ruby red poinsettias were set on either side of the blazing fireplace. A gold garland was strung across the mantel. Everything looked strangely familiar.

Amazed, her gaze returned to him. "Michael, where... How..." She shook her head. "I don't understand."

Unable to keep his hands off her a moment longer, he laid a hand against her cheek, so grateful she was alive, well, safe.

Soon, she'd be his.

He hoped.

"Gabriel, Ryce and I drove to your apartment and transported everything back here." Grinning, he looked quite pleased with himself as his eyes traveled around the room. "It took some doing, several trips, not to mention two stops for food to keep your kid's motor going. But we managed." His eyes came back to hers. "You didn't think we'd have Christmas without you?" he asked softly, stroking a finger down her cheek.

"Oh, Michael." Burying her face against his shirt, she let the tears come. He held her, savoring her warmth, her scent, her smell.

"You scared the hell out of me," he whispered. "Don't you ever, *ever* do that to me again." He didn't think he could take it if anything happened to her. He'd almost lost her once. Never again.

He tightened his arms around her. It was only when he was holding her—when his arms were actually around her—that he knew she was safe.

And so was he.

"Me?" Alex's head came up and she lifted her good hand to whack him on the arm. *"Me!"* Infuriated, she was tempted to whack him again. He grinned, rubbing his arm. She was going to be all right. She was back to normal, back to sass and spit. He wanted to laugh with joy. "Michael, when I woke up in that hospital to find Ryce was there and you were gone, I...I...I..." She couldn't finish.

"You what, Alex?" Grinning, he tilted her chin, forcing her to look at him.

"I wanted to whack you," she admitted with a grin. He rubbed his arm.

"I think you just did." Mindful of her injuries, he gently pulled her close, tucking her into his shoulder. Alex clung to him, once again feeling that wonderful sense of calm, of safety. Her eyes slid closed and she inhaled deeply, inhaled his scent, his presence, her heart leaping in joy.

Michael sighed. He didn't know if he'd ever be able to tell her of the anguished hours he'd spent, when he didn't know if she would live or die. Hours that he'd cursed himself for being so foolish, for wasting so much time, for almost losing her. He'd vowed that if she made it, if she lived, he'd make up for all the things he'd never said, never done.

Drawing back, he suddenly grinned, making her suspicious again.

"What, Michael? What?"

"I guess I . . . uh . . . should probably explain why Ryce picked you up from the hospital instead of me." His grin turned sheepish and she groaned.

"What did you do, Detective Tyler?"

"Me?" He did his best to look offended. He failed miserably. "Why are you assuming I did something?"

"Because I know you." She laughed. "All right, fess up."

"I threatened to shoot your doctor." Gently, he nudged her shoulders back down on the couch. She'd been sitting up too long. He didn't want her getting tired out.

"You what?" She struggled to sit back up and keep a straight face. "And?" One blond eyebrow lifted expectantly.

"And they sort of banned me from the hospital." He tucked the blanket higher around her waist. She tugged it down. If he didn't stop fussing over her, she was going to whack him again. He was making her nervous with all his fussing.

"With good reason." She smiled at him, filled with love, filled with hope, giving in and letting him fuss over her. "Detective, you are impossible—as well as a few other things," she added with a laugh.

"So you've told me." He brought her hand to his lips for a kiss. "I . . . I . . ." Words failed him. "Do you want to open some presents?" he asked abruptly, and she laughed.

"You sound just like Gabriel on Christmas morning."

"Well, it is Christmas. At least in this house." Michael turned his head, making her wonder where Gabriel had gone off to. Something was up. The two of them were definitely up to something. No good, probably, she decided, with a smile. "Gabriel," Michael called. "Come in here."

Muttering under his breath, Gabriel came bounding into the living room, chomping on a cookie. "Ryce says he's cooking dinner. Tell him he can't cook dinner." He stuffed the cookie into his mouth.

"Ryce," Michael called. "You can't cook dinner." He looked at Gabriel. "Satisfied?"

"Yep." Gabriel plopped down on the end of the couch.

"Don't talk with your mouth full," Michael scolded. "And didn't I tell you to save some of those cookies for your mother?"

"I did, I did. There are two left."

"Two?" Michael's eyes widened. "That's it? I've been baking all morning—"

"You baked *cookies?*" Alex's voice edged upward in surprise. "Oh, Lord," she muttered, realizing Michael was taking this Christmas thing *seriously*. Now she knew what that heavenly aroma was drifting through the house.

"Of course, I baked cookies," he said, adjusting the blanket around her again. Playfully, she slapped his hand away. "You can't have Christmas without cookies."

"They're good, too," Gabriel piped in. "Ma can't bake," he offered helpfully, making Alex groan. "Tried cookies once." He pulled another one of Michael's cookies loose from his pocket and shoved it into his mouth. Whole. "We couldn't eat Ma's cookies, but they made great Frisbees."

"Frisbees?" Laughing, Michael shook his head. "Don't worry, Gabriel, I'll be in charge of the cookie baking from now on." He hesitated a moment. "Want to open some presents?" he asked, making Gabriel bound right off the couch again.

"Sure." Gabriel looked at his mother, rolling his eyes. "He wouldn't let me open anything until you got home. Not even one little thing."

"You lived," Michael said with a smile. "Go under the tree and you'll find three small boxes all wrapped in the same paper. Bring them here."

"Do we have to open the little ones first? Couldn't we open that real big one over there with my name on it?"

"No. The three little ones first."

Grumbling, Gabriel rooted around the bottom of the tree until he found the three boxes. Stacking them one on top of another, he carried them back to Michael. "Sure are small," he said, wishing he could shake the boxes to see what was in them.

Michael handed one box to Alex, one to Gabriel, then kept one for himself. Holding his breath, he looked at Alex.

"Open it," he said softly.

Gabriel didn't need another invitation. He tore into the paper, ripped open the box and lifted the little cardboard gift out. He frowned, turning it around and around and upside down. "What is this, Tyler?" He bit on the corner. It wasn't anything to eat.

Alex lifted her gift out, just as Michael ripped open his package and lifted his.

"Ma," Gabriel said impatiently, frowning and still trying to figure out his gift. "What is this?"

Alex's gaze met Michael's. Their eyes clung, held, saying more than words could ever say.

"Oh, Michael," she whispered, sitting up with his help, touching his face, wanting, needing to touch him. Michael smiled at her, a smile that reached his eyes and touched her soul.

"Bring it here, Gabriel, and I'll show you." Michael lifted his piece, connecting it to Gabriel's. He looked at Alex. She reached over and fit her piece into place. It fit perfectly right in the middle of theirs.

"Ma, what is this?" Confused, Gabriel wondered what was going on and why his mother looked like she was gonna cry. Again.

Michael draped an arm around Gabriel and drew him close. "What these are, son, are puzzle pieces."

"Yeah, so?" He still didn't get it. Why did he want three pieces of a puzzle for Christmas? He didn't even like puzzles. Tyler sure had a lot to learn about buying Christmas presents.

"They're puzzle pieces that fit together perfectly," Alex explained, understanding immediately. She remembered that night she'd told Michael about what she'd always thought love should be: two people who were like jagged puzzle pieces that had finally found the right fit.

"I finally found the pieces that fit," Michael said softly, hopefully. "I finally know where I belong." His eyes, scared and hopeful, searched hers. "I love you, Alex."

She moved into his arms, laughing and crying. "It sure took you long enough," she complained, planting kisses all over his face.

"Is that all you've got to say?" he groused, holding her by the shoulders and trying to look offended.

"Could we open some more presents?"

Michael laughed. "I'm not talking to you, Gabriel. I'm talking to your mother."

"I love you, Michael." She hugged him. "I love you." She stopped kissing him and Gabriel rolled his eyes. Tyler had already explained to him about how he was going to hang around, and now they were going to be a family of three. It was cool. But did they have to get all mushy? The least they could do was let him open more presents. Maybe there'd be some good ones under the tree.

Alex shook her finger at Michael. "But if you ever—ever take off on me again—"

"Us," he corrected, glancing at Gabriel, who was happily scrounging around under the tree.

"Us," she said softly. "I swear, Michael—"

"Don't swear, Alex. Your mother won't like it."

"My mother's not here."

Michael's eyes lit with a wicked grin.

"Is she?" Alex asked hopefully. The man was full of surprises today. She'd wondered why she hadn't heard from her folks except by phone for the past few days. She should have known something was up.

Wiggling his eyebrows, Michael leaned his forehead against hers. "Do you think I want to eat any more of Ryce's cooking?" He shook his head. "I'm no fool. Your mother will be here—" he glanced at his watch "—in about half an hour."

"Michael, why is my family coming? I don't understand."

He laughed. "I'm not up to eating any more of Ryce's food." Michael leaned close. "The man can't cook, but no one will tell him."

"Is it time to eat, yet?" Gabriel's head popped out from under the tree. He was on his hands and knees, still scouting out presents.

Michael laughed. "We've got to do something about that kid's eating habits or we're gonna go broke before he's grown."

"Will you mind?" she asked quietly. "I'm a package deal, Michael. Gabriel and I come together."

He laid the three connected puzzle pieces in her lap, then smiled into her eyes. "I wouldn't have it any other way."

"Michael?" She hesitated for a moment. "You know I can't...can't..." Unconsciously, she laid a hand across her stomach, an unbearable sadness touching her heart. "I can't have any more children. I can't give you your own child."

He kissed her forehead. "We already have a child, Alex. Gabriel. Remember what you said about families?" She nodded. "I think...I think I finally understand. You and Gabriel...you mean everything to me. I don't know what I'd do without you. Don't even want to imagine it. When you were..." He couldn't put into words what he'd felt when Webster had her. "During all this time, all I could think about was protecting you and Gabriel. Then when you were...shot, I knew Gabriel needed me, needed my love and support. I finally understood, Alex." He swallowed hard. "I don't know what I'd do if I ever lost you. Either of you."

She looped her arms around his neck and drew him close. "That's something you don't ever have to worry about."

"You and Gabriel are my family." The ache in his heart had finally healed. Sealed over by love. Alex's love. And Gabriel's. He'd spend the rest of his life showing them his love. And how much they meant to him.

He was finally, blissfully at peace. The panic was gone, banished forever in that place in his memory where it had always belonged. Someday, maybe he'd tell Alex all about it, but not now. Now, he had too many other things to tell her.

Gathering her close, he just held her, savoring the peace that filled his heart and warmed his soul. "I love you, Alex," he whispered again, still getting used to the sound, the words. "I love you."

"I know, Michael. I think I've always known. I was just waiting for you to realize it."

"Guess I can be pretty thick at times." She grinned, and he brushed his lips against hers. "Well, you didn't have to agree with me, did you?"

"Yes, I did," she said with a laugh. "All right, Michael. You've decorated this house like Santa's castle. We've got presents, a tree and I think you've even got my mother hidden around here somewhere." She glanced around. "What else have you got up your sleeve?"

"Not up my sleeve, Alex. In the bedroom."

"Are you inviting me to your bedroom?"

"Absolutely not. Not until you're fully recovered."

She tugged on the front of his shirt. "I'm beginning to feel much, much better, Michael." Pressing her lips against his, she sighed happily as his mouth seduced hers, taking her places she'd never been with anyone else.

"You're not that much better," he scolded, pulling away. "And besides," he whispered, "your father might not appreciate me taking his daughter to my bedroom. At least not until I make an honest woman out of you."

"My father?" Confused, she shook her head. "Michael, please, tell me you don't have my father stashed in your bedroom, do you? You didn't kidnap him at gunpoint or anything." Nothing would surprise her at this point.

"I certainly did not," he huffed. "He's coming willingly."

"You're confusing me." She touched a hand to her head. "Michael, what's going on? Let's have it—all of it—" she specified, knowing he liked to go about things in his own slow, meandering way just to drive her nuts. "I want to hear everything that's going on. Exactly."

He sighed, tapping her on the nose. "All right. Today is Christmas, at least in this house, and since you said you always spend Christmas with your family, I invited your family—"

"*Our* family," she corrected softly, reaching for his hand and making him smile. He kind of liked the sound of that.

"Our family to Christmas dinner, which your mother graciously is bringing."

"The entire family is coming here. *Now?*"

He pretended to inspect her head. "Did something happen to your hearing? I could swear you're going deaf." He kissed her on the nose. "It's Christmas, remember? Do I have to buy you a calendar?"

She laughed. He was impossible. Endearing, wonderful, but totally impossible. "Michael, the only thing I remember is that Christmas was nearly a week ago—"

"No, Alex," he said gently, glancing down at the puzzle pieces, still connected, lying in her lap. He lifted his gaze to hers. "I've had a lot of time to think the past few days. A lot of time to put things in perspective, and I realized something I guess you've been trying to tell me for a long time." He shrugged. "I guess I just wasn't listening."

"What, Michael?"

He smiled at her—a beautiful, brilliant smile that sent her heart soaring with hope, with love. He took her hand, held it close. "Christmas isn't a day on the calendar, Alex. Christmas is in your heart."

"Oh, Michael." She laid her head on his shoulder and she felt his arms surround her. The tears came then—tears of joy and happiness—for him, for her, for all of them.

Michael held her, touching his lips to the top of her hair. He felt a tap on his shoulder.

"Tyler?" Gabriel was hovering over them.

"What?"

"Did you make her mad again?"

"Nope. Not me, not this time."

"Did you make her cry?"

Michael laughed. "Yeah, Gabriel, I guess I did." He glanced down at Alex. "Again."

Gabriel sighed. "That's what I thought." Training a father was going to be just as hard as taking care of a mother.

"But these are happy tears, son." Michael looped an arm around Gabriel's shoulders, drawing him close. He held them both, Gabriel and Alex. His family. Michael's eyes slid closed.

*His family.*

They belonged to him, and now he knew he belonged *with* them.

Sniffling, Alex lifted her head, smiling at the sight of Michael and their son. "My mother's going to have a fit when she finds out what I want for dinner instead of her home-cooked meal."

"And what do you want for dinner?" Michael and Gabriel looked at her curiously.

"Pizza," she announced. "Frozen pizza. And grape soda." She laughed. "Lots of grape soda."

"All right," Gabriel whooped, jumping to high-five the air. "Pizza and grape soda for Christmas dinner." This was gonna be even better than his birthday. "So what do you think, Tyler? We finally got her to eat the good stuff." He grinned mischievously. "Think we should keep her?"

Michael glanced at Alex, a wicked gleam in his eye. "I think so. Especially now that we've almost got her trained." He wiggled his eyebrows, making Gabriel giggle. "Next thing you know, she'll be asking for Twinkies."

"Not on a bet," Alex grumbled.

"You're right," Gabriel agreed. "Let's keep her." He looked up at Michael. "Can we eat *now?*" He rubbed his stomach. "I'm starving."

Laughing, Michael scooped Alex up in his arms. "Lead the way into the kitchen, Gabriel. I've got a pizza to bake." And a Christmas to celebrate.

With his family.

*His family.*

He liked the sound of that.

*His family.*

Now he knew that right here, with them, was where he'd belonged all along.

## Epilogue

*Christmas Eve, two years later...*

Wrapped in darkness, surrounded by Michael's arms, Alex planted soft kisses along his jawline.

"Alex," he moaned softly, catching her wandering hands under the sheet. "I think you can get arrested for doing that to a cop."

Propping herself on her elbow, she grinned wickedly at him. "Want me to get your handcuffs?"

Laughing, he hauled her close, rolling her on top of him, wrapping his arms around her. "So, what's on your mind?" He knew something was. She'd been acting weird—even weird for *her*—the past few weeks.

"Christmas," she said, playing with the thatch of dark hair on his chest. "I want to give you your present early."

He lifted his head to look at her. "Yeah?"

"Yeah." She grinned.

"So?" He glanced around the room. There weren't any presents; he knew. He and Gabriel had been searching the house for weeks. She'd really hidden them well this year. They couldn't find a single, solitary thing. It was driving him nuts.

Slowly she smiled at him. "We're going to have a baby."

For a moment, Michael was stunned, unable to comprehend her words. His head came up until it was inches away from hers. "You're *what?*"

She tapped him lightly on the head. "I think you're going deaf, Lieutenant. I didn't say *I* was having anything. I said *we* were going to have a baby."

"You...uh...want to explain that?"

Absently trailing a finger across his chest, she looked down at him. "Do you remember that homicide bust you made about eight weeks ago?" She remembered how torn up he'd been. For a few days his eyes were haunted and bleak, but it wasn't until a few weeks ago that she'd finally understood why.

Michael frowned, wondering where she was going with this. "The bust at the crack house?"

She nodded. "The one where you arrested the guy for killing his wife?"

Michael's jaw clenched. "He almost ki' .d their eight-month-old daughter as well."

She was quiet for a moment. "Michae! how many times have you been to the pediatric intensive ( .e ward?"

He grinned sheepishly, his hands caressing her back. "A few times I guess."

"A few times?" Alex laughed, adjusting herself more comfortably atop him. In spite of the difference in their sizes, it still amazed her that they fit together so perfectly. "I believe, Lieutenant, that going to the hospital every day qualifies as more than a few times."

"Yeah, well, she's just a baby, Alex." He looked so sad, Alex felt her heart ache. "She doesn't belong anywhere to anyone."

"I know, Michael," she replied softly, laying her hand over his heart. "As of tomorrow, though, she's going to belong somewhere to someone."

He frowned. "What do you mean?"

"You *are* going deaf," she said with a laugh. "Our agency has been in charge of her case. Five weeks ago I put in for temporary emergency custody. I found out this afternoon, it was granted."

His smile could have lit up their bedroom, but considering where her hands had started wandering, she was glad it hadn't.

"We can pick her up in the morning on the way to my folks'. They only kept her in the hospital pending placement. She's fully recovered from her injuries, so as of tomorrow she'll belong somewhere to someone." Cradling his face in her hand, she met his gaze. "We can adopt her. She's going to belong to us, Michael. To us."

He bolted upright in bed, nearly dislodging her. He caught her at the last minute, and held her naked body close to his. His eyes once so sad, so very, very bleak, were now so hopeful and overflowing with love. "She's going to be ours?" Stunned, he shook his head. Alex never stopped surprising him.

She grinned. "Would this face lie?"

"Never," he said with a laugh, hugging her tightly. "Just in time for Christmas," he said, awed again by his wife, his love, his family.

"She's one little girl who won't become just another child of midnight."

"Not our daughter." *Their* daughter. He liked the sound of that. A lot. Michael brushed his lips against hers. "I love you, Alex."

"I love you, too."

He started to climb out of bed, but she grabbed his arm, stopping him. "Where are you going?"

"To call your folks and tell Gabriel he's going to have a sister."

"He already knows. How do you think I found out about you going to the hospital?"

Michael shook his head. "That kid of ours can't keep a secret worth a damn." *Ours.* He was still getting used to it, still getting used to the thrill he felt every time he thought about it.

Alex tugged on his arm, dragging him back to bed. Settling herself comfortably over him, she began planting kisses across his face. "You can call my parents... later," she murmured, settling her mouth against his.

"Much later," Michael happily agreed.

"Merry Christmas, Michael," she whispered in the darkness.

His throat tightened as he thought of tomorrow, their daughter, their son, their future.

His family.

He smiled in the darkness. "Merry Christmas, Alex. I love you." His arms tightened around her and he rolled them over so he could look down into her beautiful face. His heart filled with love and he nestled his face against her neck, inhaling deeply of her wonderful scent. "Oh, how I love you."

"Yeah?" She grinned seductively, trailing her foot down the back of his calf. "Prove it." Her hands slid over his body, slowly, gently, until his eyes slid closed and he groaned again. "You're a cop, Lieutenant," she whispered. "You should know all about... evidence."

Laughing, Michael nibbled on her neck. "I'll give you evidence," he threatened, making Alex's eyes twinkle mischievously.

"That's exactly what I was hoping for, Lieutenant."

She pulled him close until they fit together perfectly—like two puzzle pieces that had finally found the one place in the world they belonged. She knew where she belonged; where *they* belonged. Together.

Still laughing, Michael moaned softly as her hands caressed him, seduced him, loved him. Grabbing the sheet, he dragged it over their heads, engulfing them in their own private world of love.

Michael sighed happily. He had a feeling tomorrow was going to be a wonderful day.

But then again, weren't they all?

Especially when you realized Christmas wasn't a day on the calendar; it was a feeling in your heart.

\* \* \* \* \*

*Silhouette*®

SPECIAL EDITION®

# COMING NEXT MONTH

### #1015 SISTERS—Penny Richards
*That Special Woman!*

Cash Benedict's return meant seeing the woman he'd always wanted but felt he had no right to love. Skye Herder had never forgotten Cash, and now he was about to find out that Skye wasn't the only person he left behind all those years ago....

### #1016 THE RANCHER AND HIS UNEXPECTED DAUGHTER—Sherryl Woods
*And Baby Makes Three*

Harlan Adams was used to getting his way, but feisty Janet Runningbear and her equally spunky daughter weren't making it easy for him. Janet sent Harlan's heart into a tailspin, until he was sure of only one thing—he wanted her as his wife!

### #1017 BUCHANAN'S BABY—Pamela Toth
*Buckles & Broncos*

Not only had Donovan Buchanan been reunited with Bobbie McBride after five years, but he'd just discovered he was the father of her four-year-old daughter! Now that he'd found her, the handsome cowboy was determined to be the best father he could be—as well as future husband to his lost love.

### #1018 FOR LOVE OF HER CHILD—Tracy Sinclair

Erica Barclay always put the needs of her son first. But when she fell for Michael Smith, she was torn between passion and her child. Could she still protect her son and listen to the needs of her own heart?

### #1019 THE REFORMER—Diana Whitney
*The Blackthorn Brotherhood*

Strong, loving Letitia Cervantes was just the kind of woman Larkin McKay had been waiting for all his life. And when her son's rebellious spirit called out to the father in him, he wanted to bring them together into a ready-made family.

### #1020 PLAYING DADDY—Lorraine Carroll

Cable McRay wasn't interested in taking on fatherhood and marriage. But Sara Nelson made those thoughts near impossible, and her son was proving irresistible—and Cable was soon playing daddy....

# Take 4 bestselling love stories FREE

## Plus get a FREE surprise gift!

## Special Limited-time Offer

**Mail to Silhouette Reader Service™**

3010 Walden Avenue
P.O. Box 1867
Buffalo, N.Y. 14269-1867

**YES!** Please send me 4 free Silhouette Special Edition® novels and my free surprise gift. Then send me 6 brand-new novels every month, which I will receive months before they appear in bookstores. Bill me at the low price of $3.12 each plus 25¢ delivery and applicable sales tax, if any.* That's the complete price and a savings of over 10% off the cover prices—quite a bargain! I understand that accepting the books and gift places me under no obligation ever to buy any books. I can always return a shipment and cancel at any time. Even if I never buy another book from Silhouette, the 4 free books and the surprise gift are mine to keep forever.

235 BPA AWSY

| Name | (PLEASE PRINT) | |
|------|------|------|
| Address | Apt. No. | |
| City | State | Zip |

This offer is limited to one order per household and not valid to present Silhouette Special Edition® subscribers. *Terms and prices are subject to change without notice. Sales tax applicable in N.Y.

USPED-695                    ©1990 Harlequin Enterprises Limited

## SILHOUETTE® *Desire®* CELEBRATION 1000

### is on its way
### in April, May and June 1996!

Join us for the celebration of Desire's 1000th book!
We'll have

- Book #1000, *Man of Ice* by Diana Palmer in May!

- Best-loved miniseries such as **Hawk's Way**
  by Joan Johnston, and **Daughters of Texas**
  by Annette Broadrick

- Fabulous new writers in our Debut author
  program, where you can collect <u>double</u>
  Pages and Privileges Proofs of Purchase

Plus you can enter our exciting Sweepstakes for
a chance to win a beautiful piece of original
Silhouette Desire cover art or one of many
autographed Silhouette Desire books!

**SILHOUETTE DESIRE'S CELEBRATION 1000**
...because the best is yet to come!

DES1000TR

What do women really want to know?

Only the world's largest publisher of romance
fiction could possibly attempt an answer.

## HARLEQUIN ULTIMATE GUIDES™

# How to Talk to a Naked Man,

## Make the Most of Your Love Life,
## and Live Happily Ever After

The editors of Harlequin and Silhouette are
definitely experts on love, men and relationships.
And now they're ready to share that expertise with
women everywhere.

Jam-packed with vital, indispensable, lighthearted
tips to improve every area of your romantic life—even
how to get one! So don't just sit around and wonder
why, how or where—run to your nearest bookstore
for your copy now!

Available this February, at your favorite retail outlet.

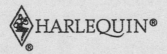

HARLEQUIN®

NAKED

# Are your lips succulent, impetuous, delicious or racy?

Find out in a very special Valentine's Day promotion—THAT SPECIAL KISS!

Inside four special Harlequin and Silhouette February books are details for THAT SPECIAL KISS! explaining how you can have your lip prints read by a romance expert.

Look for details in the following series books, written by four of Harlequin and Silhouette readers' favorite authors:

**Silhouette Intimate Moments #691**
*Mackenzie's Pleasure* by *New York Times* bestselling author Linda Howard

**Harlequin Romance #3395**
*Because of the Baby* by Debbie Macomber

**Silhouette Desire #979**
*Megan's Marriage* by Annette Broadrick

**Harlequin Presents #1793**
*The One and Only* by Carole Mortimer

Fun, romance, four top-selling authors, plus a **FREE** gift! This is a very special Valentine's Day you won't want to miss! Only from Harlequin and Silhouette.

VAL96

# As seen on TV!
## *Free Gift Offer*

With a Free Gift proof-of-purchase from any Silhouette® book,
you can receive a beautiful cubic zirconia pendant.

This gorgeous marquise-shaped stone is a genuine cubic
zirconia—accented by an 18" gold tone necklace.

(Approximate retail value $19.95)

## Send for yours today...
### compliments of ▼ *Silhouette*®

To receive your free gift, a cubic zirconia pendant, send us one original proof-of-purchase, photocopies not accepted, from the back of any Silhouette Romance™, Silhouette Desire®, Silhouette Special Edition®, Silhouette Intimate Moments® or Silhouette Shadows™ title available in February, March or April at your favorite retail outlet, together with the Free Gift Certificate, plus a check or money order for $1.75 U.S./$2.25 CAN. (do not send cash) to cover postage and handling, payable to Silhouette Free Gift Offer. We will send you the specified gift. Allow 6 to 8 weeks for delivery. Offer good until April 30, 1996 or while quantities last. Offer valid in the U.S. and Canada only.

## *Free Gift Certificate*

Name: _____

Address: _____

City: _____ State/Province: _____ Zip/Postal Code: _____

Mail this certificate, one proof-of-purchase and a check or money order for postage and handling to: SILHOUETTE FREE GIFT OFFER 1996. In the U.S.: 3010 Walden Avenue, P.O. Box 9057, Buffalo NY 14269-9057. In Canada: P.O. Box 622, Fort Erie,

---

**FREE GIFT OFFER**                                     079-KBZ-R

ONE PROOF-OF-PURCHASE

To collect your fabulous FREE GIFT, a cubic zirconia pendant, you must include this original proof-of-purchase for each gift with the properly completed Free Gift Certificate.

---

079-KBZ-R

Bestselling author

# RACHEL LEE

takes her Conard County series to new heights with

A CONARD COUNTY Reckoning

This March, Rachel Lee brings readers a brand-new, longer-length, out-of-series title featuring the characters from her successful Conard County miniseries.

Janet Tate and Abel Pierce have both been betrayed and carry deep, bitter memories. Brought together by great passion, they must learn to trust again.

"Conard County is a wonderful place to visit! Rachel Lee has crafted warm, enchanting stories. These are wonderful books to curl up with and read. I highly recommend them."
—*New York Times* bestselling author
Heather Graham Pozzessere

Available in March, wherever Silhouette books are sold.

CCST

# You're About to Become a *Privileged Woman*

Reap the rewards of fabulous free gifts and benefits with proofs-of-purchase from Silhouette and Harlequin books

# Pages & Privileges™

It's our way of thanking you for buying our books at your favorite retail stores.

PROOF OF PURCHASE
Offer expires October 31, 1996
SSE-PP100

Pages & Privileges ™

**Harlequin and Silhouette—
the most privileged readers in the world!**

For more information about Harlequin and Silhouette's PAGES & PRIVILEGES program call the Pages & Privileges Benefits Desk: 1-503-794-2499

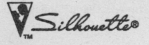

SSE-PP100